The Bedfordshire Warlock

by

Patrick R. Field

Cover Art by *Kristian Norris*

The Wild Rose Press, Inc.
PO Box 708
Adams Basin, NY 14410-0708
Visit us at www.thewildrosepress.com

Publishing History
First Edition, 2024
Trade Paperback ISBN 978-1-5092-5532-0
Digital ISBN 978-1-5092-5533-7

Published in the United States of America

Dedication

Dedicated to Edgar Allen Poe

Chapter 1

Bedfordshire, Massachusetts
October 31, 1692

A perfect image of the full moon reflects off the calm waters of Massachusetts Bay, illuminating the shoreline and the dense forest that abuts the brown sand beach. The moonlight is bright enough so that a being can move unencumbered from the shoreline through the forest to the clearing adjacent to the thick grove of trees and shrubs. There is another source of light emanating from the clearing: a circular pattern of bright lights floating above the ground. The source of light is fire, torches held by arms forming a circle around a stone well. Next to the well is a large, simply designed wooden chair with wide armrests, a wide seat, and a long plank of wood attached to the seat. The plank rests upon a raised beam of wood secured onto a wooden platform with four wooden wheels.

A man in his mid-thirties, wearing filthy breeches, is bound by thick rope on a chair. The rope burns into the naked flesh of his arms and chest as he struggles to break free. His bare feet lie flat on the muddy ground; his toes writhe on the viscous red earth. Dark hair hangs to the nape of his neck, wet and dirty, rogue strands plastered across his forehead and face. Beneath the tendrils of dark hair, there is an attractive face, albeit bruised and brandished with lacerations. Deep cuts scar his short forehead, angular cheekbones, long thin nose, thin lips, and powerful jawline. Dark, piercing eyes focus on the crowd holding the torches. His powerful, well-defined chest transitions into strong sinewy arms; the contours of muscles accentuated by his exertion to break free from the chair. Lacerations on his chest produce small rivulets of blood, coursing over the mounds of muscle and through the narrow valley between his pectoral muscles. Streams of blood flowing from the open wounds of his legs cascade over his feet and onto the ground. He is silent as he bears the pain.

The torchbearers watch the prisoner struggle as they listen to the voice of another man. The citizenry is dressed entirely in black clothing. The women wear bonnets, capes over the shoulders of dresses with sleeves that cover their arms to their wrists, and hemlines that fall to the muddy ground. The men don tall cylindrical hats with wide brims, black suits beneath long coats and rough leather boots covered with the red mud of the rain-soaked clearing. The man talking is standing next to the chair, holding an unraveled scroll of parchment in front of his face. Reading by the firelight and moonlight, his voice is deep and clear, resounding in the night's silence.

"On this day of the 31st of October, in the year of our Lord 1692, the people of the village of Bedfordshire of the Massachusetts colony hereby accuse Elias Doever of consorting with the Devil. I, Sir William Putnam, constable for the village of Bedfordshire, read the following accusation.

"Let it be known that Elias Doever is accused by the gentle and Christian town folk of Bedfordshire of supernatural acts. Levitation: as witnessed by Goody Mary Parris when she saw Elias Doever raise a broom over his head in his fields without laying his hands on the broomstick and then flying through the air when sitting upon it. Enchantment: as witnessed by Sir William Putnam, when Elias Doever made a man commit acts against his Christian nature, when he seduced John Putnam to perform unspeakable physical acts with him that were against God. Clairvoyance: as witnessed by James Corey when Elias Doever predicted that Goody Elizabeth Corey would give birth to a stillborn child with a monstrous deformity of the spine.

"As has been witnessed, he will be tested by this Christian tribunal to determine if his soul remains within his body. If he has traded his soul to the Devil for the powers of the Devil, he will float to the surface when he is placed into holy water, as he will not be able to endure the grace of our Lord and Savior. If he remains below the water, then his soul is still chaste, untouched by the Devil."

With this last statement, several men move toward the platform with wheels. Two men place their hands on the plank extending from the chair and two men stand on either side of the platform, gripping the support of the plank. Together, the two men on the plank push on the end of it and the chair lifts slightly from the ground; Elias's feet elevate, mud slowly dripping from the end of his toes. The two men holding onto the plank support pull the platform backward away from the well.

From the crowd, a man's voice calls out, "Before he is tested, does he bear the mark of the Devil?"

William Putnam lifts his right hand into the air.

The platform stops moving and the chair slowly descends onto the ground. Standing next to the chair, William Putnam places his hand on the right side of Elias's breast. Slowly creeping his bony fingers down the sinewy chest, the crawling stops above the light brown areola. His index finger moves back and forth along a raised surface on the skin as he makes an announcement, "Elias Doever bears the Devil's mark above his right teat, as this is where the Devil licked his breast with his forked tongue."

The crowd erupts. "He bears the mark! He must be tested in the ducking chair!"

Against the cacophonous roar, Elias Doever turns his head. With a scowl on his face and venom in his eyes, Elias stares directly at William Putnam. Slowly walking away from the chair and the well, Constable Putnam lifts his right hand, and the men return to their positions on the ducking chair apparatus. Pushing down on the wide board, the chair rises above the wall of the well. Struggling in the chair, Elias curses into the night as his mud-covered feet thrash back and forth. The ducking chair device rolls toward the well, the chair pivoting beyond the wall, hovering above the water. Slowly, the chair descends toward the well water; the prisoner whips about in his chair like a wild animal desperate to escape from its cage. The chair stops its descent and the voice of an older man, the rector of the Church of Bedfordshire, resonates. Holding a bible above the water, the rector recites scripture as he waves his other hand over the well, "In the name of the Father, and of the Son and of the Holy Ghost. Amen."

Elias whips about in the chair, screaming and crying, "No! No! I will not survive! I will die!"

Once again, the chair descends toward the water. As his toes touch the surface of the water, Elias screams with fury. The chair sinks into the water, Elias's feet and legs submerge, and William Putnam cuts the ropes that bind him to the chair. The rope falls into the water, and Elias slides into the well. The crowd peers into the well. He is not floating. The villagers wait patiently, but there is no sign of his body. The onlookers turn to each other, fear evident in their eyes as they contemplate that they have assisted in the drowning of an innocent man.

Suddenly, a great explosion occurs in the well and a voluminous spout of water hurls high into the air. A deep, unnatural roar echoes through the forest as the water streams higher into the air. The scene is silent, but the unearthly scream pierces the night. The spout of water bending away from the well, heads towards the nearby shoreline, plunging into the calm waters of the Massachusetts Bay with a thunderous sound. Immediately, a vortex forms in the disturbed water and swallows the spout that fell from the sky. Quickly disappearing, the water surface becomes calm again, and the glassy texture returns.

The water in the well is now bubbling, as if a gas has been released from its bowels. Within the gurgling water, a deep red color diffuses at the surface. Abruptly, Elias Doever's body rockets to the surface through the bubbling water, and the effervescence completely recedes. His body floating face down in a sea of blood. Screams from the womenfolk pierce the night air at the ghastly sight. Instinctively, men reach into the cauldron of blood to grasp the floating body and hoist it over the wall. Dropping the corpse to the muddy earth, the accidental pallbearers turn him over. Audible gasps fill the scene as the menfolk examine the body, turning their heads away from the unnatural horror displayed. A large and deep laceration perforated Elias's chest—the underlying bones of his sternum and ribs shattered as if something had exploded from deep inside his thorax. The heart and lungs macerated; the anatomy is unrecognizable, completely bloodless. William Putnam motions for a man to come forward. The man removes his coat and quickly covers the body, tightly wrapping it around the corpse to hide the grotesque display of flesh, bone, and internal viscera.

William Putnam speaks, "Let it be known on this day that Elias Doever has been found guilty of consorting with the Devil, of witchcraft. That the evil warlock died at the hands of the good Christian people of Bedfordshire." There is muttering among the crowd at this pronouncement. William Putnam signals to James Corey to approach. James Corey moves and stands next to the corpse. The constable leans over and whispers into his ear, "Take the body and bury it in unconsecrated ground, for we have witnessed the departure of the Devil from one of its brethren. Tell no one of this burial place. The location must die with you, as it will now be a place of evil and only death and destruction can come to those that disturb this unholy grave. Be quick about it and bury the corpse 'fore midnight, as that is the witching hour."

James Corey, a large and powerful man, lifts the lifeless body with his arms and drags it to a wooden working cart a considerable distance from the well. The bright moonlit night illuminates his way. As he drops the body into the cart, the cart lists slightly with the weight. Walking to the front of the cart, standing in between the two poles attached to it, he bends down and lifts the two poles resting on the ground until he is standing. The wheels move slightly with this motion. James Corey walks forward holding onto the poles, the cart carrying the mutilated cadaver follows him. He finds the road and turns the cart onto it. Walking down the middle of the road, the silhouette of a figure pulling a cart in the moonlight fades gradually until the image completely disappears into the night.

Chapter 2

Bedfordshire, Massachusetts
Doever Farm
September 1992

When my mother, Dr. Abigail Leeves, told me that she had accepted a tenure-track position in the history department at Bedfordshire College, I knew that meant that we would be moving to the "village" of Bedfordshire. It's a quaint hamlet settled on the Massachusetts Bay in the northeastern part of Massachusetts. The only question I raise to her at the prospect of this move: "How far is it from Boston?" Answer: An hour if you are driving late at night, like when the bars close, or 1 ½ -2 hours during the normal traffic travesty that is the Boston suburbs. Doable, I thought.

Why is Boston so important to me, you might ask? I am an openly gay man in the beginning of the last decade of the 20th century and this is where my people live, work, play, love and...well you get the picture. Recently, I have been feeling more optimistic about the direction of our country, as far as gay rights are concerned. America just had its first presidential candidate, Governor Bill Clinton, mention the word "gay" in a campaign speech in an inclusive manner...so we'll see. Hopefully, we'll have a change from the current administration; the president wouldn't even say the word AIDS at the beginning of the epidemic. All right, enough of that. Let me introduce myself.

My name is Dorian Leeves, and I was born in the summer of 1969; I am twenty-three years old. My mother is a huge fan of the Oscar Wilde novel *The Picture of Dorian Gray*, and thus, the origin of my first name, not a name you see very frequently on souvenir, personalized license plates. Of course, when I learned of the origin of my moniker, I jokingly asked my mother if she was hoping that if I did not age (presumably as my Glamour Shots portrait hidden in a secret stash aged into a hideous creature) then it would, in turn, be hard to tell her age (with the proper amount of plastic surgery). I thought it was funny. She did not.

My surname Leeves is of Anglo-Saxon origin, which originally meant "dear or beloved one." My father, Simon Leeves, is a British-born citizen; therefore, I have the typical British pasty white complexion. But more about that later. He and my mother met at the University of Oxford; they were both doctoral students in history. After she became pregnant with me, they married and relocated to America. Interestingly, my father's family has roots in colonial Massachusetts, like my mother's family: the Carriers. Because of that shared genealogy, and the fact that they are both history professors, they both sought and retained academic positions in Massachusetts and lived in Boston until their divorce three years ago. My father returned to England after he secured a tenure-track position at a university in London.

So, more about me. I have dark hair, cut short and over the ears, with spiked bangs that are not easy to tame because of cowlicks. As I stated, the pallor of my skin is a pale white. So, with dark hair, I look like your typical "Goth/Emo" victim. But I am not a Goth, despite my appearance. My triangular-shaped face is accentuated with high cheekbones, a long angular nose, and a prominent cleft in my chin. I have light green eyes, thick dark eyebrows (which I constantly pluck), long black eyelashes, and thick red, "bee-sting" lips. I am approximately six feet tall and have a medium build. I work out religiously. Consequently, I have big guns, a nice chest, flat stomach, and well-developed thighs and legs. Personal note: It drives me nuts when a guy has a banging upper body and skinny chicken legs. As for my personal parts, I am average. Which, sadly, can be a defining characteristic in the male gay community in many ways, but I have always believed the adage "It's not about the size of the wand, it is how you use it."

I graduated this past May from a typical, small New England liberal arts college. Unlike both of my parents, I am not a history aficionado and earned a Bachelor of Arts in Biological Sciences. Like so many who graduate with a biology degree and don't want to pursue medical school or physical therapy, I am not sure how I want to continue my education, so I am pursuing the default: I enrolled in a generic master's in the biology program.

I am currently a graduate assistant in the Department of Biological Sciences at Bedfordshire College. As the new "golden child" of the history department, my mother was able to secure this position for me as a condition of her employment. This was without knowing what kind of research was available for me for thesis work, or whether it was a match for my interests or goals. However, the assistantship includes free tuition and a small stipend. Therefore, yes, nepotism is alive and well in academia!

After learning of the possibilities for research projects, I selected the most innocuous and interviewed to work in the lab of Dr. Norris Hayden, a brilliant professor of Animal Ecology. I had a vague idea of what his research entailed. I knew his lab collected data from terrestrial and aquatic ecosystems by using something called a quadrat—a square frame made of plastic pipe. Mainly, the quadrat is placed onto a solid terrestrial or aquatic surface, and then counts of different types of slow-moving "critters" are conducted inside the perimeter and all kinds of statistical data are generated. Dr. Hayden studies how the populations of various organisms on the lower end of the food chain in the Massachusetts Bay ecosystems are affected by environmental pollutants. It is legitimate research, with a research grant and faculty privileges with Woods Hole Research Center on Cape Cod near Buzzards Bay.

My graduate assistantship also requires me to be the lab instructor for one section of the introductory biology course. This is actually okay since I have an interest in teaching as a profession. As they say, "the apple doesn't fall too far from the tree." In my case, it is two trees but not the "history" tree. A Master of Arts in Biological Sciences with teaching experience can translate into an instructor/lecturer at a community/junior college or a tenure-track position as an assistant professor at a four-year college.

Once it was settled that my mother was going to be a new faculty member, we had to find a place to live near Bedfordshire College. Human Resources at the college recommended some local real estate agents. After my mother met and interviewed a few, she settled on an agent from a local company called, get ready for it…Bedfordshire Realty. Original. Trudy Williams is an attractive, middle-aged, petite, power suit-wearing spitfire. Trudy shows us several properties in the village and the environs of Bedfordshire, but Mother and I are both curiously drawn to a property known as Doever Farm, a 300-year-old colonial farmhouse on the shoreline of Massachusetts Bay. It has been on the market for over a year, usually the death knell in real estate, but the price is very reasonable for a large Bayfront house. Older, historical homes always require more maintenance, but we are both suspicious of the low asking price. By law, the agent must reveal if there were any heinous crimes committed on the property, which could make it difficult to sell in the future.

Mother finally inquires, "Okay, Trudy, we know it's an old house, but why is the asking price so reasonable?"

In her unmistakable Boston drawl, she nervously said, "If you are asking if any crimes were committed on the property, I can assure you there were no mass murders, or the like committed in the last century."

Then she got quiet. We could tell there was more to tell us. Finally, after a few moments of hesitation, she revealed what was bothering her. "The original owner of the farm is famous, or infamous, whichever way you want to look at it. Elias Doever, the original inhabitant of the farm was executed as a witch in 1692, but he was not killed on the property. There have been reports over the centuries, as recently as two years ago, that 'strange events' have occurred in the house and the barn. But no one has ever been physically hurt as a result, thank God."

I intervene at this point. "First, isn't Elias a man's name? So, wouldn't that make him a warlock and not a witch? Secondly, what kinds of strange events?"

Trudy takes a subtle, but deep breath, and answers my query, "People have heard odd noises and…seen objects move by themselves."

"Sounds like a poltergeist, a noisy ghost, and not like the one that swallowed up Carol Anne into a TV," I state sarcastically.

This kind of information could have driven away your typical homebuyer but not an avid history buff like my mother. Her response is simply put and elegant, "What do you expect from a house that is over three hundred years old? A lot of history, both happy and sad, has happened here and the previous inhabitants have left a lot of their impressions here."

Doever Farm's acreage, a term never applicable to us when we lived in Boston proper, contains approximately 300 feet of frontage on Massachusetts Bay. Like the typical shoreline of Massachusetts, the bay coastline is a mix of coarse dark brown sandy beach and rocky outcroppings, lest we forget the term Plymouth Rock. A berm of tall sea grasses and shrubbery abuts the shallow dunes of brown sand and small boulders, which gradually disappear into the water. A wooden float is moored off the shore. The land is covered mostly with grasses and small shrubs, but a large forest of deciduous and conifer trees borders the property line to the north. It is getting near autumn so the leaves are already starting to change from their dark green color into a more faded green or yellowish green. Doever Farm and Bedfordshire will be stunning in the fall.

The house is a three-story Colonial/Georgian, the most popular type of architecture in the 1600s. It has two highly pitched roofs, known as gables, the term made famous by Nathaniel Hawthorne's novel *The House of the Seven Gables*, with an interconnecting straight roofline. Remarkably, the original wood siding is still there. Weathered to a dark-grayish hue, the elements over three centuries have had their influence on the wood and some of the more brittle boards are a stark light gray. The overall appearance of the outside of the house makes it look ramshackle, like the delicate driftwood facade could crumble in a fierce wind.

"The bones of this house are solid, wide support beams hewn from the hardest New England woods and consequently have been able to weather the course of time," Mother states as we enter the house, dispelling any doubts I had about the sturdiness of the house. We survey the first floor from the entryway.

"This was called the front room that was used to greet and entertain visitors. Very seldom were visitors allowed to roam a colonial house for a variety of reasons like spreading disease and were only permitted to enter the kitchen or dining room if they were invited to dinner," she describes as she walks through each room. We continue our tour of the first floor. Next to the kitchen is a small bedroom with windows facing the bay.

"I'll take this bedroom, if that's okay? Unless you want to hear me trudge up the stairs when I get home late from the bars in Boston or Salem."

"No, no, take this bedroom, perfectly fine with me," she states accommodatingly. Peering through the door to the left, she continues, "And this will be your bathroom then and a powder room for guests…Hmmm, the fixtures look fairly new, but the room looks like it was a tack room or a mudroom by the looks of the hardware left on the wall."

While ascending the narrow staircase, we hold onto the sturdy banister made of rough wood and come across a hallway that leads to three different doors. The middle door is opened first, and it is a bathroom. The fixtures look older than the ones in the downstairs bathroom; they are either reproductions or originals from the 1950s. There are two doors on either side of the bathroom. I open the door on the right and Mother opens the door on the left.

"Bedrooms," we announce simultaneously.

"I'll take this one," she states. "I bet this bathroom was an old dressing room that connected these rooms. Remember, there was no indoor plumbing until the late 1800s/early1900s, and this house must be two centuries older than that era!"

"That makes five fireplaces," Mother announces as she walks to the fireplace in her chosen room, placing her hand on the stone structure. "Fieldstone and mortar, fieldstone hearth, hardwood mantle. Solid materials."

I follow her through the adjoining bathroom into her bedroom and walk over to the window, multi-paned with lead-based dividers that open via a crank next to the windowsill. "Nice view of the bay. You can just make out the bell tower of Bedfordshire College."

We walk out to the hallway, and a distinctive creak is heard when I step onto a floorboard. I look down at the floor to investigate. It's loose and slightly angled upward, made like the rest of the floorboards throughout the house: wide, darkly stained planks with the original iron nails.

"It's a good thing that you took the bedroom downstairs, that board is a dead giveaway if you tried to sneak in," she declares. As we walk down the stairs, I notice the walls are covered with white stucco-like plaster and a chair rail made of thin, lightly stained wood planks like the rest of the house.

Mother opens the front door and walks outside. "Let's check out that barn I saw when we drove up." We walk toward a one-story barn on the southwestern side of the property. Mother grasps the side of the large rectangular wooden door and slides it to the left.

"Oh, a loft, I didn't expect that. The roof also has a higher pitch than it looks from the outside. Same large, support beams and stucco."

"This will make a great garage for the Mercedes," I say, referring to the Mercedes-Benz 280 SL I inherited from Nana Grace.

"My Volvo station wagon as well," she reminds me.

Doever Farm is ours.

****

A haunted farm? An executed warlock? I have to confess: I have a strange fascination for the supernatural, the occult. Since I was a little boy, I have been drawn to all things paranormal. It started when I heard my first ghost story, and rather than being scared, I wanted to know more about what ghosts were and what powers they possessed. *Casper* may have been a cartoon to some children, but for me, he was not just a "friendly" ghost but also a launching point for understanding the spirit world.

The Encyclopedia Britannica had sparse content, so I became an experienced researcher at our local library. From there my fascination grew. When I saw the movie *Dracula* with Christopher Lee, I was an instant fan of vampire folklore. I voraciously read all that I could about Vlad Tepes, the original ruler of Transylvania (now called Romania) from the house of Dracul (dragon in ancient Romanian), the man that Bram Stoker based his novel *Dracula* on. It was a big disappointment, as he was just another wacko, a bloodthirsty human barbarian who impaled his victims on stakes. However, the ancient legends of blood drinkers in the Carpathian Mountains of Transylvania piqued my interest enough to watch more similar movies made by the Hammer film studio from England. Watching other horror movies on the "Creature Feature" show on Saturday afternoons and late-night television led me to discover the films of Vincent Price, some loosely based on Edgar Allen Poe stories. Poe also became an obsession of mine in my early teenage years when I could understand his prose and poetry. The diabolical characters that Vincent Price portrayed, sustained my thirst for the macabre. The abundance of horror-genre movies produced from the early 1960s through the 1970s kept me busy in front of the television when I was a kid and at the art house theaters when I was older. However, this was just the tip of the iceberg.

When I watched these movies and read the supernatural lore, I not only absorbed this knowledge like a sponge and became an expert on all things supernatural; I also started to practice what I learned. Let me explain.

When I saw a movie or a television show with a character with special powers, like a witch or a warlock, or a Devil-worshipping zealot, I tried to emulate what I observed. Not in the sense that I was going to cook up a potion in a cauldron to poison an enemy or make someone fall in love with me or stick a pin in a doll to hurt someone. I am referring to the special "gifts" these characters possess to alter their space in the world. Telekinesis or psychokinesis—the ability to move objects with the mind, for example. When I learned about this power after watching movies like Stephen King's *Carrie*, I was instantly fascinated. I read as much as I could about the history of this power, concentrating on the books in which the authors gathered first-hand knowledge from folks like witches and gypsies who supposedly possessed this power. Apparently, if one had the ability, all they had to do was to concentrate without any distractions on the object they wished to levitate. Sounded easy enough.

When I was thirteen-years-old, I moved to the bedroom on the first floor that had an adjoining bathroom, so that I could have more privacy to do teenage guy things. One morning in late autumn, I overslept, and I awoke to hear my mother banging on my door to wake me up for school. I was having a particularly hard time getting out of bed that morning. It was still dark outside, and I was exhausted, probably from growth spurts (I grew four inches over three months). I knew the best way to wake myself was to turn on the light. In this room, the source of light is a hurricane-style lamp with an elaborate key-like switch located on the base of the lamp. The lamp sits on an antique dresser next to the door, so it will require me to get out of bed, walk over to the dresser, and turn the switch. In my sleepy daze from my comfy pillow, I stare at the lamp in the pitch-black darkness, concentrating on the switch, wishing it to turn clockwise. Suddenly, the sound of the switch clicks, and the room is illuminated. In total amazement, I jump out of the bed and walk over to the lamp to examine it. Turning the switch clockwise, I hear a clicking sound and the lamp's light is extinguished. Another turn, another click, and the light bulb illuminates again. I then turn the base over to see if there are any loose wires. Nothing is obvious. Setting the lamp down on the table, I concentrate on turning the switch again. In front of my own eyes, the switch moves slowly and methodically in a clockwise direction.

"Dorian, you are going to be late for school! Get in the shower!" my mother barks through the door. The switch stops moving. This is the beginning of my burgeoning telekinetic powers.

However, this power is not consistent. It seems to work only when I am alone and when I can concentrate without any distractions; much like the thought process of someone dealing with Attention Deficit Hyperactive Disorder (ADHD). Full disclosure: I have been diagnosed with ADHD, but I refuse to take Ritalin and cloud my thought process.

My present telekinetic ability also involves movements of small objects, almost like the way a strong magnet attracts small metal objects. After practicing for years, the best I can do is levitate a book or a candlestick about an inch above a flat surface. I have never shown anyone my ability, not even to impress a hook-up when we were both high and I could claim plausible deniability. "We were both baked, dude! Of course, I didn't levitate the bowl to your mouth"

The other power I discovered that I have is clairvoyance. Textbook definition of clairvoyance: perceiving things or events in the future beyond normal sensory contact. I also observed and read about this ability in my Saturday afternoon movies and library books, respectively. I am especially impressed with Edgar Cayce, the sleeping prophet. I forced my family to go to Virginia Beach, Virginia, one summer when I was fourteen years old, just so that I could visit and learn more about Cayce at the official Edgar Cayce Visitors Center and Association for Research and Enlightenment library. The library contains the archives of over 14,000 Cayce Readings and is one of the most revered metaphysical libraries in the world.

My favorite Cayce story involves the diagnosis of a young woman who was gradually going insane. A normal, healthy young woman progressively started to lose her mind and doctors could not determine why it was happening. Her family, desperate for answers as they watched the young woman descend into madness, consulted Edgar Cayce. After learning her name and concentrating on her presence, he told the family that she had an abscessed tooth in the upper row of teeth on the left side of her mouth. The infection and swelling are pushing against a critical blood vessel in her brain, preventing it from providing blood to her prefrontal cortex (the intelligence center of the brain). The family had her examined by a dentist. The dentist found the infected tooth, removed it, cleaned out the infection, and within a matter of days, she was back to normal.

My clairvoyant abilities started as minor displays of psychic ability that could easily have been explained as a coincidence. We are on vacation somewhere in Maine, when I was eight years old, and my family goes on a tour of an old historical mansion. As part of the tour, the docent explains how people in colonial times would deal with the long, hard winters in Maine, including the use of doors built on the second floor that led onto the first-floor roof that allowed the residents to escape from enormous snowdrifts blocking the ground floor. When we move into the master bedroom, the docent is about to explain how people kept warm in their beds during the winters when I impulsively interrupt her. "You use a bed warmer, a pan attached to a long handle that holds the embers from the fireplace. You close the top on the pan, and you slip it in between the sheets to warm them."

The docent is visibly impressed. Before she can retrieve the bed warmer to show the people on the tour, I interrupt again. "It is in the hidden cabinet next to the fireplace, hanging inside the door."

Apparently, this knowledge of an 18th-century antique and house disturbs the people on the tour, and they sort of exorcise me from the rest of the tour. We leave shortly thereafter. My mother surmises that I, at eight years of age, must have seen bedwarmers in one of my horror movies or read about them in one of my many journeys to the library. She has a harder time explaining why I knew that the bedwarmer was in a secret cupboard disguised to look like part of the woodwork around the fireplace. There are other instances as well. Besides the usual parlor tricks like guessing cards during games like solitaire, blackjack, or simple five-card stud, I can also find missing things and know when people are coming for a visit when they are near.

There is the case of my dad's missing watch. On my thirteenth birthday, I wake up to the sound of my dad tearing the house apart. He was searching for his favorite gold-plated Boucheron wristwatch he had bought in Paris while on their honeymoon. Suffice it to say, it has great sentimental value in addition to the monetary value of replacing it. He is late for a meeting with the dean of his college when he finally gives up and tells us to keep an eye out for it. It is at this time I have a vision. A brief glimpse pops into my head of an intersection of streets in our suburban neighborhood.

I then instruct my father how to find it. "When you are driving to work, stop at the intersection of Collins and Winchester and look around the curbside area of the roads. Your wristwatch is somewhere in the vicinity. The leather wristband is loose and when you held your arm out of the window when you came home last night, it fell off your wrist."

He looks at me in amazement and then asks me in his most polite British accent, "How do you know this, Dorian?"

"I just do."

Dad calls me an hour later to report that he found the wristwatch in the location I had described; it has a broken crystal, but otherwise, it is still working.

I was four-years-old when I first displayed the perception of knowing when people are near me when they are not visible. My mother's mother, Nana Grace

Carrier, was coming to our house in Boston for a visit in the latter part of the day, but Mother didn't know the exact hour; and I can't tell time at that age so that is irrelevant to me. When I sense she is near our house, I walk out onto our porch and sit on the swinging chair to wait for her. When Mother realizes I am not in the house, she eventually finds me on the porch. When she asks why I am sitting on the porch swing, I state that I am waiting for Nana Grace. As soon as my mother tries to explain that she isn't expected this early in the day, Nana Grace pulls up in her black Mercedes-Benz 300SL 4-door sedan. Years later, my mother told me that Nana Grace had called her the day before, saying she had an appointment at the beauty parlor in the afternoon and would be over after that. What Mother didn't know was that Nana Grace had the opportunity to have a morning appointment and booked it to have a longer visit with her adorable grandson, me. Nana Grace said that she tried to call to let us know, but the line was busy, and she was pushed for time to make her appointment. Coincidence? Perhaps. However, this wasn't an isolated incident. When my parents realized that I could predict the arrival of people and voiced concerns about this ability, I stopped sharing my knowledge. Unbelievably, my parents seldom ask me to use my special talents, not even for beneficial purposes. It is obvious that my unique abilities worry them.

Suffice it to say, I use my gifts for my own purposes. Telekinesis is quite handy when you want an out-of-town hook-up's keys to disappear from his jacket when you want the young man to stay longer than they had planned. Mysteriously, his keys reappear in the morning. Who needs to be the wiser?

****

My bedroom in the northeast corner of the house with one sash window on each of the northern and eastern walls gives me gorgeous views of the shoreline and the bay. The small fireplace is on the northern wall and the western wall is the common wall between the bedroom and the bathroom. I was able to get my Mission-style full-sized bed frame in the corner of the room, next to the bedroom door, which affords me a view of the shoreline while lying in bed. A tall bookshelf is next to the fireplace and a shorter one holding my boom box and tapes is in the corner between the windows. A wardrobe sits next to the tall bookshelf on the western wall; like all old houses, there is no closet in the bedroom. The off-white stucco-like plaster walls don't have any framed prints, paintings, or posters. Overall, my room looks more like a monk's cubicle than a gay 23-year-old man's, but my sparseness suits the house's era.

The only drawback is that there isn't enough space for my roll-top desk. That had to be placed in the family room. I have a few photographs in wooden picture frames on the desk: myself in my undergraduate regalia with my parents on either side of me; as a teenager with my parents in front of the Pemaquid Point Lighthouse in Maine; and at 11 years of age with my Nana Grace sitting on the porch of our house in Boston.

Nana Grace died when I was 15 years old. I really loved her. I think sometimes more than my parents. She understood me and had recognized my abilities when I was very young, but never mentioned them to my parents. She told me that I had inherited my "special" abilities from the Carrier side of the family. Nana told me that Grandpa John, who died from pancreatic cancer before I was born, could tell when someone was coming to the house and when someone was going to die. He predicted his cancer before it first appeared, but because it was such an aggressive type of cancer, standard treatment could not cure it even in its earliest stage. Because treatment would only buy him a few more months, he decided against chemotherapy and died three months later. Nana Grace said he was at peace with his choice when he passed and told her that he would see her on "the other side." She said he talked about the afterlife as if he had seen it himself. I felt comfort from that.

After a long morning of moving stuff into the house, I realize that I have worked up a sweat, the kind of stink reminiscent of the odor emanating from old men playing chess in the back rooms of Parisian cafes. A shower is in my near future, and I am curious to try the rain showerhead. Finding the box with my bathroom stuff, I pull out my toiletry bag, my towels, and a white, thick cotton robe. I love the feel of thick, lush cotton against my naked skin; I often lounge in my room or the house in a robe, with nothing else on underneath. I slip off my t-shirt, cargo shorts, boxers, and flips, and put the robe on. Hanging my towels on the towel rod mounted on the wall next to the pedestal sink, I place my toiletry bag on the sink. Retrieving my shampoo, conditioner, soap, and face scrub from the bag, I walk over to the bathtub, pull the white linen shower curtain and liner back and place my toiletries along the rim of the tub. I make a mental note to buy a shower caddy.

Turning the taps clockwise, the water comes

gushing out of the faucet. I test the temperature of the water with one hand and adjust the hot and cold controls to find the perfect temperature. I like it on the hot, steamy side. Once done, I turn the handle above the faucet and the water shoots forcefully out of the showerhead. It looks like a mini rainstorm. I slip the robe off, lay it on the toilet seat, and proceed to get into the tub, carefully raising my legs above the high rim of the tub.

My entire body is under the wide showerhead, the water gently pelting my body—amazing. I feel like I'm standing naked in a summer rainstorm. I apply a generous portion of shampoo to my hair. While massaging it into a thick lather, the water pressure suddenly increases. The pelting action becomes more intense, but not uncomfortable. The water pressure is massaging me more deeply and it feels good. Really good. As the water bullets the sensitive areas on my body, I start to feel light-headed, but not in a dangerous way, like I might faint. Rather, I feel ecstatic; like my cares are being lifted away and all I feel is pleasure. It reminds me of the euphoria I get when I smoke pot. Whatever is happening, I'm enjoying it.

As I caress my body, the sensation increases with my touch. Like small jolts of electricity. While lathering soap onto my chest, I notice my nipples have become fully erect. The stimulus is overwhelming, almost painful. I stop touching them and continue to soap my upper arms, shoulders, neck, and abdomen; the electrical stimulation radiating across my skin. Bending at my waist, I work the bar of soap down my thighs toward my kneecaps and onto my legs, cupping my calf muscles with the lather. The same intense tingling sensation spreads through my legs. Finding my ankles, I massage the heels of my feet, and the pain from my cracked heels dissipates with each touch. Lifting my foot into the air, balancing my helium-like body on my opposite lower extremity, I rub my hand along the sole of my foot. Waves of pleasure roll over the stressed muscles of that foot, making me smile and laugh quietly at the sensation. I repeat the same for my other foot, feeling the same waves of relief.

Lowering my foot, and standing in the tub, I don't feel any pressure exerted against my feet. I bend backward from the middle of my trunk, allowing the stream to continue to pelt the front of my body, thumping against my chest and abdomen. The water bouncing off my skin, laced with electricity, is becoming overwhelming. I sit down on the floor of the tub toward the faucet end to collect myself, the water still dancing over my legs and feet. I reach around and turn the taps off, and the water stops coursing through the showerhead, slightly dripping as the last few drops electrify my skin. As soon as I regain my composure, I stand up using the high rim of the bathtub and the wall to aid my ascension. Climbing out of the tub carefully, I achieve my footing and reach over to the towel rod to retrieve my towel. I gingerly dry the sensitive skin to avoid as much pain as possible. I grab the robe, walk out of the bathroom and into my bedroom. Collapsing on the bed, I instantly fall asleep.

I awake several minutes later exhausted and confused. I sit up in bed. I have only one thought: What just happened to me?

Chapter 3

Bedfordshire College
1st week in October 1992

I have had exactly five of those experiences in that shower since we moved to Doever Farm, which I now fondly refer to as my "Happy Showers." Initially, I thought there might be something in the water that might be harmful, like an abnormal concentration of heavy metals or something radioactive, but I eliminated that possibility soon after the first experience with two separate observations. First, the euphoria doesn't happen every time I take a shower—it has only happened a fraction of the time that I have taken a shower in this house. Secondly, I asked my mother if she had had similar experiences in the shower or bathtub. The conversation went something like this:

Me: Mother, when you have taken a shower or a bath, have you felt anything unusual in the water?

Mother: Define unusual.

Me: A strong tingling sensation.

Mother: Have you felt a strong tingling sensation, Dorian?

Me: Yes, but I am asking you right now.

Mother: No, I have not. There is a little iron in the water, but that is to be expected when you have a well.

Me: Yes, that's true. Okay, thank you.

Mother: Do you need to go see a doctor, Dorian?

Me: No, Mother, I am fine. Thank you.

During my analysis of this phenomenon, I have been trying to be objective, non-biased, and evaluate my situation as a scientist. In addition to the data I have already revealed, this is what I have deduced thus far:

1—The experiences are random. There has not been a pattern, like it happens every seven days or every twelve hours. Two of the experiences were days apart, and another two were weeks apart.

2—The experiences are not dependent upon my diet. I was concerned that maybe what I ingested may influence the symptomology, like consuming foods with high concentrations of digestible metals like zinc, magnesium, and iron may affect electronegativity. They had no effect.

3—The experiences have nothing to do with my current mood.

Maybe it is my unique physiology that interacts with whatever it is in the water? We are just as different on the inside as we are on the outside. What is clear is that I am exhausted after a "Happy Shower;"—all I want to do is collapse and go to sleep. Which makes it tough to go to school or work or do anything except sleep. Because of this, I have gotten into the habit of taking showers at night, or take a shower at school in the locker room before I get home. I am still planning on taking a water sample into my lab and testing for anything unusual. I need to figure out how I should broach the subject with Dr. Hayden.

****

It has been a month since the fall semester commenced. I am fully meshed into my graduate courses, my research with Dr. Hayden, and my job as a laboratory instructor for a lab section of Bio 101. Most of the students are freshmen, with a few sophomores repeating the course, and a few transfer students. This brings me to one student I have been watching: Tobias Blessing, who prefers to be called Toby. He's a junior who transferred to Bedfordshire College because he earned a partial athletic scholarship to play on the rugby team. What is remarkable is that he was not required to take a science course at his previous school, not even as part of the general education curriculum as a non-science major. That is not the case at Bedfordshire College. Every student must take one science course as part of the general education requirement, and like most non-science majors, the students elect to take biology instead of chemistry, physics, or earth science. I think it is because they had more biology in high school than any other science and because of the diversity of sub-disciplines.

Physically, Toby Blessing looks like he fell off the cover of a spring break catalog for Abercrombie and Fitch. He is shorter than me but built like a brick shithouse. From my examination of the tight t-shirts he favors, he has huge, broad shoulders, an impressive chest with "gum drop nipples," well-developed upper arms with deltoids that could cut cheese, and a flat stomach. His fondness for cargo shorts, so typical for our generation, reveals tree trunk-like thighs and muscular calves. His dirty blond hair is cut short in the back and on the sides, but the long slightly curled bangs in the front swoop down onto the right side of his face, just above his light brown eyebrows. Impossibly long eyelashes surround his ice-blue eyes. A broad nose, thick but well-defined, sensuous lips, an oval-shaped face, and a strong jawline complete his facial features. His overall complexion is a dark tan, but his cheeks retain a ruddiness when it is warm, which makes me think that he has some Irish blood. My "gaydar" pings when I've had to interact with him. I'm not sure why because he has said nothing that would suggest he's gay, and he certainly doesn't have any overt feminine characteristics. He's "straight-acting," a term that I loathe, but that doesn't mean he isn't a "Friend of Dorothy," as I've met plenty of butch boys who were eager to throw their legs up in the air.

Today's lab is the first animal anatomy and physiology laboratory: pithing and dissecting frogs. Let me explain what pithing a frog means. Amphibians have small brains, with a tiny thinking part of the brain; they primarily exist via a reflexive nervous system. In other words, they respond to stimuli instead of being proactive in their surroundings. For example, frogs do not go in search of their prey, like flies, rather, they wait for a fly to travel near them and then respond by extending their tongues rapidly to catch the fly. This reflexive type of nervous system is through the brain stem that is connected to the spinal cord. Inserting a needle into the back of the skull of a frog and wiggling it around inside the skull destroys the cerebrum of the brain, making the frog unable to control its body or feel anything, including pain.

However, the rudimentary brainstem connected to the spinal cord is intact and the reflexive part of the nervous system continues to signal to the respiratory, circulatory, and digestive systems. Making an incision from the base of its throat to the abdomen and then pinning the skin away from the frog onto a dissecting pan beneath reveals lungs inflating and a contracting heart. It's amazing to see how little the cerebrum of a frog controls its nervous system. This lab can make some students squeamish. I have a list of conscientious objectors who despise cruelty to animals, who identified themselves during the first lab and subsequently signed a statement that excuses them from their participation in the animal labs. Instead of the dissection, they must label and color illustrations of dissected frogs I provide for them.

Because we have three objectors, I have an odd number of students for a lab that requires partnerships. As my freshmen students pair up voluntarily, Toby is left without a partner. In order to investigate my intuition about Toby's sexual orientation, I quickly volunteer to be his lab partner. After distributing the anesthetized frogs in the dissecting pans, the dissecting kits, safety glasses, latex gloves, and the dissecting manuals to the others, I sit down next to Toby. With latex gloves on, Toby extracts the pithing needle from the kit and flips the anesthetized frog onto its abdomen.

Turning toward me, his hand is shaking. "I'm very grateful that you are my partner, Prof, but I'm not sure how much help I'm going to be during this lab."

Extending my gloved hand toward the one he's holding the pithing needle; I gently grasp it from his hand and answer his query. "You'll be fine. I am going to demonstrate how to pith the frog to the class; you will be doing the dissection." An expression of relief comes over his face.

At this time, I announce to the class, "Okay, everyone, come over here to this lab table. I am going to demonstrate how to pith the frog."

As I insert the needle into the back of the specimen's skull, the typical backdrop of voices expressing their displeasure rings out. Or the "scholar" who utters brilliant expressions like "gnarly." After moving the needle back and forth in the skull, I lift the frog above the dissecting pan so the students can see the uninterrupted respiratory movement in the belly. This prompts more geniuses to utter expressions like "rad" and "dope." I instruct students to try this on their own.

"Okay, Toby, it's your turn."

Toby lays the frog on its back onto the dissecting pan and picks up the scalpel. While reading the manual to determine where to make the incision, he places the scalpel blade at the base of the frog's throat and pushes it into the skin. Bloody fluid pours out. Abruptly, Toby drops the scalpel. Moving away from the lab table as he covers his mouth with his ungloved forearm, he runs out of the lab room.

"All right, everyone, continue with the lab. I will be right back," I shout while moving toward the door.

I look up and down the hallway to find Toby. He's not in the hallway. Entering the men's bathroom next, I realize he's not in here retching in the toilet, so I venture further down the hallway to the entrance of the science building. There, I discover him sitting on the steps, dabbing his face with his t-shirt, exposing his naked abdomen and chest. Seeing his amazing, flat tan stomach unclothed for the first time, his well-formed six-pack is as spectacular as I had envisioned from the impressions of his tight t-shirts. I'm desperately trying not to gawk. "Are you okay?"

"I'm really sorry that I ran out of there, but I don't

have a strong stomach. I hate killing anything...I just don't see why we must do something like this to any animal. I guess I should have signed the objector statement, but if my dad found out, he would have...well...it wouldn't have been fun," he explains as he struggles slightly to breathe.

"It's okay. Do you need to lie down? There's a couch in the graduate office," I state as I put my hand on his shoulder, platonically patting the top of his muscular deltoid. Toby shakes his hanging head. Sitting next to him on the steps, I go into lecture mode. "As to why we dissect animals, well, this is the only way we can find out how we work inside. If we understand the anatomy and physiology of less complex animals, then we have a better understanding of human anatomy and physiology. That leads to research that finds cures for diseases, conditions, and treatments for accidents that result in physical harm. Have you ever had antibiotics or an immunization? That was a result of animals being sacrificed for the good of science."

"Oh, I never thought about it like that. Hey, thank you for the offer to lie down, but I think I can sit with the other...objectors." He stands up, looking me in the eyes.

He stares at me, waiting for my response; I swear his beautiful blue eyes are staring into my soul. I am momentarily mesmerized looking at this Adonis. Quickly recovering my composure, I shake my head affirmatively and walk back into the science building. Toby follows me back to the lab room. I give him the diagram and colored pencils and tell him the room number where he can find the other students. Making the rounds to check how everyone is doing with the brain pithing and dissecting, it's obvious these students need a lot of guidance. I spend the rest of the period guiding them through this lab until it ends at 4:30 p.m.

After doing an initial sweep of the dissecting lab room, I walk to the room where the other students are completing their diagrams. Looking through the window in the door, the only student in the room is Toby. I enter.

Toby smiles and waves at me. "Hey, Prof! I'm almost finished coloring and labeling the dissection diagram. The other kids finished earlier as they had more time to do it, so I told them I'd bring their diagrams to you when I finished."

"That was nice of you!"

"I'm a nice guy," he responds, staring at me with those amazing eyes and grinning at me with that mega-watt smile. We are having a moment. Feeling slightly uncomfortable with what I'm thinking at the moment, I change the subject. "Don't you have rugby practice soon?"

"Yeah, I need to go," he states as he gathers his books into his knapsack.

I sense an opportunity. "Hey, are you going to have time to get something to eat before practice?"

"Maybe a sports drink, but I won't have time to get any food from the caf and eat."

"Well, you can't go to practice without having something to eat. What are you going to use for energy when you are fighting out of a scrum?" I scientifically, but sympathetically explain to Toby.

"Scrum? I'm impressed. Well, I don't have much of a choice."

"Yes, you do. We could get something quickly off

campus," I suggest.

He looks at me with a quizzical expression. I soon realize that I just crossed a line, and I momentarily forgot that he didn't have time to go off campus if he couldn't make it to the student cafeteria. I quickly recover.

"Wait here," I instruct as I leave the room.

Returning a few minutes later with my lunch sack, I hand it to him, "Here, you can have my lunch. I didn't have time to eat today because I was setting up the lab. I'm going home now, and I can get something on the way. It isn't much, just a ham and cheese sub and some potato chips, but it's better than an empty stomach."

Toby graciously accepts my lunch bag, smiling and staring at me, "Geez, Prof, that is really nice of you."

"Call me Dorian."

"Okay, Dorian," he bashfully concedes as he continues to dazzle with that smile. "I really appreciate it, but I need to go." He hastily picks up his knapsack and bolts out of the doorway. Then, stopping in his tracks, he turns, smiles, and waves to me. "Later."

"Later," I parrot back. I then think to myself: the ball is now in your court, Mr. Blessing.

Chapter 4

Doever Farm
1st week in October 1992

As a result of skipping lunch to set up the frog
dissection lab, and then giving it to Toby, I am
famished as I pull out of the faculty parking. This lot is
one of the few privileges graduate students have, as we
do not have to fight for spaces with the student
commuters. I have only lived in Bedfordshire for a
month, so I don't know where all the best eateries are,
but I do know about the local pizza parlor, Puritan
Pizza. It's an ironic title for so many reasons, the least
of which is that the Puritans were not Italian. But who I
am to condemn any business that exploits the incredible
hardships of a religiously persecuted people so that we
can have a slice at midnight when we get the munchies
from primo chronic? I stopped for a couple of plain
slices; this would hold me until dinner, which I was
having with Mother tonight.

It was a beautiful, crisp fall day, the kind of day in
New England when the autumnal colors are at their
most vibrant. All roads that lead to Bedfordshire are
lined with deciduous trees, including the streets in the
village. There are square plots of soil every ten feet in
the slate sidewalk, and a planted tree in each plot.
Planters, hanging baskets, and window boxes full of

orange, red, and yellow chrysanthemums adorn sidewalks, storefronts, and residences in town. Of the color palette displayed by the trees, I have two favorite leaf colors: the deep cherry red of the red maple and the fluorescent burnt orange hue of the bald cypress. I also like the intensity of the golden yellow leaves of the ash trees and the chocolate brown shades of the oak tree variety. The fall colors saturate the botanical offerings of the village of Bedfordshire and its environs so intensely that it almost looks like you are living in a surreal painting of the fall foliage. Or driving through one as I made my way onto the main highway out of town.

As I admire the landscape of the outskirts of the village, the brilliant colors of the trees contrast with the light and dark grays of the rocks composing the short walls bordering the back roads; the walls that were used by colonists during the Revolutionary War to hide from the Redcoats during impromptu battles. These stone fences crisscross all over New England and the original colonies, the most visible ones parallel to public roadways, acting as the original property borders. Doever Farm has three prominent granite rock walls: one to the west of our lot that borders the property along the access road, Granite Hill Road; one to the north on the edge of the forest; and one to the south beyond the barn that marks the property line with our southern neighbor. The stone fence bordering the access road is broken into two halves by the driveway. Each end of the fence bordering the driveway is punctuated with a column made of a variety of indigenous rocks and mortar, topped with a metal and glass lantern that originally held a columnar candle. I purchased orange columnar candles for Halloween.

Despite my admiration for this cascade of beautiful colors, I cannot get Toby Blessing out of my mind—his brilliant, toothy smile, the ice blue bedroom eyes peeking out from under the swoop of his dirty blond bangs, those impossibly broad shoulders, and that rippled six-pack that I would love to count over and over again. Truth be told, I fall hard for the all-American Abercrombie and Fitch type. It started back in college when I had my first sexual experience with a fraternity brother.

It was freshman year during the fall semester rush. I don't like to talk about my fraternity, as it was a dismal experience, but I will talk about Cal. Cal, short for Calvert, was a guy that I rushed with during the fall of 1987 at the college I attended in the southern United States. He was a big, handsome dude. Six foot three inches tall and built like a linebacker, which he was in high school. We were both biology majors and lived in the same dormitory but on different floors.

We met during freshmen orientation and teamed up for the scavenger hunt, a clever way of introducing the location of buildings and services on campus. We hit it off and decided that we would check out the fraternities together. We both liked one of the houses, known for its propensity for partying, and developed a closer friendship as part of the same pledge class and eventually as fraternity brothers. I always knew when he was coming to visit my dorm room by the sound of his flips smacking the floor as he staggered toward my room. We hung out while he smoked a cigarette, never talking about school or the fraternity. The conversations were usually about drugs, the music we liked, or the places we wanted to visit someday. Every Saturday night, we would meet at the frat house for our usual pledge class bullshit duties, and typically get drunk, high, or both and hang with and off each other by the end of the night.

For fall break, he invites me to go with him to visit his sister's university for an R.E.M. concert; they are supporting their new album *Document*. I jump at the chance, as R.E.M. is one of my favorite bands. After getting baked, we go to the concert. It's excellent, playing tracks from their new album, but also giving due diligence to previous masterpieces like *Fables of the Reconstruction.* When it's time to crash, Cal decides to sleep on the couch in the common room of his sister's apartment and I choose a sleeping bag on the floor next to the couch. We are both wasted, so it doesn't take long before we fall asleep.

At some point during the night, a six-foot-three-inch, 225-pound behemoth rolls off the couch and onto my right shoulder from the height of the couch. Suffice it to say, I woke up immediately. He slips behind me after he falls and doesn't get back on the couch. The next thing I know, a large tree branch-sized arm comes plopping over my waist. Then this arm moves so that it's pulling me closer to him. I wonder if he's still asleep and doesn't realize he's spooning me on the floor. His hand then moves across my abdomen and under the elastic band of my boxers. I don't resist him. His hand moves down between my legs. Again, I don't resist. The next thing I know, I'm on my back and my boxers are down around my ankles, being kicked away from my feet by his enormous foot. My thighs are apart, and he is lying in between them. He's fumbling with his shorts, pulling them down past his thick thighs, his legs, and his enormous feet. He lifts my thighs in the air with his hands. The sensations I'm feeling are amazing.

After he's done, he quickly gets up, pulls on his shorts, and lays back down on the couch, his face turned away from me. No kiss. Nothing. There's no kiss that night or anytime after that.

This is the beginning of a sexual relationship that lasts a few months. He would come to my room—since my roommate moved out after the first two weeks of the semester—chat, smoke a couple of bowls or a joint until we're both high, and then have sex. Afterward, he was always remorseful. Often crying and confessing that he's not acting like a Christian and that he's going to hell for what he did. He would eventually leave, not saying a word to me. He may have been ashamed of what we did, but I wasn't. I liked the sex. It was at this time I realized that I'm a full-fledged homosexual. What I didn't enjoy was his self-loathing and the crying. But as long as the sex was great…

Cal avoids me when we are at fraternity parties or in class, but always shows up at my door when he's feeling horny. This avoidance and the "not kissing" thing gets old quickly. I decide to end it, but my way.

On the night of the Founder's Party at the fraternity, he gets plastered on cheap keg beer. I get him back to my room where I easily convince him to smoke a bone with me to help his bed spins. He's totally inebriated and high, so I make my move, quickly getting his pants and boxers off. He looks at me quizzically as I part and lift his tree trunk-like thighs off the bed and drape his meaty calves on my shoulders. I grab my bottle of lube and a pack of condoms from under the mattress...when I stop. I look at him. He stares at me, confused as to what is happening. I then ask him if he wants me to proceed, telling him that I will stop if he doesn't. He continues to stare at me. I could see he is thinking about it. I pick up his right leg off my shoulder and lay it down on the mattress, intending to get off the bed, when he grabs my arm. Looking at me, he shakes his head in the affirmative and says, perfectly sober, "I want to know what it feels like."

I didn't do it, but I am curious about what a kiss will feel like. After I quickly plant a kiss on his thick lips, he turns his head away in protest and says something insulting about kissing and fags. I knew this was the end. We never talked again, not even at fraternity functions. He left school after that semester. Someone told me he's a state cop in Florida, his home state. I didn't care as I had moved on to the school I eventually graduated from: Boston Proper University.

****

Pulling the Mercedes-Benz sedan into the entrance of Doever farm requires a wide-angle turn as the driveway to the house is the original path used by horse-drawn carriages from the original path to the village. Mother doesn't have an issue with her Volvo since it's smaller than my car. I must slow down significantly to make the hairpin turn and then up and over the hill that somewhat conceals the façade of the two-story colonial. The driveway then makes another turn to the right as it passes along the barn that has become the impromptu garage when it rains and, more importantly, when the inevitable snowstorms we will have in the coming months. For now, we park both of our cars in the circular driveway in front of the house.

Walking through the front door, I am greeted with a distinctive, delicious smell. This delectable odor transports me to my childhood, watching my mother prepare and cook this luscious soup. I am speaking of the original Carrier family recipe for New England Clam Chowder. The Carrier family "chowda" is a recipe that has been passed down from its earliest carnation from generation to generation. This cream-based soup is popular in the Massachusetts Bay/Cape Cod area, but also one that has been a staple for the denizens who have had to survive the long harsh New England winters. Mother tends to make a batch of the chowder weekly during the colder months as it does not sit well or freeze well. Fresh Quahogs, also known as "chowder clams," are the biggest of the hard-shell clams and have the meatiest centers, which make them ideal for soup and for fried clams. Clams can be harvested all year long during low tide if the coastal area for clamming/clam digging is accessible. Clams provide an important source of protein and are low in calories, which is a good balance considering the excessive caloric content that butter, milk, and potatoes add to the chowder. I don't know what the secret ingredient is in the Carrier recipe, as Mother has been sworn to secrecy by members of the current generation; this ingredient will be passed on to the next generation only when the present generation is not able to make it for their families. I don't know if this is typical, but it is in our family.

I walk straight into the kitchen. Mother has set the large breakfast table for the two of us: large soup bowls with plates underneath, large soup spoons and knives, wine glasses, water glasses, a basket of sourdough bread and, of course, home-made oyster crackers in a small bowl next to each soup bowl. Mother is stirring the pot. "Dorian love, can you open the bottle of Chardonnay, fill the water glasses, and then go wash up so that we can eat? The chowder is ready."

I complete my tasks without hesitation and sit down at the end of the table. The chowder is in a china tureen designed with a slot on the side for a ladle. Setting the tureen between us, she sits down. "How was your day?" she asks as she ladles the soup into each of our bowls.

"We did the frog pithing lab today, and we had a guy, a big guy, almost faint on me. Had to run out of the lab room. You know what they say: 'the bigger they come, the harder they fall.' But he was really cute, a rugby player named Toby Blessing," I explain as I pour wine into each of our glasses.

"Oh yes, I heard some of the faculty talking about him. He transferred to Bedfordshire this semester, right?" Mother inquires as she takes a sip of wine.

"Yes, he's in my BIO 101 lab section because his previous school didn't require a science course to graduate. Can you believe that?"

"That is hard to believe," Mother responds incredulously.

"Anyway, I was able to take care of the situation, and no one got hurt. He was late for his practice and couldn't get any dinner, so I gave him my lunch. I wasn't able to eat because the lab setup required more time than I thought, anesthetizing the frogs was a bitch!" I elaborate.

"Language, Dorian! That was very considerate of

you but be careful. You are considered part of the supportive faculty, and the administration frowns on undergraduate-graduate relationships, especially when you are the instructor," she states in a serious tone.

"Warning taken," I sarcastically reply. "I will be careful." I didn't lie. I am going to be careful, but I intend to pursue whatever this is between Toby and me. Bold, I know.

After our scrumptious and satisfying dinner, I retreat to my desk in the front room to grade lab reports. The reports involve drawing the thoraco-abdominal viscera that students observed inside the dissected frog. The lab participants also had to answer questions about why they thought the lungs continued to inflate and the heart continued to beat. Most of the diagrams are spot on, indicating to me that most of the students were successful in their dissections. Lab questions are answered correctly, although, as per usual, the spelling of the anatomical terminology is vastly incorrect. Typically, successful lab reports, papers, and exams take less time to grade, and that is the case tonight: I finish earlier than expected.

I am pretty beat tonight. My low energy probably has something to do with waiting so long to eat after I missed lunch. When I mess with my metabolism, including my blood sugar levels, I usually pay for it with sleep. I decide to go to bed early. Undressing and then putting my cotton robe on in my room, I walk into the bathroom. Crossing to the bathtub, I set the water temperature in the shower: hot, but not scalding, as I feel a slight chill in the air. Flipping the handle clockwise to divert the water to the showerhead, I slip my robe off and hang it on one of the hooks I installed next to the toilet. Stepping into the shower, I close my eyes as the pulsating water strikes my face. There is no intense tingling sensation, just the usual pressure of the water jets. I'm not surprised as I had one of my "Happy Showers" the previous night. I never have them on consecutive nights. The steam from the hot water pounding out of the showerhead envelopes my body. As I lather my hair with shampoo, I think about Toby. Today, I pursued him in such an overt way that my mother even recognized my actions could be construed as crossing the ethical boundary between teacher and student. But I didn't care, and I don't care now…which is not like me.

I finish showering, dry myself off inside the tub, and grab my robe. I quickly cross the cold bathroom floor with bare feet and leave the steam-filled bathroom. Swiftly, I close the bedroom door behind me, walk to the short shelf and check to see that my alarm clock is set for 7:00 a.m. and at the appropriate volume. Dropping my robe to the floor, I quickly jump into bed naked to escape the chilly air coming through the ancient bedroom windows. I like the feel of flannel sheets next to my naked flesh, and since I am the only one on the first floor, it won't matter if I am commando when I walk to the bathroom to take a piss in the middle of the night. I turn over and lay on my stomach, with one leg extended outside the covers to regulate my heat-natured body temperature. The heat from the shower is still radiating within my skin, diffusing into, and warming the pocket of air my body creates under the covers. I quickly drop off to sleep.

****

I'm on the shore of the bay, and it's night. There's

a full moon illuminating the bay, the moon's visage reflecting beautifully on the calm, glass-like water. I spy the shape of the high-pitched gables of the house on Doever farm just over the berm. I look down at myself and realize I'm completely naked. I'm not cold, even though I feel the wind whipping off the water, sending small ripples across the smooth surface reflecting the moonlight.

Suddenly, I hear a quiet splash, and the smooth surface of the water is disturbed as something emerges. Straining my eyes to focus on the object, I'm surprised to discover it's a head, a human-like head. It is hairless as the moonlight reflects the smooth surface of the entire cranium, glittering underneath the moon's rays. The head turns toward me, and now I can see two small fluorescent blue lights emanating from the location of the eye sockets. The lights cast a deep aqua-blue color into the water surrounding the creature, like the glow that exudes from bioluminescent algae in the warm waters of tropical climates. There's a deep melodic sound that echoes in the air and sea. I am curious to see what this creature is, so I wade into the water.

I descend further into the bay, walking along the sandy bottom until I can't touch anymore. Now treading water, every crevice of my naked body is immersed as I propel upward to keep my head above the water. With a closer look at the creature, I realize the glowing lights are coming from aqua-blue irises. The being is swimming in the water, the light from its eyes illuminating the water so it can navigate the bay. I move even closer, and it quickly turns its head to look at me.

The contours of the being's striking, flesh-colored

face illumed in the light of the aqua-colored eyes. I can now discern more of its facial features. The hairless cranium is matched with a hairless face— no eyebrows or eyelashes. The facial features are reminiscent of the pleasing face of a young man: high cheekbones, a small nose with prominent nostrils, and a large mouth with very thin lips. It also has a weak triangular jawline and a delicate neck. I am now within feet of the being as I effortlessly tread water next to it, seeing my own nakedness bathed in the warm aqua light. The hairless head sparkles when the moist skin mixes with the aqua light and the moonlight. I can now detect that the skin on the cranium has a subtle scaly appearance, with layers of fine scales glittering in the light. He is perfect in an otherworldly sense.

I'm within a few feet of the being. Dropping its jaw, the mouth slightly ajar, the low-pitched melodic sound I heard before is now emitting from the creature's pursed lips. I stare into the luminescent eyes as it approaches me slowly, closing the space between us. Its face is now inches from mine. Diverting my eyes away from the light emitting from the intense aqua-colored irises, I study the delicate bone structure. It's now moving its mouth toward mine. The being is going to kiss me on the mouth. I don't resist its intentions. Its thin smooth lips finally touch mine and I feel a mild electrical stimulation passing on my lips. This buzzing sensation is reminiscent of the tingling sensation I have recently experienced in the shower. After several seconds, its lips move from mine, discontinuing the crackling sensation on my lips. I look at its mouth, still diverting my eyes away from his irises, and I attempt to kiss the being back. It backs its head away. I move closer. The expression on the being's face has not changed but we are moving further apart. Then suddenly it submerges, the glow of its eyes radiating under the water. I dive underwater, following the beacons of light created by the eyes. Getting closer to the luminescence in the water, I can now see that it has a human-like torso, and human-appearing upper and lower extremities. I reach into the water to touch the foot, the closest part of its body to my position in the water. I can almost touch it; my fingers are within inches of the heel and then…

****

I am on my back, a thin coating of water on my face and all over my body. I believe it must be perspiration. Becoming aware of my body's position in the bed, I notice the leg I use to regulate my body temperature is inside the sheets and quilt. Did I just have a fever dream? As a drop of liquid on the tip of my nose finds its way into my mouth, it doesn't have the familiar salty taste like my sweat. Lifting the covers to get a sample of my body odor, the scent emanating from my torso doesn't have the familiar pungent, musky smell. Instead, I smell the faintest odor of… seawater. Wiping my forehead, I place my fingertips onto my tongue. The mild taste of fresh bay water. I now remember my dream of being in the water off the coast of the bay, but…nonsense.

I pull the covers over my body and roll onto my belly. I extend one leg outside of the quilt, fluff the pillow under my head, close my eyes, and attempt to go back to sleep. Thoughts are racing through my head. It was only a dream. Of course, this is sweat on my body. What else could it be?

Chapter 5

Bedfordshire College
1st week in October 1992

Waking to the sound of the alarm this morning, there is no detectable odor in the room except the smell of my own body odor, remedied easily with cologne and or deodorant. I attribute my hallucination of a seawater smell and taste as an example of a powerful suggestion, created by the watery environment in my dream.

I quickly dress, dousing myself with deodorant and cologne, eat a quick breakfast of coffee and granola with fresh fruit, and roll out to school. Pulling the sedan into the Bedfordshire College parking lot at 8:45 a.m., I have plenty of time to make my research meeting in Dr. Hayden's lab. We are to discuss the location for the quadrat collection to support Dr. Hayden's latest research proposal. I take my seat at the table in the conference room. The lab team is composed of Dr. Hayden, a post-doctoral student named Jack Viceroy, who is studying Dr. Hayden's methods of data collection and analysis to set up his own lab in another research institution someday, two undergraduates who are on work-study scholarships in Dr. Hayden's Advanced Applied Ecology course, and me.

Dr. Hayden walks into the lab conference room. He

has a full head of gray hair with bangs that tightly curl sideways, a rather bizarre-looking trait, but it's completely natural. A silvery grey beard and mustache accentuate his round features. Gold-wired spectacles frame his kind brown eyes. A pipe in his mouth is a constant, whether he is puffing on it or just chewing on the end as he thinks about the next step in any facet of the research process.

"We are going to collect specimens from Witch Well Park, just outside of Bedfordshire, at the end of the week, Friday. I want to do as much quadrat collecting as possible, paying specific attention to the snail population on the rocks along the shoreline. We are looking at the abundance, distribution, density, and diversity of traits from marine snails. According to my models of pollutant spread, there is a secluded section of beach in the northern part of the park that is protected from the currents and will be an important collection point for species being adversely affected by pollutants in the Massachusetts Bay and Cape Cod environs. Dorian will head the collection team composed of our undergraduate research students and a few other students selected from my Advanced Applied Ecology course. I will meet with you at the end of the day to look at our results. I have directions to the park and maps as well for plotting quadrat distribution. Any questions?"

The room is silent. "Good, I will see you on Friday. I have to leave today for Woods Hole to discuss new grant proposals for the coming academic year, so I will be out of the lab until Friday."

For the rest of the morning, I work on the graphs for an article accepted in a peer-reviewed national journal, pending revisions. I decide to break early and get some lunch. The school cafeteria is a couple of steps above a high school cafeteria, but it does have a nice salad bar with lots of proteins like grilled chicken, chilled shrimp, chicken salad, tuna salad, egg salad, bacon, nuts, and seeds of all varieties to top off your vegetable masterpiece. I opt for a salad topped with bleu cheese crumbles, grilled chicken, tuna salad and Roquefort dressing, and a bowl of seafood bisque. One of the advantages to living close to the Mass Bay is that it is just as cheap to eat fresh seafood as it is to eat fake crab or lobster meat made from whitefish. I sit at a table and thumb through the latest version of the student newspaper, the *Bedfordshire Beacon*.

I am taking a bite of my salad when my vision suddenly goes blurry. I instantly recognize this visuospatial symptom. This is the precursor to a premonition. Just as quickly as the blurriness begins, the visual field becomes sharper, and then the subject comes into focus. It is Toby Blessing. He is walking in the quad outside with some of his fellow rugby players, heading toward the student center. I watch him and his friends walk up the stairs, through the double glass doors, and then walk down the hallway toward the cafeteria. Then my premonition stops. Looking at the doors to the cafeteria in anticipation, Toby and his friends finally make their appearance. I quickly look away, but not before Toby notices that I've seen him. Turning my head slowly back in his direction, I subtly study his form again. He's now peering at me, saying something aloud to his friends. Walking in my direction, I weirdly feel like an insecure 15-year-old being judged by the captain of the football team.

He saunters over to my table. "Hey, Prof!"

"Hey, Toby," I respond nonchalantly.

"I just want to say thank you again for giving me your lunch yesterday. That was really nice of you."

"I was glad I could help. I know what it's like to go to practice on an empty stomach." I lied; I never played team sports of any kind.

"Hey, are you eating alone?"

I nod.

"Do you mind if I join you?" he politely asks.

"Sure."

"Great, let me tell the guys to eat without me, and I'll get in line."

As Toby waits in line, I wonder why I had a premonition of him coming to the cafeteria. In the past, I have only had visions about blood relatives or family friends who were close to me since I was child. I did have a vision about the mailman once, but it was because he was sick and dying. I've never had a premonition of someone I knew for less than 24 hours, and it's obvious Toby is not ill or in danger, at least not right now. I speculate on the possibilities. Are my powers getting stronger? Or does this mean Toby is going to become very important to me in the future?

Toby returns with a mountain of food on his plate, a large salad and at least three beverages on his tray.

"Wow! It's hard to believe that sandwich and chips I gave you were enough!" I say as I look at him and his lunch.

"Yeah, well, to tell you the truth, your lunch got me through practice, but I went to the sub shop after practice and got a 24-inch grinder and a bag of salt and vinegar chips. I eat a lot of calories, but I also burn a lot of calories. It works out, right?" He thumps his tight abdomen.

I bashfully smile at him and shake my head slightly in the affirmative. He smiles back at my reaction, but then a serious expression comes over his face. He sits next to me at the table. It looks like he wants to say something but is having a difficult time getting it out.

"So, I was thinking, to pay you back for your kindness, I was wondering if you weren't doing anything this Saturday around eleven a.m., I have a rugby match, and then we, the team, the coach, some of the professors and parents…family members are going to Puritan Pizza afterward. I would like to invite you to be my guest."

Staring at those crystalline blue eyes, I can't believe this stunning man asked me on a semi-date. Smiling back, without thinking too long, I reply, "Sure, sounds like fun. I have never been to a rugby match." His face breaks out into a huge grin; there is that megawatt smile that first caught my attention.

"You said there would be parents there—do your parents ever make it to your matches?" I innocently inquire.

The grin on his face fades and completely disappears within seconds. He sits there in silence with the gravest expression, staring at the table. He glances at me a couple of times. Appears he's contemplating something. Gathering the courage to tell me something but struggling with how to say it.

"My mom died a couple of years ago, and I don't get along well with my dad. He cut me off last year, and threw me out of the house. That's why I transferred to Bedfordshire; they offered me a partial athletic scholarship, so I don't have to borrow the full amount to pay for tuition, books, room, and board."

"I'm so sorry about your mom, Toby. Were you close?"

I clearly see tears welling in his beautiful blue eyes as he shakes his head affirmatively. He quickly wipes the corners of his eyes and clears his throat. I contemplate if I should ask the next obvious question.

"Why did your dad cut you off?"

Toby looks me straight in the eyes. "Because I told him I was gay."

I am sure my expression may appear as taken by surprise, but I am not. I already knew the answer to my question before I asked it.

Abruptly, Toby stands, grabbing his tray with both hands. "If you don't want to come Saturday, I understand…I…"

I grab his arm gently before he leaves. "I would love to come Saturday," I state, looking him right in the eyes as I say it. We are having another moment.

That megawatt smile cracks through his serious countenance into an expression of joy. "You would? Okay, great!" He then releases his tray and sits back down.

We enjoy the rest of our lunch together, chatting about innocuous things, getting to know each other better. I now have an idea why I had a premonition about Toby entering the cafeteria. I also knew I would have many more. The question I was now asking myself: Is Toby Blessing the love of my life?

Chapter 6

Bedfordshire: Witch Well Park
1st week in October 1992

This morning, Mother and I traded cars, but just for the day, as I was not going to drive the Mercedes-Benz sedan into a waterfront park that is possibly swamped with muddy, soft earth. Like all fine-tuned motor vehicles, they can be quite temperamental, and I don't need sand or mud to find its way into the motor or other vital parts. The car is a classic and I want to keep it that way—at least until I sell it someday. The Volvo is perfect for this kind of rugged terrain, which turns out to be manageable.

Driving to the extreme end of the park to get as close as possible to the shoreline, I pass the structure that is the namesake of this park, presumably the "witch well." A circular well about ten feet in diameter bordered by a short wall of stone and mortar about three feet high. Next to the well is a large weeping willow tree with a circular platform built around the circumference of the tree with benches. The platform also houses a sturdy iron and wood stand, to which a metal engraved plaque is attached. Next to the plaque is a display box made of wood and iron with a glass front. The box contains mounted diagrams of a contraption that I can't identify and text that is too small to read from the road. I make a mental note to stop and investigate this display on my way out of the park after we finish collecting our data.

The undergraduate students are waiting for me in the parking lot closest to the shoreline where we are to conduct our quadrat study. Taking the map of the park's coastline, I divide the designated area into sections for each partnership to collect the data. There are ten students, so we have five teams. Being the experienced researcher, I will work alone. The northernmost section, approximately 90 square feet of rocky shoreline inside of a natural inlet, the most sheltered region (from the current of the bay) and consequently, the region we are most interested in collecting within, is the region I assign to myself. This is also the largest of the plots on the map and the most secluded naturally.

I refresh everyone's memory of how we collect our samples. Using the square quadrat made of PVC pipe (three feet by three feet in length), lay it as flat as possible onto the rocky shoreline and make counts to determine density, diversity, abundance, and distribution of marine snails. Once everyone understood the parameters of the research method, I assign the plots to each partnership.

Walking toward the northernmost part of the rocky shoreline, I cross over a large dune of seagrass and shrubs that virtually hide the cove I am studying. Looking at the bayside as I climb over the dune, I unexpectedly see a bald head bobbing above the surface of the water. Surprised by the sight, I misstep on the soft, uneven terrain, causing me to shift my focus to the topography of the dune to gain my balance. Quickly, I recover and look toward the water, but the bobbing head is no longer there. At the apex of the dune, I look up and down the shoreline searching for the person who could be in distress. I stride quickly to the edge of the shore and look out onto the inlet. Nothing. I justify that it was an optical illusion, a reflection on the water, and continue with my prescribed task.

My clipboard for recording data is attached to a thick piece of nylon cord tied to one of my belt loops. A large horseshoe-shaped boulder that juts into the water will be my starting point. I drop the quadrat onto the rocky shoreline next to the large boulder. I record my counts. As I extend my hand to flip the quadrat over to record data from the consecutive square, the quadrat flips over without my touching it. There is a mild breeze; however—these quadrats are built with small weights in the pipe to anchor them to the underlying surface. I reach for the quadrat again; it flips over again without my touch. I think about flipping the quadrat backward toward me; the quadrat moves as I mentally command. I look around to see if anyone is in the area witnessing this extraordinary event. No one is visible. I spend the next thirty seconds flipping the quadrat in multiple directions using my mind, only to have it return to the original area next to the boulder. This is the most impressive display of my telekinetic powers to date. To add to my amazement, I realize there is a certain frisson in the air; the hair on the back of my neck is standing on end. I continue to collect data using my powers of suggestion to place each quadrat, making sure the coast is clear before executing each move. Needless to say, the process of recording data from the quadrats is progressing rapidly.

As I am recording from my sixth quadrat, my

vision gets blurry. Another premonition is imminent. My visual field sharpens. I am looking at myself on the shore, as if I were in the water looking toward the shore. My vision stops. Quickly, I turn my head toward the water. There is no one there. There's a sense of excitement in the air that I felt before. I continue to stare, waiting for someone or something to emerge. Nothing appears in the water for the rest of the time that I am collecting data.

I finish collecting data for ten quadrats, 90 square feet, covering the entire area of the rocky shoreline in the cove. Leaving the inlet, I go in search of the other five teams. Each team had smaller plots of shoreline to record from, so they should be completing their counts soon. The teams are conversing in the parking lot. At this time, Dr. Hayden's Volkswagen bus arrives in the parking lot. Noticing that the sun has dropped in the sky, I look at my watch; it's 5:30 p.m.

"Dorian, how is the collecting coming?" Dr. Hayden inquires.

"I think we are finished."

"Really? We're finished with the data collection in that northern cove?" he asks, with doubt in his voice.

"Yes, the shoreline was relatively even, so that made it more conducive for the quadrat placement. I did it by myself"

"Color me impressed. Okay, I am eager to see what we got, especially in your section."

I collect the quadrats, clipboards, and species keys and place them on the front seat of the Volvo. After I congratulate the teams of students, they load into their vehicles and leave the parking lot. Dr. Hayden and I are alone.

"Your counts look good, but we'll know more when we crunch the numbers. See you on Monday. Good work," Dr. Hayden comments to me.

"Thanks. Hey, I'd like to check out the plaque and display near that stone well before the sun goes down. Do you know anything about it?"

"Yes, that is a must for every new resident of Bedfordshire. You must check out the ducking well."

"Ducking well?"

"Hmmm, meet me over there and I'll explain," he answers.

I drive a half-mile or so until I spy the well and the willow tree and park. There are no other cars in the parking lot next to the well. Dr. Hayden parks his bus next to me. We walk over together to the platform around the tree, step up onto the platform, and walk over to the glass case with the mounted diagrams. Looking into the case, a series of drawings mounted to the back of the case look rather ancient, as if they were extracted from an old book. In the first drawing, there is a crowd of people surrounding a body of water, and a chair extends above the water at the end of a pole. There is a person tied to the chair; it looks like a woman, as the being is wearing a dress, but it has a beastly face.

In the next drawing, the woman tied to the chair is submerged in the water up to her chest. Her mouth is open as if she is crying out in pain. In the third drawing, the pole and the body of water are present, but she is no longer visible. Presumably, she is under the water, most likely drowned. After I survey the drawings, I read the banner at the top: "The Ducking Stool and its Dark History." There is a lot of text accompanying the drawings, which I begin to read when Dr. Hayden chimes in with his synopsis.

"The ducking stool was used to determine if someone was a witch. They would tie the person accused of witchcraft to the chair, lower the person into the water by the pole attached to the chair, and see how the accused responded to being ducked under the water after a man of God blessed it. According to the practice, if the accused was in league with the Devil, the individual would not be able to stay submerged in the holy water and float to the top of the water when the ropes were released from the chair. If the accused did float, then the person was found guilty and branded a witch or a warlock. The guilty were then sentenced to death and eventually were either hanged, crushed to death under a board loaded with stones, or burned at the stake. If the accused stayed submerged, then the soul was pure but, unfortunately, the individual most likely would drown. As you can see not a lot of good options. This horrible practice was famous in medieval Europe, and as most Americans know, Salem Township. Bedfordshire has a small part in this dark history of religious hysteria. That plaque over there lists the names of the unfortunate souls that lived in the village of Bedfordshire and died at the hands of the religious zealots."

I walk over to the plaque and read the inscription:

This memorial is erected for those citizens of Bedfordshire who died during the religious hysteria that swept through the colony of Massachusetts from April 1692 to February 1693. Let us never forget those who died from religious persecution so that we may never repeat the mistakes of the past. May God have mercy upon those souls that died at this well: Sara Goode, Abigail Warren, Elias Doever, and John Putnam.

Dr. Hayden comments on the plaque: "Elias Doever, he is the original inhabitant of your house. His is the saddest case. Legend has it that his reaction to the water was so violent that William Putnam, the constable, and judge of the witch trials in Bedfordshire, ordered that his body be buried in secret in unconsecrated ground. This was very bad, as Puritans believed that being buried in ground that was not blessed would prevent the soul from ascending into heaven, provided the person deserved to go to heaven. The story of Elias Doever and his secret burial spot of "sour ground," where pure evil exists, has been a story that has been told many times over a campfire to the Bedfordshire children to warn them of what can happen if you stray from a Christian existence."

Something draws my focus toward Elias Dover's name on the plaque. Suddenly, my vision blurs and I feel an intense pain in my chest.

****

The picture sharpens and I am now looking at the stone well before me, but it is dark; it is nighttime. There is a crowd of people holding torches surrounding the well as a dark-haired man stripped of his shirt is being lowered into the water of the well, tied to a ducking stool. Without warning, there is a massive eruption in the water, a waterspout explodes into the sky. A body, face down, surfaces to the top of the bloody water. The mutilated body floating in the water turns over and I can see the macerated anatomy of the chest cavity and the distorted face of the man. Suddenly, his eyes open and are horribly bloodshot

62

with black irises. His mouth opens, and a high-pitched shriek escapes from his throat…

****

I faintly hear Dr. Hayden's voice. "Dorian, what's the matter?"

I am lying on a wooden platform. Dr. Hayden's face is hovering above mine. I feel nauseous, and about to be sick. Rolling over, I vomit over the side. Recovering, I place my hands on the platform and push down to sit up. Dr. Hayden grabs my shoulders firmly, lifting me to my feet.

"Here, let's get you over to the bench."

Standing on wobbly knees, he gently directs me toward the tree, to one of the benches circling the willow. I drop down to the bench, leaning my head against the back of the bench and the trunk of the willow. My head is spinning. However, the nausea is gone. Lifting my head, I wipe a speck of vomit from the corner of my mouth. A few minutes later, I am feeling better.

"I don't know what came over me. I was reading the plaque as you told that story, and I got tremendously dizzy and felt nauseous."

"Do you need to see a doctor?"

"No, I think I'm fine now. Must have been something I ate…or maybe I'm coming down with something. But I think I can get home. I only live a few miles from here. I wanna get out of here. I just need a few more minutes," I reason.

"All right, I'll wait with you until you're ready to leave."

"Thank you, Dr. Hayden."

A few minutes later, I was able to walk on my own.

Dr. Hayden insists on following behind me as I drive home to ensure that I arrive safely. I don't have to worry about the wide turn into the driveway, as I am not in the sedan, which helps my queasy stomach. I hear the singular beep of his horn as I maneuver the driveway around the barn. I glide the car quietly into the circular driveway. Once through the front door, I make a beeline into my room where I collapse on the bed, asleep in a matter of seconds.

Chapter 7

Bedfordshire College
Rugby Pitch
1ˢᵗ week in October, 1992

I awaken much later than I normally do this morning. There are a few reasons I will sleep later than 7:00 a.m.: sickness, a hangover, or still under the influence of drugs, like weed. Even though I got sick, I would not consider what happened to me at the witch well as a sickness. The dizziness, nausea, vomiting, and other symptoms characterize a vestibular imbalance. Anyone who witnessed me collapsing at the well would say that I'm in dire condition, suffering from something serious, and would need to go to the emergency room. I scarcely think anyone, except maybe another psychic, would equate my condition to the aftereffects of traveling back in time to see a man being drowned in a well. That was a first, by the way.

I've had flashbacks of things or events that have happened in the past, but I was never in the story like the psychic occurrence that happened yesterday. The bed warmer incident, for instance. I could see the scenario in my head of the live coals being dumped into the pan of the bed warmer, the pan's top being closed, and then inserting the bed warmer in between sheets, but I wasn't in the bedroom in a past era. Nor was I next to the fireplace in the past when I told the docent the bed warmer was stored in the secret cabinet next to the fireplace. However, I was at the well when Elias Doever, I presume he's the man on the ducking stool as my vision started when I read his name, was murdered. I was there when his chest exploded in the water, and present to see the expression on his face post-mortem. I was part of the crowd holding the torches, and I became nauseous after seeing the horror of the mutilated chest anatomy and the terrible contortions of Elias Doever's face.

I spent all night recovering from the nausea and disequilibrium I experienced at the well. I ate nothing after I got home, and slept all night long. I'm now left with the question of why? Why did this happen? I expect to pick up vibrations of tragic events from old houses and other historical places. Being sensitive to tragedy isn't out of the ordinary, but physically reacting to the vivid emotions of tragic events is new. Again, why there? Are the impressions left behind by Elias Doever and the other unfortunate villagers so strong that they pierce the barrier between the past and present? Perhaps, but I've visited sights that were much more tragic, including World War II concentration camps in Europe, and never felt and lived what I did at the witch well.

It was 9:00 a.m. and I had two hours to get ready and be at the rugby pitch for Toby's match. Doable. I take a shower, not a "Happy Shower," unfortunately. Time to select my outfit for the day. Picking my clothes is taking longer this morning. Lots to contemplate. Was he inviting me as a friend? Or was this a date? Semi-date? Or was this simply an invitation to a group event to repay a nice gesture? I decide not to think about his invitation and dress the way I would go to any outdoor event in autumn in New England: acid wash jeans, duck boots, a flannel shirt, and a wide-striped rugby pullover. Like most guys in the late 80s/early 90s, I have at least one Ralph Lauren rugby shirt, even though I never played rugby or desired to play rugby. This is a wardrobe essential for any young gay, or straight man for that matter, not unlike the Abercrombie and Fitch cargo shorts being a necessity. I look the part of a rugby fan. I bring a gray hooded sweatshirt with Bedfordshire College embroidered in big block letters on the front, just in case it is colder than I expect. I'm still queasy, so breakfast isn't high on my list. I manage to down a mug of coffee and a couple of blueberry Pop-Tarts.

"Where are you going so early on a Saturday morning?"

Gulping down most of my Pop-Tart, I answer, "Rugby match."

"Oh, what has brought on this surge of school spirit? Is it Toby Blessing?" Mother asks with a tinge of annoyance in her delivery.

"He invited me to go and then to a pizza party afterward…for giving him my lunch."

"Dorian, you must be careful! People will get the wrong impression, even if it's all innocent. Which it is, right?"

"Yes, of course." It is technically true, even though I'm not being completely truthful about my intentions.

"This is just not like you…and I don't mean being interested in sports. You are always careful about…the rest of the world isn't as liberal as we are. Not to mention the ethics of a teacher-student relationship that is outside the academic…please be careful."

"I will." Now I'm slightly annoyed. Not just about what she said but that she's right. Mother sees I'm coming close to crossing a line and yet I'm still pursuing Toby. I'm surprised at myself…but I don't care.

I fire up the sedan and ride into the village. There are a couple of games going on at the same time at the college practice fields, but the match is on the rugby pitch that was built especially for the Bedfordshire Braves rugby team. Bedfordshire College's rugby program has a very good reputation, one of the better teams in the small liberal arts college league in New England. It's widely accepted that the only way to make a living in the sport of rugby in America is becoming a coach for a collegiate rugby team. Perhaps that will change in the future, but as it stands, the only chance to play professionally and make a living wage is to play on a team in Europe. Consequently, competitive rugby in America is solely an amateur collegiate club sport, but it carries a certain amount of gravitas with preppy young men attending the Ivys, New England liberal arts colleges, and selective high schools.

I make my way into the Bedfordshire cheering section, recognizing a few of the faculty, predominantly from the Physical Education, Recreational Therapy, and Physical Therapy Departments. Faculty, undergrads, parents, and other family members are holding their banners and pennants emblazoned boldly with the Bedfordshire Braves mascot, the head of a Native American warrior. I greet those that I recognize. To prepare for my first rugby match, I skimmed a few books in the school's library. I know something about how American football works, so it helps somewhat when trying to understand rugby.

After settling in my seat next to faculty members, I spy Toby on the pitch. If you're thinking: "What does a typical rugby player look like?" Your answer: Toby Blessing. Strapping wide shoulders fit perfectly into the navy and yellow striped rugby jersey with the blue Bedfordshire Brave mascot face embroidered over the left breast. Navy shorts with yellow stripe piping on the side vents snuggly hug his thick thighs and backside. Black shin guards, cleats AKA "boots," and a white mouthguard complete his uniform. I'm happy to see he's protecting that million-dollar smile. His dirty blond hair bounces just above the white collar of his rugby jersey as he runs up and down the field. Toby's fellow teammates are also stunningly handsome young men. There must be an unwritten rule that you have to be drop-dead gorgeous to play this sport. Seriously, it looks like there are future Abercrombie and Fitch models auditioning on the Bedfordshire rugby pitch. I am half expecting to see Bruce Weber clicking his 35 mm on the sidelines, creating his artistic black and white stills for *fashion* catalogs or one of his infamous homoerotic coffee table books.

It's near the end of the second period of the match, and it's tied. The crowd is electrified at the possibilities of the last few minutes. It's the last play of the match when the ball is thrown to Toby. He manages to catch it, but unexpectedly, it bounces out of his hands. Desperately trying to recover the ball, Toby's fingertips are fumbling to grasp it. With all my might, I concentrate on the ball, making a trajectory back into his palms. Suddenly, he's holding it again and running toward Bedfordshire's in-goal area. He reaches the first line and places the ball on the ground just before the goal line. He scores! The Bedfordshire crowd erupts into cheers. Fans scream with glee and hug each other. I turn to a few of the faculty and give the customary hand slap. Toby's fellow players are jumping up and down around him, patting him on the shoulders, head, back, and buttocks. Bedfordshire has a goal kick which could add another two points to the five points. Toby scores. The conversion kick is successful. Bedfordshire wins the match 14 to 7.

Everyone from the stand rushes onto the pitch, hearing the official final score announcement. Students, faculty, parents, and other family members greet, hug, and exalt the players. Many come up to Toby to shake his hand or hug him. I stand back and watch Toby collect his accolades from his fans and his public, but he's looking around for something or someone on the pitch. He locks his eyes on mine, adoring his grandeur. Smiling at him, I raise a pretend champagne glass in the air while I mouth "Well done." He makes his way toward me through the crowd, accepting praise from his fans along the way. He's finally in my space. I gleefully extend my right hand to shake his when he collides into me with that barrel chest and wraps his arms around my back, pulling me close to him with my right hand sandwiched in between us. I instinctively wrap my free arm around his broad back and shoulders, feeling the contours of his muscular back.

He whispers into my ear, "That last goal was because of you."

Suddenly, I'm feeling disbelief and shock while still in his embrace. How did he know that I helped him psychokinetically with that last catch? Or is he just making a gesture? I pull slightly away from him. "What do you mean?" I ask innocently.

"Because I knew I had someone that was here just for me…it makes all the difference," he sweetly explains.

"Oh." A sigh of relief escapes me.

"I need to shower and change. I already told the coach that you are my guest, so you can go over to Puritan Pizza with the rest, and I'll meet you there. I'll get a ride with one of the guys."

"Okay, I'll see you over there. Great game, by the way."

He smiles slyly toward me. "Thanks!" He then walks back into the throngs of his adoring public.

After dropping off some research data in Dr. Hayden's office, I arrive at Puritan Pizza to faculty and family members celebrating at their selected tables. As I wait for Toby, I'm approached by two of the Physical Therapy (PT) program's faculty, one of the few clinical master's programs we have at Bedfordshire College, about my role as a graduate student in the biology department. I sense they are curious why I'm here and who invited me. I play along. After telling them of my work with Dr. Hayden and my assignment as a lab instructor in Bio 101, I explain that Toby is in my lab section, and he's the reason I was invited to this party. They seem a little disappointed by my answer regarding Dr. Hayden's research. I get the feeling they were hoping that I was working in clinical research related to health sciences. The PT school has a decent reputation and many of our biology majors select the PT track option in hopes of being accepted into the program. To amuse myself, I inform the PT professors that I plan to pursue a Ph.D. so I can teach biology courses to students interested in pursuing health science programs like PT. It's not entirely false, but it's not entirely true either. I have not thought that far ahead.

Toby eventually shows up with some of his compatriots. He's wearing a gray Bedfordshire Athletic Dept. t-shirt tightly secured to his broad chest, a pair of camo cargo shorts, black flips, and an army green baseball hat, turned backward of course. The typical athletic frat boy gear. We called these guys "jockstraps" in high school. There are the usual high fives, congratulatory handshakes, and pats on the shoulder from people who had not been able to connect with Toby on the rugby pitch. I'm enjoying the sight, ginger ale in hand when he finally makes his way over to me,

"Sorry it took me so long to get here. They wanted to take pictures for the school paper and yearbook, and…"

"You have nothing to apologize for!" I state emphatically. "This is your day; enjoy it."

"Did you get something to eat? I see you have a drink."

"I woke up this morning with a queasy stomach, so I don't think pizza is the best thing for me right now. Hence, the ginger ale," I explain.

"Oh, I am sorry to hear that…are you coming down with something?"

"No, I don't think so, more like…something didn't agree with me. I actually might cut out of here soon to recover from…whatever it is."

"I wish you would stay, but I understand. Hey, do you like movies?" Toby asks, changing the subject. I nod.

"Would you like to go to a movie tonight? The Bedfordshire Regal Theater has only one screen, but it plays like six movies at a time, and tonight's choices are *A River Runs Through It* and *Army of Darkness*. Did you want to see either of those? It would also give us more time to…talk, not so noisy like it is in here right now."

My better judgement tells me I should just call it quits here, but there was the premonition in the cafeteria and something else that's pushing me to get to know Toby Blessing better.

"Sure. Let's go see *A River Runs Through It*. I've heard it's good."

"Great, I'll find out the time and call you. What is your phone number?" he says as he fishes a piece of paper and a black ballpoint pen out of his duffle bag. Turning his head away from me I can finally make out the emblem he has on the front of his baseball hat: the head of the Bedfordshire Braves mascot.

"Listen, let's meet for dinner before that, and not pizza, cafeteria food, or my limited culinary skills. Maybe we could go to an 'All You Can Eat' buffet," I suggest after I give him my phone number.

"Yeah, that sounds great."

"I was kidding! Let's go somewhere where we don't have to carry a tray or order by a number. My treat to celebrate your triumphant goal today," I propose enticingly.

"Okay. I'll ask around to find the nice restaurants in town, and we'll figure out when to meet when I find out the time the movie is playing."

"Great," I say, subtly parroting Toby's earlier

response.

****

As soon as I walk into the house at Doever Farm, the phone is ringing. I walk into the kitchen, looking around to see if Mother is anywhere in the vicinity, and then pick up the receiver. "Hello, Leeves Residence."

"Can I speak to Dorian please," the voice inquires.

"Speaking."

"Oh, hey! This is Toby, I didn't recognize your voice on the phone. I was checking the movie times on the bulletin board in the dorm when I saw an advertisement for a showing of *The Rocky Horror Picture Show* tonight in Salem. First, do you know what movie I'm talking about? If you have, would you be interested in seeing it with me tonight?"

"Yes, I'm familiar with *The Rocky Horror Picture Show*. I've seen it twice; and yes, I would like to see it again with you. Hopefully, it's not a midnight show," I state, as it will be a late night after driving back from Salem Township.

"No, it's at ten p.m., which means we'll be out of the theater between eleven-thirty or twelve, depending if it starts on time. We can catch dinner in Salem. A teammate of mine from there told me to go to an Irish pub called Clancy's. Is a pub, okay?" Toby hesitantly inquires.

"Yeah, I love pub food, and if they have Guinness black on tap, I'll be happy as a leprechaun," I say in my cheesiest Irish accent.

Toby laughs. "That's awesome! Great accent! So, it takes about thirty to forty minutes to get to Salem, and Clancy's is close to the Salem Bijou, the theater where it is showing, so how long do we need for dinner?"

I take control of the plan. "All right, I'll pick you up at seven-thirty, which will give us two hours to get tickets, in case they sell out, and eat before show time. How does that sound?"

"Awesome! Where do you want to meet?"

That is a good question. Did I want other students to see me with Toby for the second time in one day? Meeting him outside of class cannot be easily explained away like the pizza party after the rugby match. I decide it's better if we meet in a neutral location that's also not necessarily a Bedfordshire College hangout. "Toby, why don't you meet me at the post office in town at seven-thirty? I think it's about a mile from campus, and on the way toward Salem."

"Okay, I'll see you then, dude!" he blurts out excitedly.

I burst out laughing. It only dawns on me at that moment that he looks exactly like the kind of guy that would use the word "dude," the ubiquitous term for a guy who can be used as a term of endearment between men or the perfect response to any question asked of you when you're stoned. As soon as I stop laughing, I respond, "See you tonight."

I hear him laughing as well. I've never heard him laugh. It's a nice laugh. Higher pitched, like his speaking voice. I think to myself, if he sings, he is definitely a tenor. I hear the click on the receiver as Toby hangs up the dorm phone. I move into my bedroom and lie down on my back on the bed. I'm still recovering from yesterday, but my stomach feels better. I can't help but think about my date with Toby Blessing, the star player for the Bedfordshire Braves rugby team. Yawning a couple of times, I drift off to sleep.

Chapter 8

Salem Township
1st week of October

An hour later, I'm up and in the shower, anticipating a "Happy Shower," and dress for my rendezvous with Monsieur Blessing. Accordingly, for *The Rocky Horror Picture Show*, depending on how interactive the audience would be, I dress in my best "Time Warp" outfit that will also not be too conspicuous in Clancy's Pub: black jeans, white button-down long sleeve broadcloth shirt, black leather bomber jacket, wide black leather belt and black lace-up army boots. After using the requisite amount of mousse in my hair to keep my bangs vertical, I'm ready. Mother is not home yet from Boston, so I don't have to explain anything to her about where I'm going, or who I'm going to meet. A relief of sorts. But I also don't have anyone to critique my look. Looking in the mirror next to the front door, I approve. I bounce out the front door, down the steps, and into the sedan. Firing up the engine, off I go into town.

I pull up next to the curb outside of the post office. Toby, sitting on a bench outside the post office, quickly jumps up when he recognizes me behind the steering wheel. He's wearing the standard A and F uniform: a tight "muscle" short-sleeved white polo shirt, tan cargo shorts, a navy-blue web belt, and brown leather Docksiders. He looks perfect. As he approaches the sedan, I lean over the passenger seat and open the door.

"Whoa, is this your car?"

"Yes, my grandmother left it to me when she passed," I state as I peer through the open door.

Toby steps into the car and carefully slides inside while looking at the dashboard and the fixtures, searching for the seat belt. Watching his face as he absorbs the nuances of the Mercedes-Benz, I start to laugh.

"You're cracking me up, Toby. I don't think I've ever seen anyone react to this car quite like you are right now."

"Dorian, this is a classic! I've never been in a classic car," he says with awe in his voice.

"It's a classic all right, which means it sucks in gas mileage. Good thing I live close to the college, or I would spend all my stipend on gas!"

"Yeah, I see your point, but, dude, you're always in style when you go anywhere in a car like this," Toby states with a decidedly serious tone as he deliberately rubs his hand along the smooth wooden dashboard.

"All right, point taken. Let's go, I don't want to have to rush when we get there." I pull the sedan away from the curb and head down the main street to the coastal highway.

****

After parking on the street about a block from the theater, we get our tickets and walk to Clancy's, which happens to be a block in the other direction from the theater. Clancy's is your typical Irish pub. The entrance is dominated by a long ornate bar made of some type of dark wood, probably walnut or oak, with a large mirror mounted on the wall behind the bar that reflects the labels of all the different brands of liquor and the five beer taps, including the unmistakable brand of Guinness. The booths and tables are made from the same dark wood as the bar; the banquettes and chairs are fitted with green vinyl seat cushions. The rustic look is complete with exposed brick walls, large wooden chandeliers with electric candle holders hanging from the ceiling, and opaque glass sconces. With my appetite finally returning, as I've not eaten all day, we order a generous amount of typical Irish pub fare: pints of the black, soda bread, two orders of thick-style onion rings, and a Shepherd's Pie with a gravy made from Guinness draught for each of us.

While we eat, Toby and I engage in conversation that one would consider typical for a first date or first acquaintance (I'm still not sure what to call this evening) for college-aged people: Toby's proposed major, the research subject of my graduate studies and most importantly, our future aspirations after we finish our education. It turns out that both of us have ideas about what we'd like to do but are without a clear path. Toby tells me about his options.

"I'm majoring in Physical Education, surprise, surprise, and I'm not sure if I want to continue with graduate studies to become a collegiate rugby coach, or just finish my bachelors and become a high school rugby coach, which a pretty narrow field. I've also thought about applying for the Physical Therapy program at Bedfordshire. The PT professors who come to the matches have hinted to me that if I pass the pre-requisite courses in biology, chemistry, and math, I'll be accepted with at least a partial scholarship, regardless of my GPA. So that's something else that could be on the horizon."

"Ah yes, favoritism is alive and well at Bedfordshire," I contribute in a snarky manner and then suddenly I remember I also benefit from this generosity. I change my demeanor.

"How about you?" Toby asks with a hint of curiosity.

"Well, I think I would like to teach biology at the collegiate level, whether that means I pursue a Ph.D. or not, is still up in the air. I can get a full-time position at a junior college with a master's degree in biology for sure, but if I want to pursue any kind of tenure-track position or research program, I must get a Ph.D., if not post-doctoral training. That's another three years minimum after I finish my master's degree in two years, provided the doctoral institution will allow me to transfer the credits from my master's degree. I'm not sure if I'm ready for that kind of commitment," I explain matter-of-factly.

"I hear you!" Toby exclaims.

From our conversation, it's clear that we're both "journey" types, instead of "destination" types. After we finish eating, there's an uncomfortable silence that develops between us. When we're discussing topics like life goals, or our favorite movies, while we ate, we do well. However, there's a subject that neither of us has broached yet, and it's obvious that it's coming to a head. I finally break the glass, "So…. if you haven't figured it out and are still wondering, I'm gay as well."

With my announcement, Toby lets out a big sigh, vocally expressing what's on his mind through his exhalation. "Oh my God, thank you! I didn't know how to ask you. I haven't known many gay men, authentically gay men, and not bi-curious dudes, so I haven't had a lot of experience with the coming out stuff."

"Well, to tell you the truth, I've never technically come out because I've never considered myself 'in' the proverbial closet," I state haughtily.

"What do you mean?"

"Like a lot of boys going through puberty, I messed around with other boys, and liked it. Whereas most of my partners grew out of our mutual masturbation sessions and began to pursue the 'pussoir,' I did not. I liked the sex I had with boys and didn't treat it as the convenient outlet that pubescent boys regarded it as. You know, it's a 'phase,' or some other kind of bullshit explanation. I didn't see any reason to stop having sex with boys, and I certainly didn't see any reason to start having sex with girls. I…"

"So, you never dated girls?"

"Oh yeah, I dated girls. I just didn't have sex with them. I would go with friends who were girls to all the major dances like Homecoming or Prom, but it was purely platonic. I made sure they understood that from the beginning."

"You never felt up a girl, or you know…?"

"Nooooo, I'm what is called a 'Gold Level Gay' in the gay subculture. I've never touched a 'vayeena,'— sorry, that is my word for a vagina, much less had my 'boy' in one. But I'm not a 'Platinum Level Gay:' a gay man that was born via Caesarian section, so he can claim that he never touched a vagina, not even at birth!"

Toby is staring at me in amazement, wondering

what I've just revealed, scarcely able to say anything. "Wow! I didn't know…just, just wow."

"What about you? What level are you?"

"If you are asking if I've ever touched a 'vayeena,' as you call it…oh yeah! I was captain of the rugby team, BMOC. I was expected to have many girlfriends. I've touched quite a few and had intercourse as well. So, I guess I'm a what…a bronze-level gay?"

I burst out laughing at his assessment. Toby looks confused at first at my reaction, but then he gradually smiles that mega-watt smile and blurts out laughing, air noisily rushing out of his wide nose. He continues his diatribe about his experience with the other sex, "It actually feels pretty good… being inside of a girl. That part I didn't mind, it was the affectionate part that I didn't feel. I never wanted to hold her before or after sex, just have my orgasm and…leave. Oh, I also didn't like…you know…going down—"

"Stop!" I interrupt. "I get the idea."

"I actually had a pregnancy scare with one of my girlfriends, but she was just late. After that scary dose of reality, I've worn a rubber every time whether it's with a girl or with a guy!" Toby confesses.

"So, you had sex with guys in high school?"

"Yeah. I joined in quite a few circle jerks with my teammates when we were drunk and horny enough. I gave a couple of my friends oral, multiple times, when we were stoned, and one of them returned the favor a few times. I did it because I liked it; they did it because they claimed they were horny and drunk or stoned or both. You know, the usual justification/explanation of shame afterward, 'It feels good, man, you know a mouth is a mouth, but that's all it can be.' Their attitudes sucked, but the sex was amazing while it lasted."

Fascinated by this revelation, I ask Toby, "Do you see these guys anymore when you go home?"

Suddenly, Toby's smile is gone, and he gets very quiet. Bowing his head, he stares into his pint of Guinness. After a few moments, still staring at his beer, he breaks his silence. "I can't go back home anymore. My dad threw me out of the house last year."

"Oh shit! That's right, you told me your dad cut you off. I should've remembered. You don't have to—"

"It's okay. I...strangely, in the short amount of time I've known you, feel comfortable enough to talk to you about it. It was during winter break, and I hooked up with that teammate that I messed around with in high school. We were in my bedroom. Thinking that my dad would be out of the house for the afternoon, we got stoned first and then started to get into some intense messing around. Unfortunately, Dad forgot something he needed for work, came home, and heard us laughing in my bedroom. He opened the door to see what we were doing and caught us naked in bed. He closed the door immediately and yelled at us from behind the door to get dressed and for my friend to get the hell out of the house. He then told me to pack whatever I needed and to be out of the house by tomorrow night. He told me...I was no longer his son." Toby stops talking. Tears form in his eyes, spilling over his eyelids, rivulets streaming down his face.

"Luckily, it was toward the end of the break, so I went back to the dorm one day early. The school let me stay, but they also informed me that my dad had called and told them he was not going to be paying for whatever was left of my tuition or room and board. The school arranged for a work study program for me to cover the expenses that he had not paid for, but it was too much…you know the rest."

"Do you have any family who you can stay with during the holidays?" I inquire gently.

"I have an older sister who lives in Maine, in Damariscotta, a little town on the intercoastal. She works in Bath, in the Naval Shipyard. She's an engineer who works on battleship design. I stayed with her during spring break and this past summer. I worked as a camp counselor for, what else, a rugby camp, so I only slept in her guest room for a few weeks. She's on my side in all of this, but it's still hard for her because she wants to maintain a relationship with our dad. He's not in great health."

Now I was the silent one after hearing Toby's tragic story.

"Do you have a relationship with your dad? Do you have a sister or a brother?" Toby inquires, wiping the remaining tears from the corners of his eyes and cheeks.

"No, I'm an only child. I still talk to my dad, but he lives in England. My parents are divorced, so it isn't easy having a long-distance relationship," I answer. Toby is silent, lightly bobbing his head up and down in quiet agreement with my statement. I sense he's not interested in talking about any of this anymore.

"Okay, enough of the morbid talk. Let's order another pint and…." I stop talking when I notice the time on my wristwatch. "Oh shit, the movie starts in fifteen minutes. We need to get the check." I motion for the waitress, and she brings the check over on a small black tray. I pull my credit card out of my wallet and place it on top of the check. "Dinner is on me."

"Oh no, you already bought the tickets, you can't buy me dinner too!" Toby reaches over to grab the tray.

I hold his hand to stop him from getting the paper check. "Please, let me do this," I state as I look directly into his eyes.

"Can I leave the tip?"

"All right, if that'll make you feel better. Do you have seven dollars, that should be enough?"

Our meal was hearty and satisfying, with no residual stomachaches as a result of the intense conversation. Toby jokes that I ate as much if not more than he did, and that I can never make a joke about how much he eats ever again. I laugh with him. It's our first "thing."

Walking to the theater from Clancy's, we are surprised to see there's a line about halfway down the block from the Salem Bijou. "Wow! I'm glad we bought our tickets in advance. I hope we can get good seats," I state.

"As long as we're sitting next to each other, I don't care where we sit," Toby comments. As I turn my head to look at him, he's already looking at me. His sincerity is genuine. I smile. He smiles. We're both smiling as we enter the packed lobby of the theater. I spy two seats together on the aisle, about seven rows back from the screen. Pointing in the direction of the seats, I say, "Let's get those two seats over there. I like to sit on the aisle." Realizing I am suggesting what I want, I query, "Is that okay, or is that too close to the screen?"

"Sure, I don't mind being that close," Toby answers as we make our way to claim the seats. Toby moves into the row first and then lets me have the seat on the aisle. We sit down together on the cracked leather seats, and I position my legs slightly into the aisle. Observing my posture, Toby comments, "I can see why you like the aisle seat. I never noticed how long your legs are, because they look like they are in proportion to the rest of your body. I don't have to worry about that. I have stubby legs."

Looking at his powerful thighs, partially concealed by the cargo shorts, I examine them to see if they are as short as he asserts. They're not out of proportion to his stocky, tight body, in my opinion, but I decide not to say anything. Looking around at the other members of the audience, I notice that many are dressed as the Rocky Horror characters: a large proportion dressed as the dark gothic Magenta, the top-hatted chorus girl Columbia, the ghoulish Riff-Raff and a few young men in lingerie and fishnet stockings competing to be the Transvestite from Transylvania, Frank N. Furter.

"It looks like we have a lively crowd; this is going to be fun!" I state, "Okay, so I assume neither of us is a virgin…"

"Excuse me!"

Taken back by his outburst, I explain carefully while turning my head in his direction, "I mean we have both seen Rocky Horror before, right?" But instead of seeing a confused look on Toby's face, I meet that mega-watt smile. "Oh! you little shit!"

Toby chuckles. "I've seen Rocky Horror five times. You?"

"This will be my fourth time. I saw it all four times in Boston; I'm curious to see what Salem Horror fans will do."

As if on cue, the house lights go down in the

theater, and the crowd squeals with delight. The Rocky Horror patrons do not disappoint. The audience is familiar with the snarky responses and comments to key lines in the film that have become standard practice for this cultish, subcultural phenomenon that celebrates sexual freedom. During "Time Warp," most of the costumed audience members ran up to the lip of the stage in front of the screen and emulated the strange but not difficult dance, in anticipation of the arrival of Frank N. Furter, or in this case, Frank N. Furters. Watching people play the characters of the movie being projected behind them has always struck me as being both liberating and narcissistic. I've never had any desire to "bend my knees inside and let the tailwind blow" while dancing in front of a theater full of fans, but I never had any problem with anyone else doing it.

The next song in the movie, after the refrain for "Sweet Transvestite" is "The Sword of Damocles," sung by Rocky Horror, the blond muscle man creation wearing a gold lamé bikini brief that barely covers his generous anatomy. This is my favorite "visual, without being too visual" in the movie. The live action Frank N Furters are doing their part, instructing Riff Raff to throw the switch to animate the titular hero, but there is no one on stage playing the muscle-bound creation, no audience member brave enough to wear next to nothing in front of a room of strangers. To say that I'm disappointed is an understatement.

"No one is playing Rocky. You would make a great Rocky Horror!" I playfully suggest to Toby.

"You think so?"

I'm about to comment when Toby suddenly stands up from his seat and pulls his white muscle shirt off, dropping it on the seat that has snapped back into a vertical position. Before I can get a chance to assess how amazing his body is, he looks directly at me, making me feel self-conscious for ogling, and then jogs up to the front of the theater. Finding his spot on the makeshift stage, the crowd goes nuts when they see him, whistling and blurting out catcalls. I can see Toby's half-naked body perfectly as the light from the projector illuminates his form. I'm now seeing what is connected to the flat washboard abs, the guns, and his tree trunk-like thighs; and it doesn't disappoint. His naked chest and shoulders are exactly as I had imagined them: big, well-muscled and smooth with just a hint of chest hair in the valley between his amazing pecs, each half crowned with a light brown areola and gum drop-shaped nipple. His exquisitely built chest transitions seamlessly into his abs. The creases of his skin signaling the boundary between his six-pack abdominal area and the tops of his thighs are sharply defined.

I spy the top of his plaid underwear just above the draping waistline of his cargo shorts and just below a hint of blondish short curly hair sprouting from his naval. Toby's stocky body gyrates provocatively to the pop song playing on the screen when the Frank N Furters stop chasing him around on the lip of the stage. I cannot stop laughing or making catcalls as he attempts to lip-synch to the lyrics, cheekily posing his magnificent physique while showing off his guns, basking in the spotlight. The song finally ends and before the transvestites can manhandle him, presumably to drag him off to their lair, he waves to everyone in the audience and leaves the stage. The adoring audience responds with a huge round of clapping. He walks back to his seat while watching me admire him. I hand him his shirt. He sits back down in the folding seat after slipping his shirt on. I cannot stop smiling. Neither can he, as he continues to pant from the activity on stage.

"That was…that was amazing!" I compliment my date, "You continue to surprise me!"

"Yeah? Well, that was the first time I ever did that. I dunno, it just felt right," he said in between breaths.

Feeling like my smile muscles are exhausted, I lean back and focus my attention on the movie. All of sudden, I feel fingers lightly treading across my left forearm resting on the armrest, settling on the back of my left hand. Turning my head to look at Toby, I turn my left hand over so that my fingers are now curling upward. Spreading them apart slightly, his fingers slide in between mine. Squeezing my fingers to feel his, I subtly move our enclosed fingers from the armrest onto the cargo shorts covering his right thigh. Relaxing in the seat, we watch the rest of the movie holding hands.

Walking back to the car, I saunter in front of Toby when we reach our destination and open the passenger car door for him. "Your car, Mr. Horror."

Toby giggles, rotating his head in disbelief, then slides into the seat. Closing the door, I bow to him through the window and then quickly move to the driver's door, open it, and slide into the seat. Toby is about to snap his seat belt closed when I grab his hand, causing him to let it go. He promptly turns his head to look at me. Staring into his eyes, I slowly raise my hands toward his face. Cupping his jawline with the palms of my hands, I lean forward so that our noses are nearly touching each other. Looking into those azure eyes momentarily, tilting my head deliberately, I move my mouth toward his lips. My lips softly resting on his, I slightly contract my mouth, and my lips are enveloping his lower lip. Moving my mouth slightly higher, my lips are now surrounding his upper lip and his lower lip is sliding across mine. I open my mouth slightly, letting the tip of my tongue glide across his upper lip. I hear a slight moan come from the back of his throat. Opening his mouth, his tongue finds mine and lightly massages it inside my mouth. I release a quiet sigh as we explore each other's mouths slowly, delicately. Slowly breaking apart from each other, saliva glistening on our lips as we separate from each other, we stare into each other's eyes. Instantly, our lips come together again as we re-engage our kiss, more forceful than before. We continue to explore until we both feel our breaths getting more rapid.

Toby abruptly breaks away from my mouth, licks his lips, and stares at me. "That was really nice, but if you get me started up, I won't be able to stop, and I think that could be dangerous."

Breathlessly I respond, "Agreed, but I wanted to have our good night kiss here as I don't think it would be a good idea to kiss you outside your dorm. Unfortunately, we can't go back to my house, as my mother is on the faculty and…"

"Understood, and we don't want to rush things, right?" Toby inquires cautiously.

I respond thoughtfully, "Yes, I think…yes, we shouldn't rush this. By the way, you're a good kisser; bad kissing is a deal breaker for me."

"So, you want to see me again, Professor Leeves?" Toby says with a fake, almost girlish uplift in his voice.

"Smart-ass," I respond, smirking. I move in again

for another soft kiss, just lips touching lips as we both close our eyes. "That'll be the last kiss, last anything…tonight."

I move my head away from his, smiling and gazing into those gorgeous eyes. Starting the car, I check the rear-view and side mirrors and pull away from the street. After shifting the car into gear to cruise the rest of the way home along the coastal highway, I rest my hand on the gearshift as I am accustomed to doing when driving for a long time. Unexpectedly, I feel Toby's hand slide underneath mine, enclosing his fingers in between mine so that we are holding hands like we did in the theater. I look over to him. He's resting his head on the back of the car seat. His eyes are closed, and there's a slight grin on his face. I find myself grinning too as I turn my head toward the windshield. I concentrate on driving this precious cargo back to Bedfordshire.

Chapter 9

Doever Farm
2nd week of October

I pull into the circular driveway of Doever Farm at
2:45 a.m. A late night by any standard, but it's Sunday,
and I don't have any commitments, so I'll be able to
sleep as late as I want or need. I'm whipped. I had some
difficulty staying awake as we drove back from Salem,
having to roll the window down a couple of times to
keep from dozing off. I walk directly to my room, strip
off my gothic gear, and slide into my flannel sheets. As
I writhe under the sheets, the extra soft cotton
stimulating every inch of my naked skin, I inadvertently
start to think about Toby and the kisses we shared
tonight. The soft lips, his darting tongue probing my
mouth. I'm starting to get aroused. *Not tonight.*
Normally, after a date with a hot guy, and if it didn't
culminate in a "release," I wouldn't be able to sleep.
However, I know I can get to sleep with no problem
tonight. I justify to myself that I can satisfy myself in
the morning, maybe through a "Happy Shower," as I
have a new sexual totem to think of when I'm doing the
deed: Toby Blessing, Rocky Horror, rugby player
extraordinaire. I start to imagine him naked and…*No,
go to sleep.* Once I commit to this state of mind, I fall
asleep in seconds.

****

I'm standing on the shoreline of the Massachusetts Bay at Doever Farm, the silhouette of the house evident in the moonlight. I can feel the sensation of the breeze against my naked body. As quickly as I realize that I'm in the dream again, I look out into the water in search of the alien creature with the luminescent aqua eyes. Right on cue, a faint glow deep beneath the water begins to increase in intensity as something emerges closer to the surface. The smooth glittering head of the creature pierces the pool of glowing aqua light as the being breaks the surface. The head bobs above the surface. Blinking eyes extinguish the bioluminescence producing a strobe light effect in the water. The small scales on the bald head catch and reflect the moonlight as the creature shakes off the water streaming down its face. The being turns its head in my direction and opens its mouth. The same low-frequency moaning sound emits from his mouth that I heard in my other vision, and I am drawn into the water as before. I eagerly swim toward this strange, beautiful creature, using his eyes and the moonlight as a guide. The water caresses my nether regions as before, but I cannot detect any temperature in the water like the previous vision, which brings me back to the reality that this is just a dream. I'm within feet of the creature when it closes its mouth, quickly moves toward me, and kisses me as it did before. The electrical pop of its lips stimulates but doesn't hurt. Realizing it is much more forward in its actions, I attribute this to his familiarity with me from the previous encounter in my dream, and perhaps, the brief sighting near the inlet in Witch Well Park.

Gradually, it moves away, tilting its head toward

the water. In a split second, it descends into the water, the glow of its eyes submerging. I take the tilt of the head as a directive to follow it, and I dive into the water following the glowing signpost. The light is getting further away from me. I desperately try to follow the glow into the depths, but the need to exhale builds, and I swim toward the surface. Furiously, I paddle my arms and legs, slightly panicked as I realize that I'm in very deep water. Finally, reaching the surface, my lungs about to explode, I exhale out of my mouth with tremendous force; the air streams through my vocal cords producing a deep guttural vocalization. Taking a deep breath through my mouth to restore the oxygen capacity in my lungs, I whip my head to drain my face of the excess water dripping from my hair onto my lips.

As I look toward the shore, I cannot see the roofline of Doever Farm in the moonlight. I'm no longer in the bay waters off Doever Farm but have emerged into another body of water. I look up and down the shore for any sign of where I am. Searching for the creature, I cannot detect any aqua bioluminescence in the water. Realizing that I won't be able to tread water indefinitely, I swim closer to shore until I can touch the sandy bottom beneath me. With the resistance of the sandy bottom, I walk the steep incline of the shelf as my naked body emerges above the calm shallows. Walking onto the sandy shore, I continue my trek and ascend the coarse sand of the short dunes. At the zenith of the dune, looking toward the landscape for visual clues as to where I am, I spy a faint circle of lights flickering and changing shape, slightly obscured by a large structure with tendril-like arms. Refocusing my sight on the large structure, it's now evident that the tendrils are wispy branches of a tree blowing in the breeze, casting shadows against the flickering lights. The composition of the branches and trunk is familiar to me—it is a weeping willow. A weeping willow, the flickering lights, fire floating in the air. Torches! Unexpectedly, I get a sick feeling in my stomach.

Crouching, I double over and land on my knees on the soft sand. It suddenly dawns on me: I am kneeling on the dunes outside of Witch Well Park and this is the night that Elias Doever drowns in the well. But how? How did I get this far from Doever Farm, and more perplexing, how did I get transported into the late 17th century?

Without warning, an explosive sound comes from the well. My head turns toward the sound, and in the firelight of the torches, I can see a column of water rising into the air. Watching it in the moonlight, it is arcing in the direction of the dunes. The waterspout is headed directly for me! I drop to the dune, flattening the front of my naked body against the coarse surface of the sand, anticipating the impact of the heavy, fast-moving column of water. I feel droplets spraying my back, butt, and lower extremities, but there is no crushing weight of water pushing me into the dune, and drowning me on land. The intense sound of water smashing into the calm waters of the bay follows. I bend my neck slightly to see the crashing waves. A whirlpool of short waves dissipates as the source of falling water disappears. I stand on the apex of the dune to observe the aftereffect. The furious waves lapping the shore decrease in size with each succession until the whirlpool evaporates completely and the calm surface of the water returns.

Without warning, a weak glowing light emerges where the eye of the whirlpool stood. The luminescence is an aqua color, and its brilliance is increasing in strength. The head of the creature with the glowing aqua eyes emerges. Opening its mouth, its wail disturbs the quiet of the night, and I am drawn to the sound as before. Running down the dune onto the shore, and then into the water until it's deep enough to dive, I swim toward the sound and light. Toward the creature with the face of a young man, using its glowing eyes as a beacon. Desperate to reach it for answers, I want to know what has happened. Why am I here in this century?

I'm within feet of the two glowing eyes, when suddenly, the creature dives into the water, the aqua glow following it into the depths. Diving into the water, I follow the light. I can see that its human-looking foot is within my reach. I extend my hand toward its foot and grasp it. The creature snaps its leg to loosen my grip on its foot. Turning toward me, the lights from its eyes are beaming in my direction, blinding me until my eyes adjust. As the glowing lights get closer through the prism of water, I am expecting to see the face of the young man, his fine facial features illuminating in the aqua light.

It is the face of a monster!

Screaming, water pulsates into my mouth and down my throat. A grotesque face covered with large bumps of flesh and deep crevices is staring at me, hissing as bubbles float to the surface. Large, arched bulbous structures that frame the eyes glow from the aqua blue irises. The delicate cheekbones replaced with large sharp angular shelves of bony scales. Its large mouth conceals rows of razor-sharp teeth; the creature baring them as it swims closer to me. Grabbing my arm with its scaly fingers, it pulls me toward it. The grotesque face is getting closer, opening its mouth, it is going to…

****

I'm screaming on the floor in my bedroom. My head, neck, and upper body are lying on the floor. The lower part of my body is angled above me, suspended along the side of the bed in the tangle of sheets and comforter. A light sheen of moisture covers my skin. I'm hyperventilating, my glistening chest heaving in the moonlight filtering through the windows. A briny odor, reminiscent of the last dream involving the sea creature, permeates the air. Rubbing my fingertips across my chest, I taste the liquid to verify if it is the same as the previous experience. It does. The taste and smell of bay water. I take control of my breathing. Untangling myself from the sheets and comforter, I manage to stand up. Naked in the middle of my bedroom, I am shivering, and smelling of the sea. What is happening to me? Feeling weak and exhausted, I drop onto my bed, pull the comforter toward me, and wrap myself in it to form a cocoon so I can go back to sleep. I instantly fall asleep.

Chapter 10

Doever Farm
2nd week of October 1992

What is happening to me? This is the central thought that I awake to this morning. I can still smell the strong, stale sea odor emanating from my body, wafting from the pocket of sheets I lie in. Why do I have seawater traces on my body after the dreams? Have I crossed into a new stage of my psychic abilities where my body is now manifesting physically what I am mentally picturing, like producing perspiration that is more like seawater than typical sweat, indicating a new degree of mind-body connection? Am I having out-of-body experiences like people who practice transcendental meditation and report they leave and float above their bodies or travel to other locations? In essence, the soul leaves the body and experiences what is termed "spirit travel." Is my spirit/soul moving through space into the water?

Speaking of watery environments, what is the connection to the sea creature? I now have had two vivid dreams of the sea creature and two hallucinations in the area of Witch Well Park. Before last night, I had dreamed that the creature appeared to have the face and body of an oddly beautiful young man, which might be explained as a manifestation of something in my subconscious that is sexual in nature. But now the creature has a disfigured face. What does that say about my sexual and mental health? Now there is an apparent connection between the sea creature and the death of Elias Doever in my subconscious. Is the sea creature an incarnation of Elias Doever? Did Elias Doever's soul transcend through the column of water that sprouted from the well and land in the bay at the time of his death? But I dreamed of the beautiful sea creature before I visited the witch well. Did I simply link the intense traumatic psychic vibrations that I felt at the witch well with the image of the strangely beautiful alien and the results are the horrible manifestation I dreamt last night? Is the horrible face of the sea monster an expression of Elias Doever's pain? Is my sensitivity to Elias Doever's pain because I live in his house and have seen the place where he died? Was my experience so traumatic at the witch well that the psychic aftermath is invading my subconscious? One thing I know for sure: I need to learn more about who Elias Doever was and more about his death.

I no longer tolerate the briny smell wafting from my skin. Climbing out of my sheet cocoon, I walk to the door and open it slightly to hear if Mother is awake and stirring in the kitchen. All's quiet. I don't want to contaminate my robe with the sea smell secreting from my skin, so I quickly dash naked from my doorway into the bathroom to take my shower.

By the time I finish my shower and dress casually for a relaxing Sunday morning, I can hear Mother rattling pans in the kitchen fixing our breakfast. I walk into the kitchen wearing a simple logo t-shirt, cargo shorts, flips, and a backward baseball cap concealing my still-damp hair, except the bangs peeking vertically out of the cap.

Mother starts the morning conversation. "Good morning, my love. I'm making Eggs Benedict. How many can you eat?"

"Two."

"You were out late last night. I heard your car pull into the driveway around three a.m. Did you go to Boston?"

"No, I went to Salem to see the late-night showing of *The Rocky Horror Picture Show*. It was a blast; the audience really got into it. I met some of my friends from BPU that live near there," I lie as I munch on a piece of Canadian ham.

"I'm glad that you're keeping in touch with your undergrad classmates. Did you recognize any Bedfordshire students?

"A few," I sort of lie again.

"Oh, before I forget, remember that I've that department dinner on Wednesday night, so you'll have to fend for yourself or get pizza in the village. Also, are you interested in going with me to see Aunt Alice this Saturday, staying overnight in Mendham?"

"Not if it means that I have to see her religious zealot husband!"

Mother sighs. "I understand, but she misses you."

"When her homophobic husband apologizes for all the shitty things he said to me last Christmas, then we'll talk."

"Yes, he is…an asshole, but I love my sister."

"Mother, language!" I say, pretending to be offended.

We had a nice breakfast together. Mother's Eggs

Benedict is superb, a special family recipe for the Hollandaise sauce. After I clear the table and do the dishes, I retire to the family room to read the *Boston Globe*. Mother leaves to go into town to pick up some groceries for dinner and the rest of the week. The phone rings, and I enter the kitchen to answer it. "Leeves residence."

"Dorian, it's Toby."

"Toby? Toby who? Just kidding!"

"Cute. Are you busy Wednesday night? We have an away match on Friday, so we have a longer practice on Thursday and the coach gave us Wednesday off, so…I thought maybe we could do something," Toby suggests.

"What a cowinkydink. My mother just told me that she has a history department dinner she must go to on Wednesday night, so I have the house to myself. Why don't you come over and I'll make dinner for us? I can pick you up after my lab hours, around five o'clock, have some drinks and dinner here, and then bring you back before she gets back. I can find out how long her event is, and we can plan accordingly. Does that work for you?"

"Sure, sounds great!" I hear the enthusiasm in his tone. "I didn't know you could cook?"

"Don't expect too much. I can cook to get by, but you won't starve, and I won't poison you. I'll pick up some nice wine, or would you rather beer?"

"I can do either, but if you are getting wine, I like red more than white."

"Cool beans. So, what are you doing today?"

"I have to study for two exams I have this week and read over my biology lab. I have this tough lab professor," Toby cajoles with me.

"Yeah, I've heard he's a dick!" Toby laughs loudly. "Okay. I'm gonna let you go so that you can study and read over your genetics lab protocol. I'll see you tomorrow, and we can talk more about the plan for Wednesday night."

"Sounds good. Later."

"Later," I parrot back.

Chapter 11

Bedfordshire College
2nd week of October 1992

This morning's mission, besides my graduate assistant duties, is to grill Dr. Hayden more about what he knows about Elias Doever. The dream about his death, the mysterious water column that rose from the well at the time of his death, and its connection to the sea monster is baffling me. I need answers. But I also need more information about who Elias Doever was and why he might be haunting me now that I live in his house. Dr. Hayden walks into his office connected to the lab and I immediately make a beeline to the door of his office to start my interrogation.

I lightly knock on the door and open the conversation, "Dr. Hayden, I was wondering if you have a moment. I'd like to talk to you about something."

"Sure, Dorian. Is there a problem with the protocol or data?"

"No, it's not related to the lab. It's about what happened to me at the well in Witch Well Park."

"Yes, that was strange. What do you think happened?" he asks with genuine concern in his voice.

"I dunno, but I think if I know more about the history of Elias Doever, I might get some answers.

Perhaps, something I read or heard about him triggered…my episode. Are you willing to help with this?"

"Sure, I will tell you what I know. Being a lifelong resident of Bedfordshire, I might be able to give you the nativist point of view on the dark history of this town. What do you want to know?"

I start my line of questioning, "Okay, how did Elias Doever come to be accused of witchcraft to begin with?"

Dr. Hayden begins a long diatribe. "Like a lot of the witch trials in colonial America, it was an issue like a property dispute that was the real reason behind the accusations of witchcraft. It was revealed later that William Putnam started the campaign against Elias after a property dispute; the Putnam farm shares a border with the Doever farm, and Elias inherited the farm after his father, Benjamin Doever, died. While he was alive, Benjamin refused to sell a plot of very fertile land on the Doever property that bordered the Putnam farm and that the Doevers did not plant. William wanted it and expected Elias to sell it to his family after Benjamin's death, but Elias wouldn't sell. The common belief was that William was looking for a reason to accuse Elias of witchcraft so that he could take his land.

"When citizens were found guilty of witchcraft in colonial New England, their property was confiscated by the town/church. This dark chapter of our history has plagued this town for centuries. Elias Doever was accused and later found guilty of witchcraft because William Putnam supposedly caught Elias in a compromising position with John Putnam, his brother, causing the 'moral corruption' of John Putnam. In the words of the citizenry of Bedfordshire: 'Elias Doever was found lying with John Putnam in the biblical way a husband lies with his wife.' A word of warning, be careful whom you talk to about that rumor in town. There are descendants of the Putnams who still live in Bedfordshire."

When Dr. Hayden mentions John Putnam's name, I remember that John is also on the plaque honoring the accused. "Wasn't John Putnam also tried as a witch and died in the witch well?"

Dr. Hayden explains the answer in great detail. "Yes, he was accused shortly after Elias died—accused by Mary Warren, the same Mary Warren who accused people in the Salem witch trials, forever memorialized in Arthur Miller's play *The Crucible*. The story is that she fancied John, but he wasn't interested in her or any woman after Elias died. She knew John had been implicated in a witch trial with Elias, so to take her revenge, she accused him of consorting with the spirit of Elias Doever, a blasphemous act of heresy. Because John was William Putnam's brother, they had to bring a judge from Salem, Judge Hawthorne, to oversee the trial. After he drowned in the ducking stool of the well, unlike Elias, John was buried in the Bedfordshire church cemetery on consecrated ground. William Putnam's influence in Bedfordshire was still great; he convinced the people that John was an innocent who was corrupted and that his soul could still be saved if buried in holy earth."

In hopes of finding another place to make a psychic connection to Elias, I bring up the burial question. "Speaking of being buried in unconsecrated ground, you mentioned that Elias was buried in secret after he died. Does anyone have any idea where he was buried?"

"There are three places where Elias Doever is rumored to be buried."

Dr. Hayden counts on his fingers as he explains the three locations. "First, behind the church cemetery, surrounded by consecrated ground. If Elias Doever ever rose from his grave then he wouldn't be able to cross the consecrated earth, protecting the townspeople. Second, an area known as the Backwoods near the bay coastline. In fact, we're going to be collecting data from this area on Friday. You're responsible for coordinating that fieldwork, as I will be in Woods Hole for the day. Third, on a secluded section of Corey James' farm, the man who was charged with burying Elias Doever in secret."

After hearing of our assignment in the Backwoods, I felt strangely relieved that we would be conducting marine snail research in this location. This will give me an opportunity to do my own research. Thinking he's done I'm about to thank Dr. Hayden when he suddenly stops me from leaving the office. Gently grabbing my arm, he delivers his next Elias Doever story.

"Oh! I almost forgot to tell you about the Harvard man! As the story goes, there was a sophomore at Harvard in the early part of the 20th century who allegedly slept with the daughter of the Dean of Harvard College. This angered the dean and he vowed to seek revenge on the young man. However, the Harvard man was from a prominent family and was well insulated from the dean's wrath. As the story goes, the young man was pledging one of the secret societies at Harvard, similar to the Skull and Bones society at

Yale. The dean belonged to the same society the Harvard man was pledging. The dean's influence was strong in the society, but the Harvard man was also from a very powerful family, like the Rockefellers. The society decided that the only way the Harvard man could continue to pledge was to complete a task/dare: to dig up the bones of Elias Doever in one of the three rumored burial locations. The pledge was very bright and through his research figured out which of the burial sights Elias Doever was buried.

"The pledge and a few of the society members traveled to Bedfordshire to complete his task. He kept the location of the burial a secret until the group arrived there. Supposedly, the ground was completely bare, nothing growing in the area, not even grass. The pledge planted his shovel into the barren earth and lifted the first mound of dirt. Immediately after he dumped the first shovel full of soil onto the bare ground, the student screamed in terror, grabbed his chest, and died on the spot, presumably from a heart attack. He was nineteen years old and had never had a heart condition his whole life. The brothers brought his body back to Harvard to the house of the society to cover up what had happened, never revealing the actual location where he died. The coroner's records stated that he died on campus. The autopsy confirmed he died from natural causes, heart damage, but there was also a rumor that he had an expression on his face of extreme pain or horror. Purportedly, his eyes were wide open, and had to have his eyelids sewn shut for the open casket funeral. It was also reported that there was mud found on his shoes that was not common to the type of soil found in the Cambridge/Charles River basin. It was more like the mud found along the northern coastline of Massachusetts Bay. The campfire story that evolved from this incident: The Harvard man dug up the unholy, sour ground of Elias Doever's grave and then his unclean spirit killed him. Some believe this story was used to deter people not considered worthy of Harvard from applying."

"Wow, that's quite a story!" I add.

Dr. Hayden concludes, "The Bedfordshire public library has the archives of the town. You should be able to verify many of these rumors with the known facts. The identity of the Harvard man was never revealed, thus, the reason why he is called "Harvard Man," and much of that tale cannot be substantiated, but there should be plenty of factual information regarding the legendary burial sights of the witch Elias Doever."

"Warlock, a male witch is called a warlock," I correct Dr. Hayden.

Chapter 12

Doever Farm
2nd week of October 1992

Pulling into the hairpin turn of the driveway into Doever Farm, I use my peripheral vision to see the expression on Toby's face (which is tricky when making the sharp turns) when he sees the Puritan-era house that Mother and I've made home. The impression that this remarkably preserved 300-year-old house makes upon modern citizenry is a testament to the durable, creative craftsmanship of our earliest colonial civilization. The architectural style is gothic and dark, reflective of the oppressive ideals and strict doctrine of colonial Christianity. The highly pitched gable roof lines of the houses from this era recall those made famous in Salem, Massachusetts: The House of the Seven Gables and "The Witch House," also known as the Jonathan Corwin House. Toby is slow to get out of the sedan as he absorbs his surroundings.

"Wow, I had no idea you live in a house like this. It's just like the ones I've seen in Salem and Gloucester," Toby recounts with awe in his voice.

I stop him as he moves toward the door. "Hey, we'll go inside in a minute, but let's take a walk so I can show you the property."

Following my lead, we walk toward the barn to the

left of the circular driveway. Reaching the door, I slide it back and we both peer into the ancient barn to observe the timber construction, the mud walls, the extreme height of the loft, the stalls for the animals, and the lead glass panes of the sparse windows.

"We use this as a garage during bad weather, which will be invaluable this winter," I state as I roll the door closed.

We leave the barn and head toward the beachhead. We stop in our tracks when we see two unexpected but welcomed visitors on the property. Grazing in the meadow before us are two stags, an eight-point buck and a six-point buck. Tall, strong, perfect specimens of their species majestically moving about the farm. They both stop eating when they realize we are near; lifting their heads with their enormous racks of antlers to view us. Not moving from their regal stance, the bucks are observing us as we admire them. They're not making any aggressive moves toward us. We aren't a threat. Looking around to see if they're part of a larger herd, there are no signs of any other deer, male or female.

"Is it normal for two male deer with that much longevity to travel as companions, not part of a herd," I say aloud.

Suddenly, I feel dizzy; I'm getting a premonition. Trying not to alarm Toby, my sight diminishes for a few seconds and then becomes clear again. Through the stag's perspective, I am looking at us. There is no color in this view, as if I were looking at our images through a black-and-white video. It feels like the stags are sympathetic to us, admiring two male specimens from the same species, companions as they are. The vision then stops abruptly, leaving me stunned and filled with shock from the blinding light that shoots through my head.

"Ow!"

"Are you okay?" Toby asks, his tone tinged with concern.

"Yeah, I had a twinge in my eye, I'm fine now," I say covering up for my abrupt loss of vision. I refocus on the scene. The stags remain in their stance despite my outburst. "I think we could stand here until dark and they wouldn't move, but I'm hungry. Let's go inside." Toby nods, and we walk toward the house, circumventing our deer brethren. The bucks watch us until we enter the house.

My plan for dinner is simple: sloppy Joes made with ground turkey, steak fries in olive oil, a mixed green salad, and a nice bottle of Cab. Toby said he isn't much of a cook, and neither am I, but I've learned to get by. Toby was my sous chef: he cut the potatoes, the onions for the sloppy Joes and the vegetables for the salad. I did the stovetop work. When I cook with someone I like to talk. Usually it's just meaningless banter: no politics or heavy subjects. We start with the results from the genetics/neuroscience lab.

"Remind me of your results from the lab this week?" I inquire as I brown the turkey.

"Let's see. I've attached earlobes, but I don't have a crease in my earlobe, so no predisposition for heart issues. I can curl my tongue, and I tasted the PTC paper—that was disgusting by the way. I'm predominantly right-handed and prefer the right side of the visual field, making me left-brain dominant. Everything else was normal."

"Huh? That list of traits matches mine exactly.

According to those results, we're more closely related, genetically."

Toby chuckles. "Lucky we can't have kids, or we might not be able to…" He stops talking. Realizing he made an implication about sex, his eyebrows are broadcasting concern, "I didn't mean…I mean…"

I grab his hand. "It's fine, dude. I want to take this slowly too. Not only do we need to be cautious as far as what the public knows, I want this to…you know," I finish my sentence with a shrug of my shoulders.

Toby shakes his head affirmatively. He starts to say something but stops. Hesitating for a split second, he finally continues, "I really like you, Dorian. I feel the same way."

Trying to break the serious tone, I exclaim, "Good. It should be just a few more minutes. Can you set the table? I laid everything on it already."

Dinner turned out well. We went through two bottles of Cabernet Sauvignon; neither of us feeling any pain. Thoroughly satiated as well.

"Hey, I can clean this up later. Let's go relax in the family room." We proceed into the family room. I walk to the stereo and pop in a cassette of The Smiths.

"How about some Morrissey?" I state as Morrissey wails "This Charming Man". "It's always amazed me how much straight guys like this band, singing along with the lyrics when all Morrissey writes about is his frustration and longing for guys he can't have or had and screwed it up!"

Toby laughs. "I hear ya!"

Pouring the rest of the bottle of wine into our glasses, I sit down to the left of Toby, nestling myself into the seat cushions. Because we are both wearing shorts, our naked thighs rub against each other on the couch. I turn to look at him. Moving my face slowly toward his, I kiss him lightly on the lips. I put our glasses down on the coffee table and kiss him again, with slightly more force, cupping his jawline with both of my hands. He lays his hands on my shoulders, his thumbs resting on the top of my breastbone. As our kiss intensifies, our tongues break free, exploring the contours of lips, and massaging each other's tongues. I lean down on the couch. Toby, following my lead and passionately kissing me, changes his grip on my shoulders. Toby lies on top of me, subtly moving his lower body so that his left thigh is in between mine. I can feel my arousal as the pressure from his thigh pushes against my groin. My arms wrap around his broad back as we continue to explore each other. I move my mouth away to catch my breath. At that moment, his body faintly gyrates and pulses next to mine. My arms encircle his back—but they're not my arms. They are covered in a greenish-blue tint and the skin is not normal—it is reflecting light as if it were wet or luminescent!

They are scales!

My arms are covered in marine-colored scales! A layer of thin aqua-colored translucent skin is in between my fingers! While examining my altered appendages, I feel overcome, as if my mind is drifting off, but also watching everything in front of my face. A sense of foreboding permeates my mind as I succumb to the feelings stirring in my brain. The sexual arousal I feel from Toby's thigh pushing against me pulsates throughout my body. I am no longer in control of my body as my hand moves toward his groin where my fingers find the impression of his erection. I hear a deep sigh from the back of Toby's throat. Inexplicably, I pull my thighs closer to my body and wrap them around his waist, curling my feet inward to latch onto the small of his back. I pull him closer, his thigh pushing into my crotch.

Toby moves his head so my head is no longer in the crook of his neck. He looks confused. He lifts his entire body off me and moves to the other end of the couch. Sitting, he then looks at me. Regaining my composure, I glance at my arms and hands as I sit up from the couch; they are no longer covered in scales and my fingers have lost their webbing. Eventually, I sit upright and look at him.

"I'm sorry, I don't know what came over me."

Toby looks hurt. "Dorian, I meant what I said before. I want to take this slowly. I want a relationship. I don't want a fuckbuddy. If I wanted that, I could get one of my teammates drunk or stoned or both… Been there, done that. I want something…*real*, and I think, or I thought we might be able to…" He stops talking in exasperation.

"Toby, I understand, and I'm sorry. I want the same thing; believe me, I do. I'm…developing feelings for you and that hasn't happened in a long time. Something came over me…I can't explain it, I…" I stop myself before I divulge too much. "You are so damn sexy! I promise it won't happen again. Please give me another chance."

Toby turns his eyes toward the floor, staring, thinking, and then gives me his answer. "Okay."

Moving closer to me on the couch, his thick, welcoming arms invite me into his space. Encircling my arms around his broad shoulders, I lay my head on his left shoulder and squeeze tightly, melding my arms into his muscular flesh. He reciprocates, burying his head deep into my left shoulder. We hug for what seems like minutes. I slowly break away, tilting my head so I'm looking directly into his eyes. Leaning in, I give him a soft gentle kiss on the lips.

He gently pulls away. "I think I should go now. It's getting late, and it is a school night and—"

"Yes, I should drive you home now." Suddenly, I remembered that I'm going to have the house to myself on Saturday. Contemplating whether I should risk asking Toby after this incident, my impulse takes over. "But before you go, what time will you be home on Saturday after your away game?"

"By, noon, why?"

"Mother is going to Boston for the day," I explain cautiously, "and staying the night with her sister. I have the house to myself. If you'd like, we can spend the day together, not the night, here at Doever Farm."

Looking at me, he doesn't answer immediately. "Yeah, that sounds nice. I'll call you when I get back to the dorm."

I smile at him. We get up from the couch and head for the front door when he unexpectedly grabs my left hand with his right hand and clasps his fingers around mine. Without looking at him, we hold hands as we walk to the car.

****

It's 9:30 p.m. when I return to the house at Doever Farm. Still bewildered by what I saw and how I acted, and not in the mood to cross-examine myself as to why I experienced the hallucination I did. Distracting myself from further analysis of the evening, I realize Mother has not come home yet from her dinner. I use this opportunity to clean up the kitchen, a diversion that should work for a few minutes at least. It doesn't take long to clean up.

After thoroughly removing any evidence of a date from the house, I notice my stench, a bit malodorous. It's 9:45 p.m., a little early for my nightly shower, but I'm feeling unusually tired after the strange events of the evening and want to go to bed soon. Removing my clothes, I put my robe on and walk into the bathroom. Taking my robe off, I place my towel for easier access, then reach toward the shower controls. Suddenly, the handle for the hot water turns clockwise on its own. When I reach for the handle for the cold water, the handle turns independently but does not turn as far. As I place my hand on the handle to redirect the water to the showerhead I feel a slight tremor in my hand, a very mild jolt. I try again and the same thing happens. I immediately touch the other handles cautiously, yet there is no sense of electrical charge. I dip my hand into the water collecting in the tub, remembering that if there is an electrical short traveling through a body of water, a quick motion of a few fingers in the water will give a shock but not enough to electrocute. There isn't an electrical jolt. I have another overwhelming feeling: something wants me to take a bath instead of the shower I desire. Too tired to contemplate the ramifications of this newest psychic occurrence, I mumble, "I guess I'm taking a bath."

Climbing into the deep bathtub, I recline my head toward the end without the hardware so I can feel the hot water on my feet. Submerging the lower half of my body into the hot water, I inhale the steamy vapors through my nose. Placing a washcloth over my eyes, I try not to think about what happened tonight. Unfortunately, I'm not successful. I cannot get the images out of my head of the scaly arms and webbed fingers that were wrapped around Toby's back. Knowing that the appendages looked marine-like, I'm convinced that this is yet another vision related to the sea creature in my dreams. I begin to wonder why I'm taking a bath instead of a shower. I patiently wait for the outcome, but nothing is happening.

Feeling drowsy, I'm almost asleep when, unexpectedly, I feel the sensation of bubbles in the water bouncing off my body. It lightly touches the most sensitive parts of my skin, but it is unmistakable. The bubbling increases in force and small waves are forming on the surface of the water. Within seconds, the water in the bathtub is churning, the small waves growing into more powerful ones, lapping along the edge of the tub. The waves collect into denser column-like spouts, spraying across my body as they jump from one side to the other, gliding along my chest, my belly, my thighs. Suddenly, the columns of water unite to form something that looks organic, like an arm and a hand, hovering above my abdomen! I am in awe as I watch the appearance of webbed fingers develop in the watery appendage. Abruptly, the fingers on the hand bend backward toward my lower abdomen, and I can distinctly feel them creeping down my pelvis. I quickly push myself upward, so my pelvis and abdomen are above the water. Grabbing the sides of the tub, I thrust myself out of the water to stand in the tub, the water level reaching my calves. The watery hand dissipates into the bath water. I step out of the tub and switch the drain to empty the tub. Grabbing my towel, I dry my face, watching the tub drain. I'm waiting to see…well, I'm not sure what I'm expecting to see. The last of the water disappears into the drain. Nothing unusual here.

After I dry off, I put on my robe and walk out of the steamy bathroom. I collapse onto my bed with my robe on. I have no energy for some reason. After a few seconds, I pull my robe off, grab a pair of mesh shorts from my dresser, put them on, and snuggle in between the sheets. I will process all of this in the morning as I can't keep my eyes open. Within seconds, I'm asleep.

****

I wake up earlier than my alarm, but I still don't have much time to contemplate what happened in the bathtub or the couch last night. I must be in early to the lab to organize tomorrow's field exercises in the Backwoods area of Bedfordshire. I approach these phenomena from a rational point of view and think like a scientist. First, organize the observations into categories.

Category 1: mental experiences. Two dreams in which I'm drawn to a sea creature or monster on the banks of the Mass Bay at Doever Farm and at Witch Well Park. Two visions, the psychic experience at the well of Witch Well Park and the hallucination of my arm becoming an appendage like the sea creature.

Category 2: physical experiences. Five happy showers, so far. The "otherworldly" movements of the handles in the bathtub that pre-determined I was going to take a bath instead of a shower, and then the resulting appearance of the watery appendage that tried to grab me in the groin. The physical sickness I felt after the vision at Witch Well Park, and the seawater residue left on my skin after the dreams of diving into the bay with the sea creature.

Category 3: the sea creature. Both dreams involved interaction with the sea creature. Then there is the possible sighting of it at the cove of Witch Well Park. The transformation of my arm into the arm of the sea creature when I was lying on the couch with Toby. This can also be placed under physical and mental experiences.

Category 4: Elias Doever. The intense psychic experience at Witch Well Park. The second dream in which I witnessed the column of water exploding from the well he died from and descending into the bay.

All right, now I have all my categories. What's the one variable that most, if not all, of these experiences have in common? The sea creature is in most of the events, but it's not present in the happy showers or the vision at Witch Well Park. Elias Doever is the next possibility. This is strengthened by the fact that I'm living in his house and have had visions/dreams where I witnessed his death and the aftermath of his death. However, he was neither in the first dream nor was there any sign of his energy in the bathtub experiences. Suddenly, the answer comes to me.

"It is so simple. It's water!" I verbalize my "Eureka" moment aloud lying in bed. Every experience, whether it be psychic or physical, has involved water. So, what does that mean?

Realizing I'll be late for school if I don't move quickly, I contemplate the lynchpin to this mystery as I get ready. Rolling out of bed, I lightly step to my dresser, pull my underwear and socks out of the drawer and slip my boxers on. I have another revelation as I dress: perhaps, the force that's causing these events travels via water.

This force travels through the water in this house as it has stimulated me physically in the shower and bathtub. An electrical-like force, evident from the first time it came through the water of the showerhead and then last night when I tried to adjust the shower handles and felt a mild shock. There was also the electrical buzz I felt when I kissed the sea creature in my dreams. They must be related. Is it the sea creature that's causing the force to travel through the water? The image of this being first appeared to me in a dream soon after my first happy shower, and because he's a being from the sea, it would make sense that he can project some kind of energy through the water. But where does Elias Doever fit into this?

As I select my blue broadcloth button-down shirt and khakis from my wardrobe, another thought enters my head: Elias Doever is the sea creature! Putting my arm through the shirt one sleeve at a time, I explore this hypothesis in my head. Perhaps, when Elias Doever died, he was transformed into this creature. That would explain the explosion that occurred when he died in the well. His soul or spirit escaped through the column of water that formed in the well, traveling toward the bay where the column landed, transferring his spirit into the water of the bay. It is here where he was transformed into the water being that I have been dreaming and/or hallucinating. I tuck the tail of my shirt into my khakis, buttoning the top button.

Stepping away from the wardrobe, I pick up the coiled, blue cotton webbed belt off the dresser. As I unroll it and place the belt through my belt loops, a new thought pops into my head: what is the obsession with my sexual release? Sitting on the edge of the bed, slipping on my socks, I think more about this piece of the puzzle. Selecting penny loafers to finish off my preppy New England liberal arts college look, I wrangle my left stocking foot into the shoe. I make another deduction in my head. Perhaps, the spirit of Elias Doever/sea creature is living vicariously through me and is trying to achieve an orgasm.

Remembering the story that Dr. Hayden told me about Elias and John Putnam, I propose a possible scenario in my head. Elias's spirit/afterlife form discovers that another gay man, a gay man with psychic abilities, lives in this house and that it can possess him to relive sexual experiences. The electrical sensation in the water is Elias's spirit traveling to unite with me and take over my body, possessing me so when I'm in a heightened sexual state it can experience those thoughts, those feelings. The energy Elias's spirit exudes not only causes me to enter that sexually heightened state but remains in my body so it can feel the physical pleasure of sexual stimulation and release, which it hasn't succeeded in doing…yet. That must be what this is all about!

Feeling proud of myself for figuring this out, I walk into the bathroom. While brushing my teeth, another thought strikes: will I be able to contact Elias Doever to stop these jarring events? I am psychic, but can I influence such a powerful entity that can affect the physical world?

Then another breakthrough moment: is this the reason why my abilities have increased since we moved to Doever Farm? Does Elias's spirit leave some of that energy behind when it leaves my body, which makes me even more sensitive to the psychic world or more telekinetic? Perhaps I'm being too hasty about trying to exorcise Elias. There are benefits from our encounters, and I probably will become more powerful if these encounters continue. As I rinse out my mouth, I think about that last thought. I could become more powerful, but at what cost?

I smooth mousse into my bangs to give it that stiff vertical look, a style popular since the late eighties. Dashing out of the bathroom, I notice Mother at the kitchen table having her morning coffee. I acknowledge her presence by kissing her on the cheek.

"Good morning, Mother. How was your dinner?"

Taken back by my atypical gregarious gesture, she comments, "Well, you're in a good mood this morning. My dinner was lovely, thank you for asking."

"It must've been, you weren't home when I went to bed. Late night for you!" I state, pouring coffee into my thermos and topping it off with my favorite hazelnut-flavored non-dairy creamer. "I'd like to hear the details, but I'm running late, and I'm in charge of coordinating tomorrow's field work," I say as I grab a banana, an apple, and a granola bar.

"Want to meet for lunch today?"

"Let me call you when I know more about my day. I might be working through lunch. Love you!" I shout as I walk out the front door.

Getting into the car, another thought crosses my mind. I am going to the Backwoods tomorrow, one of the fabled locations of Elias Doever's grave. Can this be a coincidence?

Chapter 13

The Backwoods
2nd week of October 1992

The Backwoods, a thick forest of deciduous trees and evergreens about a mile from the center of downtown Bedfordshire, is a quiet, beautiful, unblemished stretch of land. The cool gray coat of the birch trees juxtaposed against the fluorescent vibrance of the oranges, yellows, and reds of the changing leaves is striking, like giant burning matchsticks with brilliant flames brushing against each other in the breeze. There's a single lane gravel road that cuts through the forest to the coastline and the unusually wide brown sand beach from which we will collect our data. We're using the same quadrat collecting method that was used at Witch Well Park with the same group of student researchers, alleviating the need to talk about protocol. Like before, I designate an area of the beach to each partnership. Once again, I will collect data by myself. I've chosen the most secluded area of the beach in the northernmost section of the beachhead.

Data collection today is duly unremarkable. There's no apparent outside influence being exerted in this location while I'm doing my counts. To test this, I concentrate on flipping the quadrat using my telekinetic powers, moving it concentrically. After the quadrat somersaults along the beach for several revolutions, I resist tumbling the square of plastic tube any further. To my disappointment, no other force takes over. I also do not feel the presence of any psychic entity on the beach like the energy I detect when I have visions associated with Elias Doever or the alien sea creature.

I finish my counting in an extraordinarily short time. Sneaking away from the beach, I find a quiet spot to try to make a psychic connection. Finding a clearing about 100 yards from the edge of the shoreline, I sit cross-legged on a soft patch of pine needles and close my eyes. Clearing my mind of all thoughts, an opportunity for an otherworldly force to make contact is here. Meditating in the middle of this gloriously flamboyant and still forest, I feel at peace and relaxed, recharging my soul, if you will, but I never contact anything otherworldly.

I'm convinced that the only thing extraordinary about this forest is its beauty. I walk back to the beach to check on the other groups and soon realize I'm the only person standing on the brown sandy turf. Looking out across the water, I quietly declare, "I am here, looking for the burial place of Elias Doever...trying to make a connection to Elias Doever. He is not here. Is this what you want of me?"

There is no answer, psychically or otherwise. I depart the beachhead.

Chapter 14

Doever Farm
2nd week of October 1992

The day was uneventful, which is surprisingly disappointing. Considering the extraordinary events that have happened to me in the last month or so, I was expecting more of the same when I visited the Backwoods. As far as the research goes, it's a successful day for Dr. Hayden's lab. As for my own agenda, I can eliminate one of the possibilities for the secret burial site of the warlock Elias Doever.

Mother and I ate dinner early tonight as she had to get up early tomorrow for her trip to Boston. She apparently has a full schedule with her sister, Ruth. For our dinner tonight, she made one of her favorite Italian meals: lasagna with grilled vegetables, and chicken sausage with a homemade tomato sauce she cooks all day, and a Caesar salad. It's a deliciously satisfying, carb-loaded meal, which means that I will be asleep soon tonight.

****

I pull the covers up to my neck, re-fluff my pillow, clear my mind, and relax, attempting to go back to sleep. After several minutes, I am still not able to sleep. Something is keeping me awake. I open my eyes. Sitting up in bed, I scan the interior of my small room for the presence of anything unusual. Nothing out of the ordinary. Nevertheless, I cannot shake the feeling that there's a presence that has roused me out of my sleep.

Without warning, a bright aqua-colored light comes beaming through the highest panes of the window on the northern wall, intense enough to get my attention but not strong enough to blind me. Getting out of bed, I walk to the window to get a better view. The stream of flickering light is coming from behind the berm on the edge of the beach. The direction of the light stream is not just focused on the windowpanes of my room or the house. It is radiating further up the beach and at every angle in between as if the source is moving in a circular fashion. I recognize the distinct color of this beam of light; it's the same color that emits from the irises of the sea creature in my dreams. I'm amazed at the prospect of what this could mean. My curiosity getting the better of me, I put on a pair of sweat shorts, a t-shirt, and my flips and leave the house to investigate.

As I walk toward the flickering light, a low-pitched wail gets louder. It's the same droning sound from my dreams! I keep reminding myself that I'm completely awake, and lucid, yet I am now experiencing elements of my dreams in my real life! The beautiful wailing noise has the same effect on me as it did in my dreams; I feel a compulsion to follow it. Reaching the berm, and climbing the short but steep hill, I peer over the edge of it with anticipation. My deepest hopes and fears come to fruition. The sea creature with the beautiful face of a youth is floating in the waters outside of my home! The individual beams of light emitting from the irises of his eyes curiously combine into one concentrated beam of light. The gentle waves of the bay cause the concentrated ray of light to bob up and down as the creature floats along the surf. As the creature turns its head, the beam of light moves up and down the water and the beach, creating the semi-circular pattern I witnessed.

The sea creature spies me on the shore and turns its head in my direction, focusing the aqua light onto me. His mouth remains open, continuing to broadcast that deep rhythmic sound. He's communicating with me somehow through his wailing. It instructs me to remove my clothes and come into the water. I strip off my t-shirt, flips, and shorts, and then wade nude into the freezing water. I am visibly shivering from the water. The creature refocuses its light beams onto the water before me. Instantly, the water becomes warmer, like bath water, the temperature in my dreams. I follow the beams of light into deeper water, knowing that I could easily drown if this being wished it. For some reason, I trust it will not hurt me. I'm now treading water within feet of the creature, and it is even more beautiful than in my dreams. The greenish-blue gleaming tint to the skin accents the handsome but sharp features of the angular face: features, besides the bald, gleaming head, that would be characteristics of a classically beautiful youth of Greek or Roman statues. The being moves closer, continuing to shine the light emitting from his irises onto the water around me to keep it warm. I'm standing on the sandy bottom. The wailing has decreased in intensity, but I can still hear the echoing sound.

"Dorian Leeves."

I hear my name, but the creature's mouth isn't forming the words.

"Dorian Leeves."

It has said, or rather communicated telepathically, my name again. I feel that it wants me to answer the call and ask a question.

"Yes, my name is Dorian," I acknowledge aloud. "Why have you summoned me?"

"It is time. To reveal what I am. Who you are."

"Who I am!" I say aloud, my voice echoing along the shoreline.

"I existed before the first living thing made its presence known in this world. I am as ancient as the oldest sea. I am a force, a spirit, a god. The humans of this land who have witnessed my power have called me 'Hobomock', 'Widigo', 'Windigo'… 'Devil.' I am not the Devil. I am Beladon, the Keeper of the Seas. I have been dwelling in this sea for millennia, waiting for the chosen one borne of the land with whom I will share my power with. Together, we will become rulers of the sea…and the land." Beladon stops. "You think you are that mortal. You are not that mortal."

I am dumbfounded; Beladon answers the question I am thinking.

"Elias Doever was the chosen one. He was borne with gifts, but when he used his gifts, men did not understand them and killed him. I have waited for him to return, to be reborn. I have waited for three hundred years…for you. Dorian, you are the reincarnation of Elias Doever."

I'm silent after hearing this revelation. Strangely, I'm not surprised that Beladon has revealed that I'm a magical being, as this would explain why the weak telekinetic and psychic abilities I've always possessed have become stronger in the last few months. That my extraordinary abilities are part of a larger plan. However, when I hear that I'm not the original "chosen one," but the reincarnation of the chosen one, this is more difficult to understand. I break my silence. "I don't understand."

"When you entered Elias Doever's dwelling, I knew you had the same gifts of the chosen one and that you possessed his essence."

Essence? What could this creature be talking about? I quickly contemplate what the word "essence" translates into during a conversation about possession…inheritance of abilities. Inheritance! That's it! Beladon is referring to DNA!

"Do you mean there is a part of Elias Doever in me that has been passed down through his descendants?"

"Yes. Your mother and your father come from the blood of Elias Doever."

Another revelation, this time about my parent's bloodlines being connected. I will process this fact later as I have more pressing questions. "Is it you that gives me the…the electrical feeling when I'm in the shower, in the water?"

"I am the Keeper of the Seas. My power dwells in the water. I give Dorian Leeves my power through the water. Your powers are stronger."

Suddenly, this all made sense to me. Beladon was projecting his DNA (or whatever a god has) through the water so that it could be absorbed into my body, altering my DNA, and making my powers stronger. Then I thought about the watery appendage and the intense vibrations I felt from its touch.

Beladon answers this question before I ask it. "Your powers are stronger. Your will commands the elements."

I gather from this explanation that I was responsible for producing the turbulence in the water and the subsequent creation of the watery arm and hand. That, perhaps, because I was thinking subconsciously about the transformation of my arm earlier in the evening, my subconscious took over to form the appendage. When the watery fingers touched my abdomen, I felt intense reverberations throughout my body because it was loaded with the powerful alien DNA. Then another thought came to me. How was the shock I felt with the shower handles related to this phenomenon?

"Dorian Leeves is able to receive more of Beladon's essence."

Again, another cryptic answer to a question that I didn't ask out loud. The shock I felt at the handles influenced me to take a bath. Simply put, Beladon persuaded me to be submerged in water rather than stand beneath a stream of water. By diffusion, the higher concentration of Beladon's DNA in the bath water moves into the water in my body, having the lower concentration of DNA. Perhaps, Beladon's statement also meant that my body is primed enough from the transfer of DNA through the previous showers to tolerate a massive dose of DNA transfer when submerged in water. Thinking about Beladon's ability to move his DNA through water, I quickly remember my dream/vision of the column of water spurting from the witch well into Mass Bay.

"Yes, my essence cannot survive in a dying body, so I had to return it to the sea. At the time of Elias Doever's death, I returned to the sea."

I change the subject once more. "I have a feeling that there is something else that I am to do."

"We are most powerful when the essence of the three are united," Beladon cryptically states.

"The three? You mean the DNA, ah, essence, of myself, you, and Elias Doever?"

"Yes."

"But you said that I already have the essence of Elias Doever in my blood. Why isn't that enough for us to exact our power?"

"It must be the original essence of Elias Doever that comes from his remains."

"This is the reason why I have had an overwhelming feeling to find the burial place of Elias Doever. It has been you pushing me to find his remains," I say somewhat accusingly.

"Yes."

"When I find his remains…his bones, and they are combined with my blood, which contains my DNA and yours, then our power will be the greatest? Is that what you are saying?"

"Yes. The uniting of the three is to be at the time of day of Elias Doever's death."

"At night, when the sun is not seen?" I clarify.

"Yes."

"What does that mean? When our power will be the greatest?"

"We will become the rulers of the sea and the land."

I have one more question. "Are you the same being that had the…non-human face I saw in my dream?"

"Yes, that is the true form of Beladon. This body is from the thoughts of Dorian."

Beladon's appearance is mined from my own thoughts of male beauty? I study Beladon's features carefully, feeling relief that I don't have to have contact with the monstrous being I saw in my dream.

"It is time for Dorian Leeves to return to the land," Beladon abruptly states.

Before I can comment, the aqua light coming from Beladon's irises becomes fainter and I feel the chill of the water. I take the not-so-subtle signal that our conversation is done. As I quickly swim to shore to escape the decreasing temperature of the water, I feel gentle waves pushing me forward. I turn my head to investigate. The perfect image of the moon reflecting on the glass-like surface is interrupted by a swirling action forming in the still water. A whirlpool is forming in the area of the bay where Beladon is floating. From the middle of the whirlpool, the silhouette of a man slowly rises out of the water, standing upon a column of water above the furious swirl of seawater. With the light emitting from his eyes mixed with the moonlight, I see the perfect naked body of a young man, of this sea god modeled from my thoughts. A perfect specimen of male youth, reminiscent of the marble and alabaster sculptures of Greek and Roman heroes. I know this is my ideal and it is not real, but I cannot stop admiring this beautiful man standing upon his pedestal of water, Poseidon incarnate. Unbelievably, I'm becoming excited in the freezing water. Beladon's glittering head turns in my direction so that the faintly glowing irises are trained on my pupils. The mouth of this statuesque being drops and the familiar wail echoes across the shoreline. Instantly, the waterspout and Beladon are sucked back into the depths of the bay.

Within a short while, I'm in my bedroom, stripping and then drying myself off with my terry cloth robe. Jumping into my bed, I nestle my naked body into my bedclothes to warm myself. As I attempt to wipe all thoughts from my mind to fall asleep, I'm having a difficult time getting the image, my image, of the nude statuesque Beladon on the pedestal of water surrounded by the whirlpool out of my mind. A striking tableau of a creature extracted from my concept of beauty. Botticelli's *Birth of Venus* pops into my mind as I desperately try to clear my head. Eventually, my drowsiness overcomes, and I drift off to sleep.

Chapter 15

Doever Farm
3rd week of October 1992

As I awake from a good night's sleep, I'm weary of spending another morning processing all the extraordinary events that have happened to me since we moved to Doever Farm. Beladon answered many of my questions, but our meeting raised more questions, particularly concerning this cryptic notion that we will become "rulers of the sea and land." I know that Beladon hasn't revealed all the facets of his plan, or what he is, as he would not thoroughly answer that question. I suppose I will learn more when I find the bones, the "essence" of Elias Doever.

It is now obvious to me that as the reincarnation of a warlock who died 300 years ago, this is my destiny, however, the ending. My fate was sealed to be part of this plan when my mother and my father conceived me, the meeting of two bloodlines that descended from a common ancestor: Elias Doever. I fear the extraordinary abilities that I was born with and developed in the last two months, like commanding elements, for example, have a price. I just hope that it's not as devastating as I fear. Life goes on until this supernatural reality presents itself.

****

Toby and I meet at Puritan Pizza for lunch at noon, which is about a mile walk from the campus. After platonic handshaking, we order our lunch selections from the counter: Eggplant Parmigiana, baked in a casserole dish, for me, and a Chicken Parmigiana submarine and a side of fries for Toby. Still impressing me with that enormous appetite.

"I had a decent match, but I could've done better with my kicking. I bet I would've done better if I knew somebody was rooting for me in the stands, like you," Toby explains as he takes an enormous bite of his sub.

He doesn't know how accurate he is. With my new powers to command the elements, I'm sure that would include rugby balls. "You can depend on me being there for the rest of your home matches, maybe a few away games, if they aren't too far away. Just let me know your schedule."

"That would be great! My scholarship pretty much depends on how much I deliver on the pitch. Having you there would boost my confidence, make me a better player," Toby confesses.

After more getting-to-know-each-other-better chit-chat, I suggest that it's time we go back to Doever Farm, and that we should order a couple of pizzas to go for dinner later. We pile into the sedan and stop by the local convenience/grocery store to get a couple of six-packs. It's an unusually warm day for October in New England, the Mass Bay region is experiencing an "Indian Summer," so we roll down the windows. The temperate breeze feels good against my face, pleasurable and relaxing. I smile. Toby grabs my hand resting on the gearshift, enclosing his fingers around mine, squeezing them.

"I know it's only been three days, but I missed you. I've been looking forward to hanging with you for an entire day, away from campus—away from all the pressure of keeping us...secret...I'm just glad to be here," Toby states as he looks me in the eyes.

"I feel the same way, and I missed you too," I say, pulling his hand toward my chest.

As I turn into the circular driveway of Doever Farm, the pair of tall stags we saw three days ago, loom into view. I park near the front door, admiring the majestic creatures that remain unfazed by our presence as we exit from the car.

"I haven't seen these bucks since we saw them together on Wednesday. Majestic. Not another deer has crossed the yard or wandered along the road since then, including these two. They seem to only make their presence known when the two of us are together. It's as if they are acknowledging us; a male couple of one species acknowledging another."

"They are handsome animals for sure, but do you think they're a couple, gay deer, ah...bucks?" Toby asks.

"I've never heard of homosexuality in this species, but there's documentation, evidence of homosexuality in other species, like black swans and sheep, and in male penguins, pairs have been observed hatching and raising chicks together...so why not?" I respond.

We observe the stags for another minute, appreciating the anatomical features of these regal beasts: the impressive rack of antlers, the rich dark brown coat (the darker winter coat), the large brown sympathetic eyes, the strong muscular necks and bodies, and the creamy white markings on their muzzle and throat.

"Let's go inside," I suggest.

I bow my head toward the stags as we move toward the house. Surprisingly, the eight-point buck bows his head in response; then with a stamp of his enormous hoof on the ground and a subtle bounce of his head, the pair move away from us as we enter the house.

After putting the beer and pizzas in the fridge, we now contemplate what to do for the day. We've already eaten, and I am full, so I won't suggest anything involving eating. Drinking—that's a different matter; there's always room for more beer. Watching television seems to be a ridiculous idea on such a beautiful day. We could go for a walk or a hike.

"Well, whatever we decide to do, it needs to be outside. It's so nice!" Toby exclaims.

"I agree. I was thinking a hike, or maybe a drive—"

"Let's go swimming!"

"Swimming! This time of year! The water will be freezing cold!"

"Sure, but as long as the sun is out, it shouldn't be too bad. Come on, I saw that float you have offshore. That would be fun to swim out to and sunbathe on…we have this beautiful, warm day!" Toby couldn't contain his excitement.

"Do you have a bathing suit?"

"No, but I can wear these shorts or…nothing at all. I'm not shy about skinny dipping."

"Okay, naked boy, I think I have a bathing suit that will fit you," I say as I tamp down his idea of getting naked together.

Thinking about our conversation the other night,

I'm serious about taking this slow. Swimming together naked would present an opportunity to break that pact. I motion Toby to follow me to my bedroom, and I begin searching for a suitable bathing suit. I find a pair of mesh shorts that I think will fit him.

"Here, try these on," I say as I exit the room to give him privacy. Seconds later, he emerges from my bedroom, my mesh shorts snugly fitting his fully formed bottom; he looks like he's waiting for his turn for a Bruce Weber photo shoot.

"Wow. My shorts have never looked so good! You definitely have more in the backfield than I do," I state as I continue to admire the globes of muscle pushing against the nylon fabric.

"They feel great," Toby says as he ties the drawstring on the shorts.

While bending his head down to guide himself with this task, I glance briefly at his crotch and quickly look up as he finishes the task. I think he caught me looking because he's smiling.

"Cool, let me get something to wear and I'll grab some towels from the closet. Why don't you get the cooler on top of the fridge and ice down the beer," I instruct.

He nods and walks toward the kitchen as I search my dresser drawers for a pair of jean cut-offs, my usual swimming gear, unless in a public pool, which has outlawed them (something about loose threads getting in the drain?). Finding them, I slip them on commando style and proceed to check myself out in the mirror to make sure no holes are exposing my nether regions. Check. I find two bath sheets in the bathroom.

Walking into the kitchen, I notice that Toby has

successfully found the mini cooler and is packing the ice around the bottles of beer. I toss him a towel as we leave through the back door, heading toward the berm and the beach. The bay looks breathtakingly beautiful today. The sun reflecting off the calm surf is almost blinding, enticing us to bathe in the supposed warm waters that don't exist at this time of year. The gentle warm breeze bends the sea grasses, cattails, and the branches of trees displaying their fall colors.

Before I can kick off my flips, Toby has already removed his t-shirt, shoes, and is running into the surf. Screaming at the top of his lungs as his legs disappear further into the freezing surf. As he nears the drop-off, he dives into the water, fully submerging his body into the frigid depths but quickly surfaces to the water, screaming.

"AHHHH!, OH MY GOD. IT'S COLD!"

Somewhat hesitant to get in after Toby's outburst, I take off my shirt and run into the surf as well, the icy water stinging my calves and my thighs as I run into deeper water. Now submerged up to my pelvis, I plunge into the icy depths. It feels like a million needles puncturing my skin at the same time. I surface.

"FUUUCK! That's FREEZING, not just cold!" I yell.

Challenging me, Toby yells back, "Race you to the float!"

Knowing the movement will increase our circulation and warm our bodies, I accept the challenge, and using freestyle, head toward the float. We meet at the float at the same time.

Breathing rapidly, grabbing the side of the wooden float, I instruct Toby in between breaths. "You go first.

We both can't get on it at the same time or it might capsize."

With that instruction, Toby grabs the edge of the float with both hands, and using his amazing upper body strength, he easily hoists himself onto the wooden slat surface of the float. Scooting along his abdomen until his entire torso is on the surface of the float, he rolls over and sits up quickly. Now sitting, he offers me his hands. Between his pulling me up with his guns and my furious kicking, my belly is on the float's surface in a split second. Rolling over, chest heaving, I warm the front of my body in the sun's rays. Lying down next to me, I can see and hear Toby's panting for air as well. We both lie still, enjoying the sun's powerful rays dry and warm our bodies. Turning my head, I squint against the glare of the sun so I could take in the full splendor of Toby's magnificence.

Observing his perfect form, the outline of his massive chest and nipples rises with each short breath as his taut abdomen springs with each inhalation and exhalation. I can also see the outline of the bulge beneath his mesh shorts; a tight, compact mound resulting from the freezing temperature we escaped. Glistening in the sunlight, his powerful thighs, and muscular calves, transition into perfectly formed feet and toes. Looking at his face, the sun brilliantly highlights his angular cheekbones, casting shadows on the hollows of his cheeks. His wet, dirty blond hair slicked back toward his skull exposes the short, broad forehead that I have rarely seen beneath the tangle of his bangs. He's an exceptionally handsome man. He looks like a golden boy from a Thomas Eakins painting.

Turning his head in my direction, he notices me

admiring his body. Placing a hand across his brow to shield the sun's rays, he looks at me and smiles. Raising his head off the float, he rolls over onto his abdomen, so that the edge of his waist is slightly overlapping mine. Balancing on his left elbow, he places his right hand on my chest and bends his head toward mine to plant a light kiss on my lips.

"Thank you for inviting me. It's been a perfect day," he purrs into my ear.

"It has been perfect, but you know what would make it even better?"

"What?" Toby asks with a quizzical expression.

"The beer that we left on the shore."

"Oh yeah, that would be great out here. I'll swim back and get it," he states as he stands up.

"Don't worry about it…"

My exclamation, interrupted by the action of the float bouncing up and down, I watch Toby complete his perfect dive off the platform. The ice-cold splash reaches my feet, causing me to sit up quickly. Toby effortlessly swims back to shore.

Suddenly, he goes under. Not purposefully, as if he were diving underneath the water, but more as if he were being pulled. His head rises shortly above the water, but he quickly goes back under in the same location. His head briefly appears again for a split second before disappearing into the depths. He's in trouble. Instinctively, I scramble to stand up and dive off the side. Swimming furiously toward the spot where Toby went under, roughly twenty yards away from the float, he's no longer bobbing up and down. Filled with dread, I dive beneath the murky surface, but I can't see anything. I furiously move my arms in the water to feel for Toby's presence. I don't feel anything.

Abruptly, the water begins to churn, becoming choppy. The rest of the bay is calm except for this spot. A fast-moving whirlpool forms, swirling around me. Unexpectedly, a human-shaped disturbance forms in the eye of the whirlpool; it's Toby. With horror, I see a chain wrapped around his ankle, tugging him under the water. Desperate, I lunge for the chain and grasp it in my hand. It's the type of chain that is connected to an anchor. I try to break some of the links by pulling on the chain, but the rusty metal is too strong. Then I hear a voice, as if it's being whispered in my ear, "Dorian, use your powers."

Concentrating on the chain in my hand, I think of breaking the links psychically. I imagine the metal links elongating until they reach their breaking point. At my command, the links begin to elongate as I had visualized, snapping apart, the broken links floating down into the eye of the whirlpool. Placing my right arm underneath Toby's armpit, I wrap it around his chest and begin to swim us back to shore. Within minutes, I can touch the sandy bottom with my feet. I drag Toby out of the water and onto the shore. I lay him down on the sand and immediately check to see if he's breathing. Nothing. Quickly placing both of my hands, stacked upon each other, in between his mountainous pecs, I push my hands down into his chest and release, rapidly repeating this act three more times. I stop pushing and observe. There's no movement in his chest. Squeezing his nostrils together and forcing his mouth open, I place my lips over his mouth and deeply exhale. Toby begins to cough, seawater spurting out of his mouth onto his face and neck, followed by a violent choking fit. Turning his head to the side, Toby continues to cough water furiously out of his lungs. I hold his head as he vomits the remaining seawater, but all I can see are strands of mucous and salivary bubbles. Toby continues to cough, a reflex that will subside eventually. Helping him to sit up so that he can breathe on his own, I quickly look toward the area of the whirlpool; it's gone and there's no sign of Beladon.

Toby, forcefully breathing on his own, suddenly surrounds me with his arms and places his head in the crook between my neck and shoulder. Hugging me strongly to his chest, he begins to cry.

"You saved…my life…Oh, my God…I thought I was…going to die…I love you…Dorian."

Shocked by his words, I squeeze him tighter, his hard, cold, ice-like nipples piercing the skin of my chest. I rub his back gently in a circular motion.

"It's okay, Toby, I'm here. Everything is going to be fine now. Everything is going to be fine." As he sobs lightly into my shoulder, I continue to rub his back. He finally breaks his hold on me and wipes away his tears.

"I'm so embarrassed."

"You have nothing to be embarrassed about. You just had a life-and-death situation. I would probably cry, too," I say, comforting him.

"Oh, I'm not embarrassed about my crying. I'm embarrassed about what I said…about loving you…that sounds bad, I mean…"

"Shhhh, it's fine. Don't worry about it. You just reacted to almost dying. Hey, I saved your life. I'm your hero, I get it," I say sarcastically.

He immediately laughs. His megawatt smile recovers. Changing the subject, I reposition myself to look at his ankle. "Ooooh, those cuts are deep! We better get those cleaned out. It was a rusty chain that dug into your ankle."

Toby asks incredulously, "Is that what happened? I felt something wrap around it when I stopped swimming for a minute to catch my breath, and the next thing I know, I feel something strong pulling me under the water."

"The chain was most likely attached to an old anchor that was dragging on the bottom. I was able to break the chain. It was pretty rusty."

"You saved my life twice. Once out in the water and a second time when you gave me CPR. Back in the old days, that would mean I would have to be your servant for life."

"Whoa, no one is going to be anyone's servant. Just buy me a beer or something…" I say in a typical blue-collar Boston accent. Toby laughs at my ridiculous accent. "Seriously, I need to dress those scrapes around your ankle. Do you think you can walk on it?"

"Let's see."

Rolling over carefully so both of his knees are on the sand, he plants his right foot into the sandy shore. He then straightens out his right knee, thrusting himself vertically. Quickly placing his weight on his right leg, he places his left foot onto the ground lightly. He screams out in pain. I scoop his left arm onto my right shoulder and wrap my right arm around his back to support him.

"Okay, nice and slow," I state as we methodically move up the dune to the berm.

We make it to the crest of the berm when we're confronted by a sight we didn't expect: the two stags are standing on the other side of the berm, as if they were waiting for us. We both stare at the bucks for a moment as they continue to study us.

"Am I crazy, but do they look like…like they are concerned about us?" Toby states.

"No, you're not. I was thinking the same thing. But we need to get you in the house," I say emphatically, gently guiding Toby toward the house.

Holding their ground as we maneuver around them, the bucks watch us intently as we limp forward. Looking back at them, I notice them following us but keeping a safe distance. Why are they following us? What is their motivation? Are they looking to get food from us? Are they making sure we get to the house safely? Regardless, as soon as we reach the back door, they stop their approach.

I help Toby to sit down on the couch in the family room, propping his left foot up on the coffee table with a pillow from the couch. Pulling a quilt from the side, I drape it over his semi-wet, half-naked body, tucking it around the sides of his thighs and trunk to keep him warm. I retrieve the necessary first aid supplies from the bathroom: rubbing alcohol, antibiotic gel, gauze, band-aids, tape, and a bath towel. Returning, I give him the towel to dry himself. He stops moving as I examine the wounds more intently. The bleeding has stopped. His lacerations are not deep, but they are wide.

I pour the rubbing alcohol on a piece of gauze, look at Toby, and warn him, "This is gonna hurt like a bitch, but this is the only way I know to kill whatever kind of bacteria might have been on that chain. Did you have a tetanus booster when you transferred to Bedfordshire?" As he's concentrating on his answer, I quickly wipe his wounds with the alcohol-soaked gauze pad.

"Yes, I… OWWW, FUCK! That really hurts." His ankle jumps reflexively from the pain. "Man, that stings! I guess you know it's killing whatever's in there if it's killing me!"

"Exactly." I gently rub the antibiotic gel into the wounds.

To butterfly the sides of his lacerations, I cut band-aids into strips. Wrapping the gauze around his ankle in concentric circles, I hold it in place with strips of the first-aid tape. "All right, that's the best I can do. It's not bleeding, and the wounds are not deep, but they are wide. If you begin to run a fever, I'm taking you to the hospital, unless you want to go now."

"No, I'm okay. I'm a fast healer," he states, using the towel to dry his mop of hair. "Do you have a t-shirt or sweatshirt I can borrow? I left mine on the beach."

"Oh, sure, duh," I say out loud. "I can't believe I forgot to get that!" I head off into my room and pick out a heather gray sweatshirt with a hood.

"Hey, you're doing great! You're a great nurse!" Toby states as I re-enter the family room.

"Well, thank you, but that's not a career goal I've considered, Mr. Blessing. Maybe I should rethink it. I'm going to make a fire. The sun will be setting soon, and this house gets drafty at night."

I proceed to gather newspapers, roll them into tight balls, and place them below the fire grate. Placing kindling and small logs onto the grate above the rolled paper, I top off my masterpiece with a medium-sized hardwood log. After striking a match and setting the paper alight, the fire roars to life, its flames rising high into the back of the fireplace. "How does that feel?" I ask Toby but turn and realize my golden boy is asleep. Tucking the quilt around his body to keep him warm, I settle next to him on the other side of the couch.

Watching the fire, I finally take the time to process what happened today. A shiver goes down my spine when I realize how close Toby came to drowning. And Beladon saved Toby. But why? Maybe I've misjudged Beladon. Maybe he's not as selfish as I thought. Or maybe he did it to convince me that he's not a bad…god. Then another shiver goes down my spine. Did Beladon orchestrate the whole thing? Did he wrap that chain from the anchor around Toby's ankle to create the whirlpool to save him? Beladon commands the sea; he would know how to do that if he wished.

Before I can say another word, my vision gets blurry, and I pass out sitting on the couch. I'm violently awakened by Beladon's voice uttering one word, "No."

I have my answer. Beladon could have ignored me, but he answered my question: he didn't cause the accident. I feel better.

We're sitting in the dark, a few embers in the fireplace are the only source of light. Realizing it's dinner time, I walk into the kitchen and pre-heat the oven for the pizzas.

Popping the pizzas in the oven on sheets of tin foil, I set the timer for fifteen minutes and then run out to retrieve the beer and the clothes we left on the beach. Returning, I'm greeted by the sight of my sleepy-eyed, golden boy, still wrapped in the quilt but sitting at the kitchen table. I check the pizza in the oven.

"Hello, are you getting hungry? Pizza should be ready in a few more minutes."

Toby responds groggily, in between yawns, "Yeah,

I'm getting a bit hungry. How long was I asleep?"

"A few hours. We both fell asleep. Are you up for a Sam Adams?"

"Sure. Wow, I don't fall asleep like that very often."

"You don't almost drown every day either," I curtly state.

"True, or I just feel really comfortable around you and that's the only way I can sleep." I take the statement as the obvious compliment he's implying.

The pizzas are delicious. We settle back into the couch in the family room with the last of the beer. Toby rests his head on my shoulder as we watch the embers of the fire slowly die out. I then remember to look at his injury.

"Hey, let me look at your ankle." Unwrapping the bandage around his ankle I'm astonished to see that the wounds are almost completely gone.

Toby looks down at this ankle. "See? I told you I was a quick healer. Playing Rugby, my body has learned to adapt to injury."

I wasn't completely convinced of this, as your immune system doesn't quite work like that. Nevertheless, I confirm his earlier statement, "You sure are."

"Hey, it's getting late, so why don't you stay the night? You can have my room and I'll sleep out here on the couch. I'll stoke the fire with plenty of wood to keep it warm," I suggest.

"No, I can't make you do that. I'll sleep on the couch."

"No, you're a guest, and you need to keep that ankle raised, which will be a lot easier in a bed. No more objections—you are taking my bed, I insist."

Toby finally relinquishes "Okay, I think I'm almost there; I'm beat."

Walking toward my bedroom, I notice he doesn't have a limp anymore. As if his ankle is completely healed. Is this Beladon's work? Toby gives me a big bear hug. Pulling his head slightly away, he kisses me full on the mouth for a few seconds, and whispers in my ear, "Good night."

Lying down in between the sheets and the comforter, I notice he is not paying attention to his ankle at all. He pulls the comforter up to his neck and I snap the hurricane lamp off. As I leave the room, I can't help but utter what my mother always said when I was a little boy when I went to bed, "Sleep tight, don't let the bed bugs bite." Or Beladon, as an afterthought.

****

I awake to see a shadowy figure looming over me. Before I can react, I hear a soothing familiar voice, "Dorian, Dorian." It's Toby standing next to me, wrapped in my blanket. "The fire has gone out and it's freezing out here," he whispers.

"I'll be okay," I say, realizing I am shivering as well, and pull the quilt up to my neck.

"I don't want you to be cold. If you want, you can get in bed with me," he offers.

Weighing my options quickly, deciding that a warm bed with a hunk of a man who is probably an excellent radiator is warmer than a drafty 300-year-old house, I gather the quilt around me and follow Toby, who isn't limping, toward my room. Removing the blanket from around his body, Toby's boxer briefs look like a second skin around his well-developed glutes and upper thighs. I'm wearing my b-ball shorts and a t-shirt. Laying the blanket across the bed, he pulls the sheets back and slides under them. I slide in next to him, the back half of my body lying in front of his body. He places his right hand on my shoulder. "Jesus, your shoulder feels like ice. Here, let me warm you up."

Toby's warm, muscular chest is kneading into my shoulder blades, his right arm fully wrapped around my chest, resting just above the top of my rib cage. I can feel his warm breath on the nape of my neck. I can also feel my penis coming to life. His lower body is not sandwiched next to mine, so I don't know if he's feeling the same way. As much as I want to, I refrain from inching myself closer to him. I think of non-sexy things to calm my growing erection as I listen to the distinct sounds of Toby sleeping; not snoring, but a heavy breathing indicative of deep sleep. I made the right decision. I eventually fall asleep with this powerful man's muscular paw wrapped around my chest.

Chapter 16

Graveyard of the Church of Bedfordshire Village
3ʳᵈ week of October 1992

I wake up this morning to an unusual odor: a musky, strong masculine smell, and a pressure against my face. I'm being couched in something firm and pliable but a texture that does not match the soft cotton cloth of my pillowcase. Cracking my eyelids open, I detect a light brown surface, smooth and warm—bare skin. Raising my head slightly, my eyes still trying to focus on the bright morning light, I see Toby's firm, naked chest. The potent smell wafting in my direction is from his exposed armpit. Turning my head slightly upward, I stare at his boyishly handsome, sleeping face.

I lie my head back down onto the firm but inviting pectoral muscle of his chest, absorbing all the stimuli around my face: the steady, rhythmic thump of his heartbeat, the slight elevation of my head with every inhalation. I study his large left hand that drapes upon my chest. The perfect shape and length of each bronzed, curled finger resting near my collarbone. His buff manicured nailbeds and calloused fingertips. Following the natural line from his hand to the upper part of the extremity, I examine the powerful, broad forearm and the hint of the strapping mountainous muscles of the upper arm.

As I continue to admire Toby's physique, there's a subtle movement indicating Toby is waking up. Fingers are smoothing, petting my hair, digits lightly grazing sensitive skin and twisting strands that elicit gentle tugs. Closing my eyes to eliminate all other stimuli, I bask in the exquisite sensation of head massage. Then I hear and feel the vibrations of a deep, groggy voice, "Good morning."

I slide my head along Toby's chest to his left shoulder, smiling and resting my head on the cap of his shoulder so I can see his face. "Good morning."

Detecting an unpleasant odor coming from my mouth, I quickly lift my head off Toby's shoulder, and instinctively cover my mouth with my hand. "Sorry about the dragon breath." Sitting up, resting my head and back against the wall, I continue our conversation, "How are you feeling this morning?"

"Good, my lungs feel a little sore, but my ankle feels fine," Toby says, coughing slightly, as if he's confirming a self-fulfilling prophecy.

"I'm glad to hear that. By the way, your pecs make a great pillow," I comment slyly, raising my left eyebrow.

Toby grins slightly. "It was nice to wake up like that. So, what's the plan for today?"

"Well, I think we should start with a big breakfast: pancakes, bacon, sausage, fresh squeezed orange juice, and of course, coffee. How does that sound?"

"Awesome, let's do it. I'm hungry." Toby turns toward me; his musky smell growing in strength the closer he gets to me.

Swinging my legs off the bed, I stand up and immediately stretch my trunk, rubbing my belly under my t-shirt, my usual morning ritual. Trudging into the bathroom, I yell back to Toby, "I'll be just a few minutes, and then you can have the bathroom."

After my morning ritual, I exit the bathroom and head to the kitchen. Toby's waiting in the hallway. Also a victim of bedhead like I was, he's rubbing the sleepers out of his eyes, looking incredibly hot, and wearing nothing but his boxer briefs.

"Your turn," I say nonchalantly, trying to cover my lusty thoughts as I head to the kitchen.

He briefly pats my left shoulder as I pass and enter the kitchen.

I pull out the necessary ingredients from the refrigerator and pantry for our breakfast feast as well as the cooking utensils. A few minutes later, as I'm organizing the food and prepping the frying pans, Toby enters the kitchen looking refreshed and more modestly clothed; making a beeline for me. Leaning into me, he gives me a longer-than-usual kiss on the lips. Savoring the feel of his lips sliding over mine, I can taste the minty flavor of my toothpaste.

"Good morning!"

"Now that's more like it," I respond.

After we finish our delicious and deeply satisfying breakfast, we relax into more conversation over coffee. Discussing the possible activities we can do together today, the same suggestions from yesterday appear again. Thinking about the events of yesterday, I inevitably start to think about the near drowning and Beladon. Then it comes to me. I've time today to check out one of the rumored Elias Doever burial sites: the unconsecrated ground next to the graveyard of the old church. However, I'm with Toby today, so is that going to be a good combination? I imagine that conversation using my best "burnout" dialect, "So like, I need to check out a burial site for the remains of a three-hundred-year-old dude, so like, I can dig up his bones. Wanna come?"

I need to think of an alternate reason for going to the graveyard. After a few minutes of devising a reason, I verbalize my white lie, "Hey, I need to check out something in the graveyard of the old church in town. Do you want to come with me?"

Toby, as I expected, responds non-verbally with a confused, inquisitive expression.

"I'm looking for the gravestone of a relative of Elias Doever, the man who lived in this house three hundred years ago and was executed as a warlock but was not buried in the cemetery. I've heard there is a clue to Elias Doever's burial site in an epitaph on one of the tombstones of his relatives. Sound like something you would be interested in, poking around a graveyard on a crisp Sunday afternoon?"

"Why do you want to do this?"

Thinking on my feet, I conjure a mostly true answer. "Well, after we went to Witch Well Park and I learned about Elias Doever's tragic history from the memorial plaque and Dr. Hayden's story, I became interested in more details of Elias Doever's persecution and execution. He was the original owner of the house we live in, and...I don't know why, but I feel like I need to know more about him. Learning the legend of his secret burial plot and that no one has ever discovered it has made me curious to try and find it. Weird?"

"Yes," Toby says without hesitation, but then

continues, "How long were you thinking of staying there? I have to study at some point today."

"Hopefully, not long. But if it does, I can always whisk you back to campus."

"Okay, but I need a shower first before we go anywhere. I stink!"

"Dude, I noticed… No, I'm kidding. I need one, too. Here, let me show you how the shower works," I say as we proceed into the bathroom.

After I show him how to operate the various handles, testing the water with my hand to see if it has any "surprises," I grab a towel for him from the stack on the shelf above the toilet. While Toby showers, I clean up the kitchen and take care of the breakfast dishes. A few minutes later, he walks into the kitchen, drying his hair with a towel and wearing another tied around his waist, looking as if he walked out of a locker room or communal dorm bathroom. He is hot. Full confession: I have a thing about having sex after showering (probably the Virgo in me) and all I can think about is ripping that towel off and attacking him. I immediately push that thought from my mind and focus on other things.

"If you need to borrow some boxers, just grab a pair in my top drawer."

"No, think I'll go commando today," he states as he retreats into my bedroom to dress.

"Great, I'll be looking for signs of protruding anatomy all day," I say quietly.

I shower quickly. No happy shower. I slip on a pair of boxers, an old gray hooded sweatshirt, b-ball shorts, and my flips. My look contrasts Toby's gear: a t-shirt, cargo shorts and docksiders. We don't look like we're dressed for the same season. After retrieving a pen and pad of paper for the fictional reason of writing something from a tombstone, a couple of granola bars and a couple of bottles of water, I put everything into my knapsack and hoist it over my shoulder. Grabbing the keys to the sedan, I'm half expecting to see our deer couple as I open the front door, but they're nowhere in sight.

"I was hoping that we would see our deer brethren. They always seem to appear when we're together. Oh well."

Driving away from Doever Farm, Toby grasps my hand after I have shifted into high gear, and we hold hands all the way into Bedfordshire proper. The original Church of Bedfordshire Village and the church's graveyard are in a block on the eastern side of the town near the docks and public beach. The graveyard is on the western side of the church building and adjacent to a small but dense forest north of the graveyard. After scouting and studying the layout of the graveyard previously, I determined that the narrow strip of land south of the forest bordering the northernmost line of graves constitutes the unconsecrated ground. In the minds of the Puritans of Bedfordshire, the unholy undead would not be able to cross the holy ground of the graveyard but would have to travel through the thick forest, presumably to seek revenge. The Puritans probably felt that they would be safe if they stayed out of these woods.

I park the sedan on the street parallel to the graveyard. The historical cemetery is separated from the sidewalks on the southern and western sides of the graveyard by a short stone wall made of fieldstone and mortar, not unlike the walls fashioned for protection during the Revolutionary War. To enter the graveyard, you must either walk through an archway on the southern side, a stone pathway between the entrance of the church and the cemetery, or via the woods on the north side. We chose to enter via the archway made of iron and stone on the southern exposure. The iron signpost of the archway is ancient revealed by the many layers of black peeling paint and rust that cover the curved metal façade and iron lettering that spells BEDFORDSHIRE CEMETERY.

Walking along the flat stone pathway, we examine the gravestones, looking for a headstone with the name of "Doever" engraved upon it. We discover that many of the oldest gravestones/markers, with dates ranging from the 17th and 18th century are thin and small with a minimal amount of barely legible engraved words, nearly impossible to read from 200-300 years of weathering. Many are broken and chipped, revealing the marbled layers beneath.

After a few minutes of walking, unexpectedly, I experience a wave of lethargy, dizziness, disorientation, and nausea. The same symptoms I felt when I was visiting the well where Elias Doever was murdered. If this is any indication of what is to happen next, I'll lose consciousness soon and time travel to some important date in Elias Doever's life. Looking around to see if there's anything I can lean on, I calmly ask Toby for help. "Toby, I don't feel well. I need to get out of here. I'm going to pass out."

Noticing the forest to the north and the unconsecrated ground, my intuition is telling me that I need to move in that direction. I'm barely able to vocalize my thoughts as my condition worsens.

"I need to move…to that area…before the woods."

"What's wrong with you?" Toby places my arm around his shoulder, guiding me down the stone pathway toward the edge of the graveyard.

I'm losing energy quickly. Barely enough stamina to stand, I can't move the muscles of my mouth to respond to Toby. He's totally supporting my dead weight. Toby circles his arm around my waist and using his superior upper body strength, essentially drags me down the stone pathway. We're within a few feet from the end of the stone pathway, presumably marking the end of the cemetery, when Toby stops abruptly. Dropping his arm from around my waist, I instantly slump to the ground and land on my back, unable to move. Trying to make sense of why he dropped me, I can only move my eyes to look at him while my head rests on the ground.

As if on cue, Toby turns his head downward to look at me. His eyes have a faraway look—a blank expression on his face. Suddenly, he begins to speak, but it's not his voice but a deeper, more solemn, monotone.

"Elias, why did you leave me? I died inside the day you died."

I can scarcely believe what I'm hearing, but being paralyzed, I'm helpless to do anything.

With the same blank expression, Toby continues to speak with this foreign voice, repeating only one phrase: "I died the day you died."

Toby repeats this dire phrase seven times, standing above me with the same blank expression on his face for what seems like minutes, but I know is only seconds. Suddenly, the muscles in his face soften and his blank expression disappears. Shaking his head as if he has been hit by something, he staggers for a moment but then quickly gains his composure. He spots me on the ground.

"Oh my God! Dorian!"

Quickly, he kneels next to me, realizing I can't move. Cupping his hands into my armpits, he lifts my trunk off the stone pathway and drags my body. Using my telepathy, I will him to drag me toward the grassy meadow next to the woods at the end of the pathway. He does as I instruct. Seeing a tree trunk lying on the edge of the woods, I will Toby to drag me to it so he can prop my body against it. Toby gently places my upper body propped up against the tree. I'm starting to regain my faculties. The sensation is similar to the feeling of blood returning to a foot that has fallen asleep due to vascular compression. Toby sits next to me, leaning his back against the tree. I slowly turn my head to look at him. He's gradually closing his eyes. I strain to whisper my concern, "Toby! Toby! Are you all right!"

Slowly, his neck muscles lose tone, and the back of his head thumps against the hollow of the tree trunk. He's asleep in seconds. Abruptly, my arms and legs begin to awaken as if they were thawing from a deep freeze. I can bend my knees, elbows, ankles, and wrists. Folding my body into a position so that I can roll over onto my knees, I lay my hands flat on the ground and gradually stand up. Looking down at Toby, he's still passed out, lying prostrate against the tree trunk. I move his head so that the back of his skull is tilted to the right, lying against the tree trunk, to reduce the tension in his neck and larynx. As I stare at Toby's handsome face, unexpectedly, my view of his face becomes blurry, then blank.

****

I'm looking at a large gray gravestone but the engraving on the stone is worn and difficult to read. I'm able to detect the dates of 1663 and 1693, and one word: PUTNAM.

I'm now in a primitive-looking room. The walls are made of logs with a dark mud-like substance sandwiched in between. The light is low; a single large columnar candle illuminates the sparse interior. A man with a pleasing face, piercing blue eyes, long dirty blond hair, and a reddish-blond beard is lying on a wooden bed. A brightly colored patchwork quilt covers the lower half of his body. The contours of the muscles in his arms, chest and neck are well-defined but not overly developed. A wisp of light brown colored hair sprouting from his abdomen peeks out from the edge of the quilt. The tuft continuous with that growing in the valley between his sinewy chest muscles.

He's laughing. Talking to someone in the room whom I cannot see. I hear one word, "Elias." I move closer to the semi-naked man on the bed. I'm now looking at his face, into the ice-blue eyes that are staring back at me. He closes them and purses his mustachioed lips. I'm kissing him, the sensation of his wet lips on mine. I gradually move away to look at his face again. I can hear light kisses and a low groan coming from the man. The kissing sounds move to the chest, into the space between the two slabs of muscle. The masculine groaning increases in volume. The view shifts to look up to the beautiful man's face once more from the position of someone resting their head on his abdominal area. The facial expression changes on the man as a disembodied, resonant, low-pitched voice exclaims, "John Putnam, ye are my life."

****

The vision is over. Promptly, I put together what Toby was saying to me in his trance. "I died the day you died," and the surname on the gravestone, and soon realize that the gravestone in my vision is that of John Putnam, Elias Doever's male lover. The vision in the cabin was of John Putnam becoming intimate with me while I occupied Elias Dover's body.

Toby was possessed by the spirit of John Putnam!

Inexplicably, the story of John Putnam's death comes into focus in my head. Dr. Hayden had told me that John Putnam was buried in consecrated ground even though he was found guilty and executed as a warlock. Because his brother William Putnam had enormous influence in Bedfordshire, he convinced the parishioners of Bedfordshire that John could be buried in the church graveyard because his soul could still be saved. I could come to only one conclusion from this message and this vision: John Putnam was reaching out beyond the grave to contact me, a descendant of Elias Doever.

While Toby is unconscious, I decide to make use of this quiet time to try to contact the spirit of Elias Doever. After the supernatural disorientation and paralysis I experienced today, I'm hopeful that my symptoms are because I'm near Elias Doever's remains—that he's buried nearby in the unconsecrated ground I stand upon. I sit down on the grass and lean my back against the tree trunk as before. Closing my eyes and crossing my legs, I concentrate to make a psychic connection. Emptying my mind of all thoughts, I focus on my breathing, the rhythm of air flowing into my nostrils and out through my mouth.

After lying perfectly still for several minutes, I've not made any contact with any entity, nor have I felt any vibrations of a psychic force. Refusing to be discouraged, I continue my attempt to reach Elias Doever. Several minutes pass, still no sign of Elias's presence nor John Putnam's, which I had thought was a possibility after his possession of Toby. Nevertheless, I'm content to continue however long is necessary or until Toby wakes.

"Can I help you?" a deep, older voice asks, but it's not coming from a psychic connection.

I open my eyes to investigate. Standing in front of us is a tall man dressed in a black suit with a white shirt and thin royal blue tie. There is a glint of something shiny reflecting from his lapel; it's a silver cross pinned to his jacket.

"Hello, Father."

"Reverend, my boy, I'm not a priest. I'm Reverend Corwin. Are you and your friend all right?" he asks in concern.

"Yes, we both were overcome with something while we were walking through the cemetery, so we sat down here to rest. I think it might have been something we ate, but we both feel better now. I'm letting Toby sleep a little longer, but we're going to be leaving soon."

"Would you like to come into the church to get some water or maybe a cup of tea to warm up?" Reverend Corwin kindly asks.

"No, I have to get Toby back to school. He's the star rugby player for Bedfordshire," I state, not understanding why I gave him that much unnecessary information. Confession of a guilty mind? I decide it's time for sleeping beauty to wake up.

"Toby, Toby, it's time to leave," I say, gently shaking his shoulder.

His eyelids start to flutter. His eyes open widely. Simultaneously, turning his head upward and toward me, he speaks groggily.

"What happened? I was dragging you…"

"Toby, this is Reverend Corwin," I say, interrupting Toby before he says too much. Toby's eyebrows tilt downward toward his nose. Turning his head upward, he sees the man in a black suit.

"Oh, hello, Reverend, we were just taking a little snooze. I'm a rugby player at Bedfordshire—"

I interrupt him again. "Yes, I already told Reverend Corwin about that, and I also told him that I need to get you back to school soon, so…"

At this suggestion, Toby attempts to stand using the tree trunk as leverage as he's still a bit wobbly. I copy his actions and soon we're both standing next to Reverend Corwin. Toby instinctively extends his hand to the friendly stranger to shake his hand. "Reverend Corwin, I'm Toby Blessing and this is Dorian Leeves."

Prompted by my introduction, I make the same gesture. Suddenly, as I'm shaking his hand, a faint but distinct vibration like a low-level electrical shock travels through my hand and into my forearm. Reflexively, I release his hand to stop the strange sensation from traveling any further. I look at the Reverend to see if he feels anything. His facial expression gives me no indication that he's uncomfortable.

"Well, it was nice to meet you, Reverend. We'll be on our way. Thank you for the invite. Come on, Toby, let's go to the car," I say as I motion (with my still stinging hand) to walk along the edge of the woods, bypassing the graveyard. Toby looks at me with a familiar confused and quizzical expression, but he does not argue.

"Nice to meet you, Reverend. Maybe we'll come to the Christmas Eve service or sooner," Toby yells as we quickly move further away from him.

"All are welcome, my son," he shouts to us.

As we near the stone wall on the west side of the graveyard, we both climb over the shallow barrier with ease. I briskly walk down the sidewalk toward the car to continue the charade that we're in a hurry to get somewhere. Toby finally breaks his silence about my choice of departure.

"Why did you want to leave this way? It would've been easier to walk down the stone pathway through the archway. Your car is parked right next to it."

Thinking quickly on my feet, I invent a plausible explanation. "We both got ill walking through the graveyard. I lost control of my muscles, and you blacked out. I don't know what's in there, a gas leak or some type of radiation, or who knows what, but I wasn't about to go through there again."

"I blacked out?" Toby asks me as we climb into the sedan.

"Yes, you blacked out for at least thirty seconds. Don't you remember being confused as to why I was on the ground before you dragged me to that tree trunk?" I state as I start the car.

"Yeah, I remember that, but I don't remember much before that or after. Just waking up next to you, leaning against that tree."

At that moment, I'm feeling relief that Toby doesn't remember anything about his being possessed by the spirit of John Putnam. I don't even know how I would begin to explain that. "What time did you want to go back to campus to study?"

"I didn't bring my watch, but I should probably get back. I have three exams this week, including a biology lecture exam."

"Okay," I state as we near the stone gates of the Bedfordshire College entrance.

However, instead of turning into the entrance, I make a turn in the opposite direction into the parking lot of the First Presbyterian Church of Bedfordshire, across the street. I park the car. Toby turns to me with that adorable "little boy doesn't understand" expression.

"What are we doing here?"

Grasping both of Toby's hands in mine, I explain, "When I travel long distance and feel like I'm going to fall asleep, I've learned that parking lots of churches are the safest places to take a quick nap. No one bothers you when you are parked at a church, because no one patrols the parking lot like in shopping malls or public parks. I drove us in here so that I could say goodbye to you properly."

With that last part of my explanation, I gently grab Toby's shoulders and pull him closer to me. After quickly looking around the parking lot, I close my eyes and plant a kiss on his soft lips. Covering his entire mouth with mine, I initiate a dance between our tongues. It's a deeply sensual kiss. After several seconds, I slowly break away. Looking at Toby, I absorb all that has happened to us this weekend.

"This has been one of the most amazing weekends I've ever had, and I'm not just saying that."

"I feel the same way. You saved my life...twice! You cooked for me, took care of me...a guy could get used to this," Toby gushes as he gives me a dose of that mega-watt smile.

I can't resist giving him another quick kiss on those luscious lips. Before anything else can get started in the romance department, I start the sedan, drive across the street, and drop him near the gates of Bedfordshire College. Driving home, I begin to process what happened in the graveyard but decide to wait until I can be alone in my bedroom to think without any distractions. Pulling into the circular driveway, Mother's Volvo is parked near the front door. Walking in the door, I'm bombarded with the smells of something that has a tomato base and spices.

"Hey, sweetie!" Mother's high-pitched cry shrieks from the kitchen.

Peeking around the corner of the kitchen, she is stirring something in the blue Creuset ceramic and iron pot with a wooden spatula. I lean into her and give her a peck on the cheek. "Hmmm, what smells so good?"

"Turkey Chili. Can you set the table, honey? I've been waiting for you to get home so we can eat together. How was your weekend?"

"Good. I processed some data and went swimming yesterday."

"Swimming! In that freezing water?" she exclaims.

I continue the conversation as I retrieve the bowls and silverware. "It was such a beautiful day, it must have been in the seventies, I couldn't resist. Hey, have you seen that pair of bucks walking around the property?"

"No," she responds as she ladles the chili into the bowls I've laid next to the stove.

Picking the bowls up and placing them on the placemats, I simultaneously describe the stag to her, "They are enormous, an eight pointer and a six pointer. Really majestic looking, they seem to travel together on the property. I haven't seen any other deer besides these two. Which reminds me, have you ever heard of male deer coupling?"

Mother sits down at the table as she answers my question, "No, but that doesn't mean that it isn't possible. I'll have to be on the lookout for them. My visit with your aunt was nice and uneventful. Your uncle was out of town. If I had known that I would've encouraged you to come with me, but it was a surprise to me when she told me he was hunting."

I decide not to answer and continue to eat my chili in peace. The rest of the dinner conversation is school-related and light. After dinner, we settle into the family room and watch some TV. We are treated to a double dose of animal-centered programs as we find ourselves laughing aloud watching one of those informative but fun documentaries about animals in the wild. Not long after, I feel tired and give her a kiss on the cheek. As I'm about to walk back to my room, she grabs my hand.

"Is everything okay, honey? You look like you are preoccupied with something."

"Yes, I'm fine... I'm still trying to adapt to my

new life here, that's all."

"I know it's an adjustment from Boston, but you'll make new friends, colleagues, that is what we call our peers in the academic world," she gently explains.

"Sure," I nonchalantly reply as I walk toward my room.

My adaptation comment is a true statement. She doesn't need to know that "adaptation" means conforming to a supernatural way of living. Not yet anyway. I close the door, lay down on the bed, and finally start to process what happened today. Thinking like a scientist, I sort out all the elements of the day.

First, the episode at the graveyard is like the episode I had at Witch Well Park. The same strange feeling that overpowered me and disabled me at the well was present at the cemetery. It rendered me unable to move my arms and legs. Toby had to drag me out of the graveyard because I couldn't stand. Second, my loss of motor functions only happened when I was in the Bedfordshire Church graveyard because once I was dragged into the area before the forest, I regained my muscular abilities. So, what is it about the graveyard? The graveyard contains earth blessed by the church, consecrated ground, where Christians can be buried and supposedly ascend into heaven. The ground near the forest where Elias was rumored to be buried is not blessed, unconsecrated.

Wait? That can't be it? The blessed ground?

"Did I lose control of my body because I was walking on consecrated ground?"

Then I remember the weird reaction I had when I shook Reverend Corwin's hand. Was that because he's a holy man who has the power to bless things in the name of Jesus? Why am I reacting to the things that are blessed by the church? Is it because of my connection to Elias Doever? Beladon? Because I have their DNA in my physiology? I was confirmed in the Catholic church, have been to Mass and other holy places, and never had this reaction. Elias Doever was not allowed to be buried in consecrated ground for fear he may rise one day and seek revenge, and the holy ground surrounding his grave would serve as a barrier. Perhaps, he was cursed from that point to never be able to cross land blessed by the church. When the "magical DNA" I share with Elias was mixed with the "magical DNA" of Beladon, its virulence increased and that is why I cannot walk on consecrated earth.

Feeling satisfied with my initial analysis of this incident, and a possible answer to my conundrum in the graveyard, a third subject enters my reasoning circus: the presence of John Putnam's spirit.

John Putnam's spirit mistakenly identified me as Elias Doever, most likely because of the shared DNA I have with Elias. If the amplification of his DNA via Beladon's DNA is strong enough to elicit the resurrection of John Putnam's ghost, then that would verify my prior hypothesis: the DNA that I share with Elias Doever was responsible for the reaction that I had in the graveyard. In addition, the vision I received when looking at Toby was of the gravestone of John Putnam. And what about that flashback of the intimate scene between John and Elias. This would reinforce the theory that John Putnam's spirit was trying to contact what it identified as its dead lover. To express the feelings John had after Elias was executed, it possessed Toby's body to communicate that heartbreaking message of despair: "I died the day you died."

A wave of sadness rushes over me as I think about that phrase. To be in a same-sex relationship of any sort in Puritan America was heresy, punishable by death. The bravery that these men showed to try and live their authentic lives was truly remarkable, and each paid with his life. I'm teary-eyed now in my room thinking about this tragic love story. Humbled and saddened at the same time. Overcome with emotion, it's time to go to bed.

I strip and climb in between the sheets to warm myself. Obviously, I have more questions for Beladon. I must not think about them lest I get a visionary answer. I'm not in the mood. However, there is one thought that I cannot resolve as I am drifting off to sleep. I've eliminated two of the rumored locations of Elias Doever's burial site, which leaves me with one more possibility: James Corey's farm. That will require more research. A new task at hand. Lying in bed, I'm desperately trying not to think about this. Eventually, the exhaustion of my body wins, and I fall into a sleep that feels like I'm six feet under.

Chapter 17

Library and Archives of Bedfordshire Village
3rd week of October 1992

To find the original property lines of James Corey's farm, I'll have to conduct research in the archives of Bedfordshire Village located in the Bedfordshire Public Library. I plan to visit the library tomorrow as I have biology lab today and a deadline for statistical analysis for our snail study.

Today, we're conducting the physiology lab, where students will learn how to use several devices to obtain physiological data: a sphygmomanometer, also known as a blood pressure cuff, to record blood pressure; and a stethoscope to aid in obtaining blood pressure, breath sounds from the chest and back, and the contraction sounds of the different areas of the heart. In this lab, students work in pairs to obtain the data. Often, the men will remove their shirts to get accurate data, so I try to pair students into male/female partnerships. A couple of female students came close to fighting to be Toby's partner. There are some healthy specimens in the class, but no one can compare to my man's physique.

Watching Toby's female partner place the stethoscope on his chest to secure breath and heart sounds, the reflexive contraction of his pectoral muscles to the cold metal of the bell of the stethoscope and the resulting outburst make me smile. His female partner's ecstatic reaction to touching his massive chest muscles is also worth observation. I imagine how I would do this if I were Toby's partner. Foreplay to a hot make-out session? I'm starting to get wood, so I move away and focus on other pairs to maintain my professionalism. But I make a note for future dates with Toby.

After lab, I talk with Toby briefly, choosing my words carefully. "Mr. Blessing, it looked like you were having a good time in lab today, enjoying all the attention."

Toby looks around the room, leans in, and whispers, "Jealous?"

Smirking, I change the subject, talking in a hushed tone. "I'm going to the Bedfordshire library tomorrow to do some research. Want to meet for dinner afterward?"

"Yeah. My practice is over at six p.m. Is that too late?"

"No, the library closes at seven p.m. on Wednesday. That is one of the reasons why I'm going tomorrow night."

"Okay, I'll meet you there around seven p.m. I'll need to shower after practice and it's about a mile from school."

At this time, a group of students walk by, and I camouflage our conversation. "Yes, Mr. Blessing, that is correct. Breath sounds are a proper follow-up to CPR. Thank you for the question."

"Thank you, Mr. Leeves. Have a good day," Toby says, winking and smiling slyly as he leaves.

****

The librarian, Mrs. Marian Parris, of the Bedfordshire Library, is also the pro-temp archivist of the town. A woman in her late fifties/early sixties, she appears to be the stereotypical version of a librarian: short and small-boned, a studious but kindly looking face with spectacles perched on her nose with an attached chain around her neck, and gray hair pulled back into a bun. She's wearing a white blouse with puffy sleeves, a light brown sweater vest, a tan skirt, and brown suede flats. After I secure the necessary permission to observe the oldest documents, Mrs. Parris directs me to the archives room where the oldest maps exist. After instructing me to put on a pair of latex gloves to eliminate the transfer of oils from the skin that can be damaging to the ancient parchments, she lays a stack of maps in transparent laminated pouches on the desk. The gloves are an interesting request as Mrs. Parris tells me not to remove any of the cartography from the envelopes. I assume I was to put the gloves on in case I can't resist the sudden impulse to remove a map from its protector. I also request a copy of the most recent city map of Bedfordshire with the property lines drawn for each numbered residence.

The parchments are organized in a box, filed by most recent to the first records, from the mid-1850s until the late 1600s. I flip through the envelopes to the bottom of the pile and select two maps dated 1690 and 1695. Both maps are hand-drawn and in no manner are they proportional to the actual property dimensions of Bedfordshire. Rather, these maps demonstrate the distribution of the properties by surname within the confines of the village. Searching the contour of the Mass Bay coastline, I find the plot of land owned by

"Doever, William," the small, rudimentary town square and the cemetery of the Church of Bedfordshire Village. These reference points will help me to determine where the other plots might be in modern Bedfordshire.

As I scour for the name Corey, I come upon a plot to the west of the town square with the name of "Corey, Giles Matthew." A possibility. I try another tact to find the current location of the farm owned by James Corey. Starting at the Doever and Putnam farms, I make note of each coastline plot moving north: the farms that constitute modern Witch Well Park, the land that would become the foundation of Bedfordshire College, the church property, the port of the village, the backwoods (known as East Forest on the map), and then a couple of other plots north of the backwoods. It's within the northernmost limits of the village that I find a plot designated as "Corey, James."

The boundaries of the plot appear to encompass a large piece of property when compared to the other plots in the vicinity. It is bordered by the Mass Bay coastline on the east, by a large forest on its northern border, another farm at its southern border, and a road/path to the west. I place the modern map of numbered residences next to the parchment in the laminated pouch. Using the forest that is the northern border of the original farm, I'm astonished to observe that the forest on the recent city map remarkably has the same shape and expanse as the ancient map. It has scarcely been developed in 300 years. Looking at the properties on the current map bordering the southern border of the forest, there are four separate numbered lots: two of them along the coastline, and two bordering the modern highway to Salem and Gloucester. Recording the lot numbers, I leave the room with the maps and seek out Mrs. Parris.

"Mrs. Parris, I was wondering if you know how I can determine the physical and/or street addresses for recent lot numbers. I have found four lots for which I'd like to know the modern street addresses."

"Lot numbers are also the 911 numbers. We can determine the addresses in the reference room," she informs me as we move in the direction of the reference room.

She expertly finds the resource book that lists properties by their 911 numbers, and then shows me how to look up each lot number. She returns to the front desk as I conduct my search. I determine the street addresses for the four lots as 106, 108, 110, and 112 Old Salem Highway. The coastal lots are 108 and 112. Lots 106 and 110 border the highway, situated directly west of the coastal properties. I have the addresses of the lots that were part of the original James Corey farm. My mission to find the third rumored burial place of Elias Doever is going well. I'm involuntarily smiling.

Returning to the room with the maps, I'm about to return them to the archivist when suddenly I remember something Dr. Hayden had told me concerning the reason behind Elias Doever being targeted by William Putnam. I'm curious to see whether the property lines between the Doever and Putnam farms were changed after Elias Doever's death. Comparing the farm property lines between the map of 1690 and the map of 1695, I'm pleasantly surprised to notice they were not changed three years after Elias's execution. William Putnam's plan to incorporate part of the Doever farm was prevented somehow. Further investigation is warranted, but that'll be another day.

After learning the physical addresses of the four lots of the original farm, I wonder if these addresses stood out in any other way in the Village of Bedfordshire's history. Remembering the story about the young Harvard student who died when he supposedly disturbed the burial place of Elias Doever, I wonder if any unusual deaths occurred in the confines of the original James Corey property.

I approach the front desk. "Mrs. Parris, thank you so much for all your help today, but I have one more request. Is there a resource that includes outstanding deaths that have occurred in Bedfordshire?"

Mrs. Parris looks up at me strangely. "Outstanding deaths? Are you asking about accidental deaths?"

"Yes, maybe…deaths that stand out for some reason, like the cause was never determined or the nature of the demise was shocking in some way."

Mrs. Parris's facial expression and demeanor change. "Are you looking for information about the Danforth tragedy?" she whispers to me.

"The Danforth tragedy?"

Abruptly, she leaves the front desk and walks back to the bookshelves behind the front desk, searching for something. Walking back toward me, she has a book in her hands. Placing it on the counter, she continues our conversation in a hushed tone, "This will answer your questions about the Danforths. Can I get you anything else?"

"No, ah…not for now, thank you," I answer quickly, realizing she's not going to discuss the book with me. With that, Mrs. Parris looks down at her ledger and continues with her work. I take this as a subtle cue to remove the book and read it on my own.

Walking back to the map room, I glance at the cover of the book: *Tragedy in Bedfordshire: The Danforth Murder-Suicide.* Sitting at the desk in the archives room, I turn the book over to read its brief description and a few quotes from other authors. The synopsis describes the murder of Anne Danforth by her husband Jacob Danforth and then his subsequent suicide. The grisly details describe a plot that would be fitting for an Alfred Hitchcock film or Truman Capote novel:

Anne and Jacob Danforth appeared to be normal, church-going folks when they moved to Bedfordshire, Massachusetts in 1952. They had told family and friends that they hoped to start a family in the sleepy coastal town. However, soon after they arrived, the childless couple began to engage in scandalous behavior that included hosting parties involving late night drinking, illegal drugs, and adultery with multiple partners. In that same year, Jacob Danforth murdered his wife by cutting her throat with a hunting knife while she was in the bathtub. After killing her, he stripped himself naked and proceeded to get into the tub with her body, where he cut both of his wrists with the same hunting knife and bled to death. The Danforth murder-suicide shocked the nation and to this day the rapid moral degradation of Anne and Jacob Danforth has yet to be explained.

I recognize the names of famous crime detective biographers who had written blurbs for the book. Curious to see if this horrible story would be cogent to my task, I search for references to the address or location of the house where the murder-suicide took place. The first chapter alludes to the basics of the incident entitled "The Scene of the Crime." Skimming the first chapter, searching for the address, I found what I was looking for on the second page:

"The discovery of the bodies at 112 Old Salem Highway, in the quiet village of Bedfordshire, Massachusetts occurred at 9:10 a.m. on April 11, 1952, discovered by the housekeeper…"

Is this the connection I'm looking for? Unexplained moral degradation of a young, innocent couple and a grisly murder-suicide occurring on the original property of the James Corey farm. This can't be a coincidence that this tragedy took place on one of the fabled locations of the remains of an executed warlock. Was this the first lead to the last of the rumored possible locations of Elias Doever's burial place? This would require me to read about the details more intently, but I was meeting Toby for dinner in thirty minutes. I walk back to the front desk and ask Mrs. Parris one last question for the day. "Is it possible for me to check this book out?"

"Yes, but you must have a library card. Please fill out this application." She slides a form toward me along the countertop.

After completing the application, she laminates my new library card. Stamping the card in the sleeve on the inside of the back cover of the book, she announces her rehearsed but sincere pitch, "You have two weeks from today before you have to return it and there is a fine of twenty-five cents per day for every day that it is late."

"Mrs. Parris, thank you. You have been a great help. I'm leaving now, so I don't need the maps anymore. Do you need me to put them away?"

"No, I will take care of it. Please throw away your gloves," she says with a stern tone as she lifts the trashcan toward me from behind the desk.

As I step outside, Toby is waiting for me as planned in the parking lot of the library, leaning next to the hood of the Mercedes. Looking dapper in his khakis rolled up to his calf, light brown docksiders with no socks, and a short-sleeved white cotton button-down shirt, he looks every bit the preppy model for a photo shoot in Martha's Vineyard.

"Hey, you look very handsome."

"Well, when you said dinner, I wasn't sure what that meant, so I went to my default gear."

Walking toward Toby, I unexpectedly think of a way to check out 112 Old Salem Highway and go to our dinner location at the same time. "Since you look so pretty, I think we should go to dinner somewhere nicer than where I was originally thinking. Why don't we drive to Salem and go to Clancy's like we did on our first date? It'll also give us some breathing room from the inquiring eyes on this campus."

"That sounds awesome! Their onion rings were killer!" He flashes that million-dollar grin.

Firing up the engine of the classic sedan, listening to it roar for a few seconds, we pull out of the library parking lot onto Main Street. Knowing that Main Street transitions into the Old Salem Highway just north of the Bedfordshire Church graveyard, this is the spot that will be the starting point when determining where the 112 address would be along Old Salem Highway. Passing several small yards that correlate with the lots on the city map, looking subtly at the mailbox numbers, we are in the high nineties as we cruise along. Toby's hand creeps up next to mine on the gearshift handle and grasps it as per usual.

"How did your research go at the library?"

"Good," I answer quickly as I spy a mailbox with the stenciled number 106. I bring Toby into my search. "Hey, Toby, I need to check out a possible sight for our research, so help me keep an eye out for the number 112. Even numbers are on the coastal side of the highway."

Toby immediately turns his head to look out the passenger window. "We just passed a box with the number 108," he states excitedly.

I notice that the 108 mailbox is next to a long driveway that ends in a home perched on a hill. This would indicate that 108 is the coastal property as it was drawn on the city map. As we pass it, I comment aloud, "Okay, I assume 112 will have the same arrangement as that last driveway, since it's also a coastal lot. So, we're looking for the next long driveway on the right."

"There is 110 on that mailbox," Toby interjects.

Looking at it, and the short driveway leading to a modest one-floor house near the highway, there's another entrance to a driveway to the left of it, but it doesn't have a mailbox. I put the right turn signal on, slow the car down, and carefully turn into the driveway. The sedan creeps up until we reach a rusted metal slat gate across the driveway. A chain is wrapped around the frame of the door and a metal post parallel to the gate. There's a padlock securing the ends of the chain together. There's also a crude sign fastened to the top of the gate:

PROPERTY CONDEMNED NO TRESPASSING

"Damn! Now how am I, I mean, *we*, going to get to the shoreline to do our counting?"

With this statement, I get out of the car and walk to the gate. Toby follows my lead. Knowing that I could break the chain or pop the lock with my telekinetic powers, how would I explain that to Toby? Furthermore, we can't trespass. Well, not now, anyway. My plan for exploring the Danforth property is thwarted. Disappointed, I stand quiet and motionless in front of the gate, gazing into the distance, noticing an abandoned Cape Cod-style house at the top of the hill. To the right of the house, and closer to the gate along the driveway, is a barn that is almost as large as the house; and to the left of the house is a small shed, closer to the bay's shoreline.

Toby breaks the palpable silence. "Bummer, are there any other places where you can do your counts?"

"Yes, probably, but this was going to be so perfect," I state, realizing that what I said about "perfection" sounds odd. Toby doesn't respond to my strange comment. "All right, no reason to cry over spilled milk. Let's go, I'm hungry. I didn't get much for lunch today," I suggest as I turn away from the gate, walking back to the car.

Toby follows suit. Once securely belted, I slowly back the sedan out onto the highway. Switching gears, I gun the engine, tires squealing; I obviously am transferring my frustration to the car. As we drive down the road toward Salem, I notice on the right side of the highway an official-looking metal sign with a chocolate brown background and white lettering, and an image of a small green tree in the corner. I instantly recognize this as the standard format and look for signs for public parks. As the sign gets closer, I slow down to read the sign, perfectly legible in the evening sunlight:

Salem State Forest, Southern Trail Entrance 100 feet

It's accompanied by a white arrow pointing to the right. Immediately, the forest to the north of the James Corey farm on the parchment comes to mind and the modern city map indicating undeveloped land to the north of Bedfordshire proper. I signal and then pull over into the entrance to see what it looks like. There's a brown wooden gate in between two stone pillars, but it is open.

"What are we doing?" Toby asks, curious.

"This could be the answer to my access problem," I say as I lean over Toby to read the sign on the right stone pillar.

Toby accommodates my gesture by placing his left hand lightly on my back in between my shoulder blades. I read this smaller sign with a brown background and white lettering: Trail Entrance Opens 8:00 a.m., Closes 5:00 p.m.

No Alcohol

No Restrooms

Do Not Feed the Animals!

I settle back into my position behind the steering wheel. "I think this will work. We can drive to the bay shoreline on this road and then walk south along the shoreline toward the property on 112 Old Salem Highway so that I can…for making counts of the marine snail population," I explain, catching myself before I say too much.

"Okay, but why do you need to go to the beach behind that condemned house? Do you know that there are numerous snails there for some reason?" Toby innocently inquires.

"Just a hunch," I lie, "based on wave patterns and the shape of the coastline.

"I'll call the National Park Service tomorrow to find out what's needed to conduct quadrat counts along the shoreline," I announce as we back out onto the highway.

Toby and I ate at Clancy's: basically, the same bar food and beer we had on our first date. As I watch Toby carefully eat a piping hot, thickly cut onion ring, I think that Toby is consistent, if nothing else. An uncomplicated, authentic all-American boy. I signal the waiter for the check when Toby interjects.

"No, Dorian, I'm paying tonight. You paid last time. I insist," he states as he anticipates my objection.

Smiling at his gesture, I refrain from saying anything else. I quietly fold my napkin and place it on the table. I'm sipping the last of my beer when he surprises me again.

"So, Homecoming is next weekend, and we've a match on the Friday night before the parade and a football game on Saturday. Of course, I need to be there for the match on Friday, but I really don't want to go to the game on Saturday or the dance that night. I was wondering if we could go away on that Saturday, maybe to the Cape. I've never been to Provincetown, and I've heard it's nice. Open-minded. Guys can hold hands in public; kiss in public."

With this last sentence, I feel his hand on my knee, rubbing it lightly. I move my right hand below the table and place it on top of his as he rubs my knee. He stops rubbing and interlocks his fingers in between mine.

"That sounds like a great idea. It's the off-season, so it shouldn't be too expensive. I know a couple of bed and breakfasts I have stayed at before. I'll call to see if they have any vacancies."

"Oh, I didn't mean stay the night. I was thinking a day trip. I don't have the money…"

I interrupt him, simultaneously squeezing his hand. "Toby, if we're going to drive to the end of the Cape, because that's where P-town is, which is about a three-hour drive depending on the traffic, then we should stay the night there. My treat, and before you say anything, I want you to know that I respect your need to contribute, but I want to do this for you. You work hard, you deserve it…"

The corners of Toby's mouth curl slowly upward as tears fill his eyes. "Thank you, Dorian. You're a special guy."

"You are too. Now, for God's sake, stop acting like a pussy!" I blurt out in my best rural, back bay Massachusetts drawl.

Toby bursts out laughing, releasing my hand to wipe the tears with the back of his wrist. Toby pays the check, leaving a nice tip for the cute waiter. Walking back to the car, I break the ice by swinging my right leg backward and circularly so that my right foot connects with his butt; noticing that his shorter stature creates the perfect height for me to make a connection. He grabs my foot the second time I attempt it, and I lose my balance. Before I fall to the street, he instinctively scoops his massive arm around my back, balancing me. His face is now inches from mine as I regain my composure. Holding me securely, he places his slightly open mouth over mine. I close my eyes, leaning against his burly upper limb. It's a nice but sexy kiss. I open my eyes and stand up on my own.

In the silence of the night, we get into the sedan and drive back toward Bedfordshire. As soon as we exit Salem proper, seeing the sign indicating that Bedfordshire is 21 miles away, I shift into a cruising speed and Toby's hand is on top of mine as per usual. Instead of holding it in the usual manner, I grasp his hand, interlocking our fingers, and pull our hands toward my mouth. I gently kiss the back of Toby's hand and smile at him. We ride to the college entrance in blissful silence.

Chapter 18

Bedfordshire College
3rd week of October 1992

The next day, after learning of the strong possibility that the property of 112 Old Salem Highway is the burial location of Elias Doever and that the condemned property is adjacent to the Salem State Forest Southern Trail, I immediately called the Massachusetts State Parks administration for advisement on how to conduct a non-invasive research study. After being connected to a Park Ranger and explaining the nature of our quadrat study, I was informed that I didn't need any paperwork or special permission, only that we could enter the forest at 8:00 a.m. and had to be out of the park by 5:00 p.m. With this knowledge and some research conducted this morning regarding this stretch of shoreline of the Mass Bay, I present my protocol for a quadrat study to Dr. Hayden after lunch. As he studies the protocol, he has some questions for me.

"Okay, well, it looks like a strong candidate for our study, but it's a little farther north than I had proposed in my original grant application. Then again, some of our data have not been exactly what I was expecting. The counts along the shoreline of the Backwoods weren't as promising toward supporting my hypothesis, so maybe another count along a forested area could be of value, if not toward this hypothesis, perhaps a related study. When were you thinking about doing this count?"

"I was aiming for Wednesday next week. That would give me enough time to collect a team of student research assistants and volunteers. It's also on one of my non-teaching days," I answer definitively.

"How many were you thinking?"

"Well, the forest extends about a mile along the shoreline, and based on the typical composition of the coastline in forested areas, I would say that I would need five teams of two: ten students. That's within our budget as well."

"Sounds logical. All right, start putting it together. Dorian, I must applaud you for your motivation and ingenuity with this selection. The Salem Southern Trail was always a possibility for a site but your diligent research has persuaded me to give it a try. I just need to ask you this question: Why this area? I mean, what about it made you think that it could be a possibility for our study?"

I quickly respond, "Its location. Its location could answer many questions I, we, have."

****

After receiving the green light for the quadrat study along the Salem Forest Southern Trail, I move quickly to reserve a school van and secure the undergraduate assistants and volunteers from Dr. Hayden's Ecology class that don't have Wednesday afternoon classes. I post the sign-up on the bulletin board outside Dr. Hayden's classroom/lab, and by Friday afternoon, I have my undergraduates. It's amazing how much extra credit, and a little money can motivate.

Fulfilling the necessary components of my protocol, I head home feeling quite satisfied for a quiet evening. Toby leaves tonight for a match in Hartford, Connecticut, and won't be back until Sunday, so I have the next two days to read the book about the Danforth murder-suicide I checked out from the Bedfordshire Library. Mother is also home for the weekend, so we can do some mother-son bonding, if necessary.

Chapter 19

Doever Farm
The Story of Anne and Jacob Danforth
3rd week of October 1992

After catching up on all things academic during dinner, Mother and I settle into the family room to watch the evening news together, but then I decide to retire to my room as Mother starts to become invested in her nighttime game shows.

"Where are you going?" she asks.

"Turning in. I'm beat. I also got a good book I want to start."

"Oh, okay. Are things getting better at school, the lab?"

"Yeah, slowly but surely. I organized a lab outing for next week and Dr. Hayden was pleased. I like working with the undergrads."

"That's great, honey. Just remember to keep that distance we talked about. Is that rugby player one of your undergrad research students?"

"No, he has never expressed interest...busy with rugby, I guess. Why do you ask?"

Mother gets that look on her face I know so well, that "don't pee on my leg and tell me it's raining" look. "Okay, point taken," I respond.

Why is she so obsessed with this idea of Toby and I

being together? Am I being that obvious somehow?

Annoyed, I pull the book du jour out of my backpack and lay it on the bed. Fluffing my pillows and then stacking them vertically, I create a firm but soft headboard. This creation along with a cold soda and I'm ready to delve into this biography of the Danforths.

Settling my back and neck into a comfortable position against my pillows, I examine the cover of *Tragedy in Bedfordshire: The Danforth Murder-Suicide.* The grainy black-and-white photograph on the cover is an image of the Cape Cod-style house that I saw at the end of the long driveway of 112 Old Salem Highway. The lettering of the title is colored blood red with a stark font that reminds me of the crime magazines like *True Detective* or *Police Detective* popular in the 1940s and 1950s. Even the author's name elicits a noir feeling: Sam S. Crutcher. I take notes while reading, especially those associated with the property of 112 Old Salem Highway.

Jacob Danforth came from one of the original families of New England: a descendant of Thomas Danforth, the first Deputy Governor of the Massachusetts Bay Colony and the infamous judge during the Salem witch trials. Anne Danforth (nee Abernathy) could also trace her family back hundreds of years in the New England register. Jacob was an apprentice-trained carpenter but made a living mostly as a housing contractor. A big, strapping man, six feet five inches in height and weighing nearly three hundred pounds, he had a chest measurement of fifty-two inches that required him to have his shirts and coats made by hand. He met Anne Abernathy while she was a student at Smith College, pursuing a master's degree in English literature. Anne was an extremely attractive petite brunette with an hourglass figure and a "good head on her shoulders." Jacob and Anne met at the local Presbyterian Church in Northampton, Massachusetts, and were married the month after Anne secured her graduate degree in 1951.

After graduation, Anne Danforth was offered and accepted a tenure-track position on the faculty of Bedfordshire College. The Danforths moved to Bedfordshire in the summer of 1951. They purchased the buildings and property at 112 Old Salem Highway and Jacob had his first job in Bedfordshire: renovating the dilapidated Cape Cod house and barn. It seems the buildings and grounds had been vacant for over fifty years, but the "bones" of the house were good, and this would provide Jacob with a model home that would display his skills as a carpenter and builder.

Soon after, they moved into their new home and Anne settled into her position at Bedfordshire College. They sought out the Bedfordshire Presbyterian Church, transferring their membership from the Presbyterian church in Northampton. Jacob and Anne became active members in the church, especially activities involving young people (teaching Sunday School and Youth Ministry) as they were eager to start their own family.

After several months of trying to conceive and not being successful, Anne was examined by a prominent specialist in Boston. Unfortunately, it was determined that Anne would never be able to conceive and that their only option for starting a family would be adoption or foster care. The Danforths were devastated by the news. Anne distracted herself by delving into her new teaching career and research to ensure her tenure at Bedfordshire College. Jacob occupied his mind and time with his building projects: completing the renovation of the Cape Cod; reconstructing the barn into a larger structure that would double as a garage; and building a new woodworking workshop, where he could practice his carpentry skills. It was no secret in the community that Jacob was a master craftsman, as he often volunteered his woodworking services to the church. He also built original wooden toys for the children of the congregation, especially those who came from modest homes. It was said that Jacob became increasingly obsessed with creating new and innovative wooden toys for children, spending all hours of the night in his newly constructed workshop. It was reported that Anne would keep him company, working on her sewing projects huddled next to him and the wood-burning stove that Jacob had installed in the workshop to keep them warm during the bitter cold months.

The Danforths started "acting peculiar," as it was described by the members of the community, sometime in the late spring/early summer of 1952. Church members reported that Jacob Danforth, who was always friendly and outgoing, was increasingly becoming friendlier with the female parishioners, whether they were married, single, or underage. Often proposing that he meet women of the congregation for drinks after church meetings. On more than one occasion, he invited a few of the unsuspecting women to his workshop, enticing them to see the toys that he had made for the children. What they thought would be an innocent tour of his woodworking shop turned into a nightmare of sorts, in that they claimed that he made advances toward them to engage in sexual activity with him either alone or with Anne. After several of these incidents, the women eventually confided in each other and united to tell the men of the church. When word of this behavior reached the rest of the congregation, the angry husbands, and the rest of the men of the church confronted Jacob. Denying their accusations, Jacob stated that these women were confused and were reading too much into what he said. The men ultimately believed the female witnesses, and Jacob and Anne were asked to leave the church. Neither seemed to be particularly saddened by this excommunication from their parish, but many in the church were very sad to see the Danforths and their talents leave the congregation.

It was at that time, in the summer of 1952, that the Danforths became frequent visitors of the most notorious establishments in Boston, where drinking, drug use, and debauchery were common. Jacob and Anne Danforth became regulars in these underground sex dens, identified anonymously by many of the clientele that stated they were not only active in the orgies that were fueled by alcohol and illegal drugs, but also coordinated the activities, often inviting the denizens of these clubs to their home in Bedfordshire to engage in weekend long bacchanals. Neighbors complained often to the Bedfordshire police about the music and noise coming from 112 Old Salem Highway into the early hours of the night. When the police raided the parties for disturbing the peace, they did not discover any drug use or illicit sexual activity, so the rumors of orgiastic drug-fueled activities were never substantiated. However, alcohol use was documented as being pervasive, as well as the non-desirable, deplorable nature of the party attendants.

In later interviews, prostitutes from Boston identified Jacob Danforth from photographs and spoke of engaging in sex with him alone, sometimes several times in one night. On one occasion, one of the prostitutes spoke of having sex with another woman they identified as Anne Danforth. A prostitute, the author of the Danforth book referred to as "Mary," told the biographer that she became close to the couple, not only engaging in sex with both, but on one occasion, a well-known male prostitute in Boston was included in one of their sexual tryst weekends in Bedfordshire. She also recalled that Jacob Danforth, on this occasion, quoted aloud in what she assumed was Biblical verse before and during sexual activity and performed ritual-like behaviors like anointing foreheads with oils before the participants engaged in sex with each other, regardless of gender. Mary stated that all sexual activity always either included both husband and wife, or the presence of one watching while the other engaged in sexual activity.

The Danforth book author discusses this specifically because Mary stated that in her interview Jacob Danforth confided to her that he had heard a rumor that Anne was carrying on an affair with another man outside of their marriage bed. Something that both had agreed would never happen. Mary said that he was so deeply disturbed by this discovery that she heard him say he would kill her if he found it to be true.

This jealousy of a supposed affair became the hypothesized motive for Jacob killing his wife and then taking his own life. The Danforth biographer dwells upon this theory extensively in his book. When Jacob discovered his wife's ongoing indiscretion with another man, he slit her throat with a hunting knife in the bathtub while she was bathing. The biographer theorizes that the bath may have been taken after one of her liaisons with her lover. Then due to his remorse for killing his beloved wife, Jacob removed his clothes and got into the bathtub naked to be closer to his dead wife. Lying behind her in the bathtub, he held her in his arms as he sliced his wrists with the hunting knife. He bled to death while his arms encircled her nude body. Police records later validated that this was the position that they were discovered in by the housekeeper.

In the middle of the book is a series of photographs of the couple and the property at 112 Old Salem Highway. The first photograph is a wedding portrait of Anne Abernathy Danforth. She is a lovely woman with long dark hair tightly coiffed in the style of the late 1940s: bangs tightly rolled above the forehead, and the fall pulled back on the sides and curled underneath so it bounced above her shoulders. Her complexion is perfect like alabaster and her dark eyes peer beneath a translucent veil that hangs just below her thin angular nose. Her lips are generous in a Cupid bow shape. A stunningly beautiful woman.

The next image is a photograph of Jacob Danforth in a military uniform. A large man with masculine, blunt features, he reminds me of a young Marlon Brando as Stanley Kowalski in *A Streetcar Named Desire.* The third photograph is a snapshot of the happy couple in front of their new home in 1951. Anne is wearing a sundress and straw hat and Jacob is wearing a short-sleeved checkered shirt and dungarees. His arm is around the waist of his new bride. It is apparent in the photograph that the Cape Cod and the barn are in severe disrepair, the background of the smiling innocent couple that will be dead in less than a year. The other photographs are grainy crime scene pictures of the inside of the house including the bathroom and bathtub where the nude bodies were found in the murder-suicide. The last photograph of the set is a picture of the property after the crime, police cars and ambulance surrounding the renovated Cape Cod, barn, and workshop (looking like a shed behind the house). This is the photograph that also doubles as the grainy cover photograph with the heavy noir-looking title.

After perusing through the photographs, I realize I have read the entire book from cover to cover in one sitting. The time of 1:00 a.m. is blinking on the alarm clock. Realizing the late hour, I put the book and my notes on the bookshelf. Stripping off my clothes, I pull back the comforter and slide in between the flannel sheets. Not thinking about the Danforth tragedy that I consumed tonight in one read, I'm asleep in minutes.

Chapter 20

Bedfordshire College
4th week of October 1992

I'll see Toby for the first time today since our dinner last Wednesday. Today's biology lab is the zoology-based lab where students observe and describe specimens from the different phyla in the kingdom of *Animalia*, including examples of mammals (taxidermy), arthropods (preserved insects, crustaceans, arachnids), mollusks (live snails), annelids (preserved segmented worms), echinoderms (dried sea stars, urchins) and porifera (dried sponges). It is a rather odorous lab in that many of the preserved specimens and the dried samples have strong smells that quickly build up in the lab room, and fill the hallway. People entering the science building always know when the zoology lab is being conducted in introductory biology. Many of the students opt to use masks and white lab coats, giving the impression of intense research. After class, I speak briefly with Toby.

"Hey, so I got my permission to do a study in the Salem Forest Southern Trail tomorrow, so I'm not sure if I'll have any time to get together afterward, really depends on how quickly we're able to do our counts and pack up. What is your practice schedule like Thursday night?"

"Oooh, we have an intense practice and meeting afterward because we have a match on Friday afternoon. You know, when it's Homecoming, the teams are on high alert as the alumni, i.e., the big donors, are on campus and the better we look on the pitch, the better the school's chances of getting more donations."

"What time are you available after the match on Friday?"

"The match is at three in the afternoon and then we have a dinner right after, so probably not until eight, eight-thirty at night," Toby explains.

"Hmmm, then maybe we should make a plan now for Saturday. Why don't I pick you up at the gates at seven, seven-thirty in the morning? That way we would avoid most of the traffic and get to the end of the Cape by ten o'clock, ten-thirty at the latest. That would give us most of the day and that night, and then Sunday morning before we leave. Is that doable?"

"Sure, that sounds awesome! I wasn't planning on doing anything late at night after the dinner, maybe have a few beers in the student lounge. Let's definitely make it seven, I want to have as much time as possible," Toby concurs.

"Seven it is. If anything changes, I'll call. I'm looking forward to it."

"Me too!" Toby says loudly. Catching himself, he places his index finger over his lips and quickly looks around the room, "Shhh, Mister Leeves, not so loud." He shoots me a sample of that crazy grin of his as he exits the lab room.

I find myself involuntarily smiling as Toby leaves the room. Realizing that I won't see him for another four days, I find myself feeling something that I rarely feel when it concerns another human being: sad. I'm sad that I won't be able to see, talk or touch Toby until the weekend. A familiar proverb pops into my mind: "Absence makes the heart grow fonder." For the first time in my life, I think I understand what this proverb means.

Chapter 21

Salem State Forest Southern Trail
4th week of October 1992

We arrive at the edge of the Salem State Forest, the shoreline at the end of the access road, in the school van around ten o'clock a.m. I disperse the teams along the pre-determined sections of the shoreline, leaving the most southern section, which blends into the piece of shoreline belonging to 112 Old Salem Highway, for me alone. After making sure the teams are in place and counting/collecting data correctly using the quadrats, I make my way to the end of the shoreline bordering the Salem State Forest. From the marker indicating the property line of the forest, I can see the Cape Cod house and the shed workshop that have become familiar to me from studying the photographs in the Danforth biography; albeit the actual landscape is in full color as opposed to the grainy black and white photographs. However, these structures are not colorful by any means. The external building materials are severely weathered from decades of wind and salt spraying against the façade of each structure: the wooden siding on each building is a dull gray hue, the once bright white shutters have faded to a leaden color, and the roof is covered in fragile paper-like grayish-black shingles. The spindly branches of the trees in the yard are bare, sprouting from what appear to be dead, colorless limbs and trunks littered around the property. In contrast, the trees of the forest bordering the property are displaying their bright, cheerful autumnal colors. Indeed, except for the bright colors of the sky, bay, and the shoreline, the appearance of the Danforth residence isn't far removed from the grainy black-and-white portraits in the biography.

As I walk closer to the property, details come into focus that reveal nuances of the decay that were not evident further up the beach. Boards from the wooden siding are missing and or broken and splintered. Reflections of clouds in the sky are warped and interrupted by the jagged borders of broken windows throughout the house and workshop. I'm within about one hundred feet of the workshop and the house, when, abruptly, I start to feel a buzzing sensation racing through my body, followed by dizziness. Stopping in my tracks on the shoreline, dropping my research materials on the sand, I attempt to balance with my outstretched arms as I try to recover from my disorienting state. The disequilibrium is overpowering. Falling to my knees on purpose to avoid collapsing, I now feel an extreme pain resonating in my forehead. Trying to focus on the landscape, the building that I was studying mere seconds ago is blurry, indecipherable. I know that I'm going to experience a vision, as the debilitating posture I find myself in is exactly like the state I experienced in Witch Well Park, where Elias Doever met his demise. In this location that has no record in Elias Doever's history, there's only one conclusion that can be made: I'm near the remains of Elias Doever! I have found his burial place! But before I can feel elated about my discovery, my vision goes awry, and I'm now plunged into darkness.

****

I'm in the interior of an older automobile, circa early 20th century, watching the headlights beam onto an old dirt path as the car slowly moves through the darkness. It's nighttime, but the scene is illuminated, presumably by moonlight. Everything in the vision is in sharp focus. The car passes a barn like the one on the property at 112 Old Salem Highway. Then the familiar silhouette of a Cape Cod house comes into view. A full moon shines above the apparently abandoned house. The car stops. I'm in the company of three young men dressed in suits and hats reminiscent of the early 1900s, and they are carrying shovels as we walk to the left of the house. I remove something from my head, a cap, and jacket, dropping it to the ground. Rolling up my long-sleeved white shirt to my elbows, I'm looking at the ground in the moonlight, surveying the sea grasses, shrubs, and trees. I'm searching for something. A roundish area of earth near the shoreline where there's no vegetation, not even sea grass, comes into view.

Using one arm, holding onto one end of a shovel, I push the spade into the soft dirt. Then with one foot on the back of the spade, I step onto the shovel and dig the shovel deeper into the earth. Removing my foot, I then pull the handle back with both hands to loosen a spade full of dirt and then toss it to the side. I repeat this several times until I feel a resistance that I have not felt yet. Tossing the shovel to the side of the hole, I drop to my knees, and using my hands, I sift through the dirt. A long pale cylindrical object is partially unearthed. Grasping the object tightly with one hand, a bolt of electrical-like energy suddenly rushes through my hand, destroying the muscles so that the fingers grip the cylindrical object tighter. The bolt of energy quickly travels up my arm and into my chest when I feel a crushing sensation, as if an enormous weight has landed on my breast. I'm now falling toward the small hole I've created, my face landing on the soft, tilled earth. Everything goes black.

****

I'm now inside a structure. It's a small one-room structure made of wood slat walls, wooden beams crossing horizontally below a pitched roof, and a wood plank floor. There's a large primitive-looking wooden table with tools and stacked pieces of lumber of various sizes and thicknesses. There's a small iron stove heater in the corner with a wide, black metal tube ascending from the back of the stove to the ceiling. I don't recognize the interior of this structure, but my knowledge of the building type and its materials leads me to believe that I'm in a cabin or a shed or a workshop because of the tools on the table. Then it dawns on me. I'm having this vision because I'm near the property at 112 Old Salem Highway. I must be in the shed workshop next to the Danforth's Cape Cod.

There's a vibration resonating inside the structure. A low pitch humming that is increasing in sound. The humming is coming from the floor. A faint pulsating light is flickering in between the narrow spaces of the floorboards. The light dims as the humming sound decreases in strength, but then increases in intensity as the humming sound becomes louder. The tempo of the pulses quickens, as if the pulsations were replicating the beat of a heart in distress. The humming, beating sound is becoming uncomfortably loud as if any minute whatever is beneath these floorboards is about to explode. Beams of light in between the wooden planks are reaching and reflecting off the ceiling. The desperate rhythm of the overwhelming stimuli of sound and light is unbearable, a crescendo that will destroy the eyes and ears of any creature in the room, building in intensity…

BOOM! BOOM! BOOM!
and then…Darkness. Silence.

****

I awake to a deep sucking sound, my chest heaving. I'm lying on the soft, wet sand cradling my body, gasping for air. All I can hear is the sound of my own frantic breath sounds…an absence of the unbearable beating sound or blinding light I'd succumbed to. As my breathing slows to a more normal rhythm, I can hear faintly, in the distance, the sound of waves lapping on the shoreline and sea birds squawking above. My eyes gradually open to the bright morning sun, stinging as they adjust. My head thumping, blood vessels pulsing in my neck, my body calms itself from the overstimulation I experienced during my visions.

As I recover, it affords me the time to process all that has just happened. It's clear to me from my two visions that Elias Doever is buried on this property. The young man who collapses and dies as he digs into the bare earth must be the Harvard student that Dr. Hayden had mentioned, the unfortunate soul who supposedly found the burial place of Elias Doever and died that night from a heart attack. The jolt of energy from the cylindrical object that I felt reaching his heart and arresting it was presumably a long bone from Elias' remains. The second vision also made it clear that a supernatural force lies in the earth beneath the floorboards of one of the buildings on the property. Because these visions appeared sequentially, the force emanating beneath the wooden planks must be connected to the force that killed the Harvard student.

The building appeared to be a one-room structure. I only saw one door, windows on three walls, and a stove against the fourth wall. It also had a relatively high-pitched ceiling but no loft, and no ladder or staircase was leading to a second floor like that of a barn. The structure is the shed/workshop. However, my visions have left me with a conundrum. How is it that the young man died when he was digging into the ground with no building surrounding him in the first vision, yet the second vision was specific that some force lay beneath a floor made of wood? Then it dawns on me. The only logical answer is that the workshop shed was built over the same ground that the Harvard student dug into.

With that assumption, investigating the shed workshop is the next logical step. Feeling better, I manage to balance and sit up on the sandy beach. Then, with great difficulty, I slowly stand, using my hands and arms as support on the sandy shore as I move my unsteady legs. Staggering toward the dunes that lie on the edge of the barren grassland area that surrounds the Cape Cod-style house, I climb the soft hills methodically until I reach the peak of the dune, the same height as the sparsely covered ground. The buzzing sensation in my body lingers, but I'm not feeling the disorientation this time. Walking toward the ramshackle shed workshop, I stop just before the wall facing the bay that contains a small window. Leaning forward to peek through the window, the dirt-covered glass prevents me from getting a good view of the furnishings, but I can discern the layout of the building, and I'm correct in my assumption: this *is* the building in my vision, where I saw and heard light and sound emanating from beneath the wooden floorboards. Walking toward the only door on the wall furthest from the bay, the handle has been secured shut with a chain and a padlock. I know that I can probably break this lock or chain with my telekinesis. But then what would I do? I don't have time to enter, rip up the floorboards, and dig for who knows how long to get to Elias Doever's bones. I'll have to return another time. Probably, in the dark of the night.

Realizing I have not made any quadrat counts, I walk back to the beach to begin counting speciation. Fully recovered, I roll the plastic PVC square over the sand using my mind trick. Within hours, my territory is covered. I walk north along the shoreline to check the progress of the other groups further up the beach. They're progressing nicely. I ask all groups to mark where they have completed the most recent count so we can break for lunch.

While eating, I pull out the biography of the Danforths from my knapsack and open the book to the middle section that contains the photographs. I search the photos that include the shed. The first photo of the property is the day the Danforths moved into 112 Old Salem Highway: the smiling couple with the Cape Cod to the left of them in the far background and the barn to the right, about one hundred feet behind them as they stand on the driveway. The second photo of the property focuses on the renovations of the barn and the house, but there's no shed in the background in either photograph. The last photograph taken at the crime scene (several months after they renovated the house and barn), the photo used for the cover portrait, includes the left corner of the barn, the house, and the shed behind the house. This photographic evidence verifies my previous assumption: Jacob Danforth built the shed on the earth that covered Elias Doever's remains. That would explain the dual visions of the Harvard student collapsing over a plot of earth he was digging within and the strange light emitting from beneath the wooden floor of the shed, a floor that was built upon the unconsecrated ground that concealed the bones of Elias Doever.

This discovery now raised the next question: Did Elias Doever's remains somehow affect Jacob and Anne Danforth? It was stated in the biography that Jacob spent a significant amount of time in the shed working on his projects and Anne would accompany him, even throughout the colder months, thanks to the iron stove Jacob had installed. They walked on the floorboards above the remains of an executed warlock that had considerable power. Did Elias Doever's power live on in his bones and influence the Danforths, changing their personalities... their morality...their souls? This is a question that only Beladon would be able to answer.

Collating the quadrat counts covered thus far, I estimate that we have about two more hours of counting to cover the shoreline of Salem State Forest Southern Trail. After I collect the data sheets from the volunteers and the research students, Dr. Hayden's Ecology students sign an attendance sheet to receive extra credit for their day's work. I spent the next two hours in the lab feeding the data from the quadrat counts into the computer and getting preliminary statistics regarding mean, median, maximum, and minimum for the speciation report of the marine snails in the Salem Forest territory. A quick glance reveals some promising data that I'll brief Dr. Hayden about when he returns from Woods Hole tomorrow. I write a note to Toby explaining I'm going home for the night and that I'll see him Saturday morning, seal it in a plain envelope with his name on the outside, and drop it off in his student mailbox.

****

I'm exhausted. The visions, as usual, have left me drained of any energy, and I'm in bed, eager to sleep. I've only one task for this evening before I can slumber. I need to try to contact Beladon and inform him about my discovery, but I also need to ask him the question I raised this afternoon: Did Elias Doever's remains have a negative effect on the Danforths?

Concentrating on these thoughts while lying naked under my bedsheets in the quiet of my room, I begin to feel a rush of serene energy permeate my body. Beladon's here, his voice echoing in my head. "Dorian Leeves…Dorian Leeves…you have found the essence of Elias Doever."

"I believe so…my visions indicate that he is buried in a location that was part of the James Corey farm, the third location rumored to be the burial place."

"But you have not secured the essence."

"No, I could not. There was a barrier, a wooden shed that covers the earth where he is buried. I must return to dig up his bones. I am thinking that I may go back tomorrow night. It will be easier for me to pull up the floorboards and dig when it is dark."

There's no response. I surmise that Beladon agrees with my plan. I then think about my question, "Did Elias Doever's essence affect the Danforths, the people who lived on the property where Elias is buried?"

"I know nothing of this. When a powerful being's physical remains die, the power lies with the being, beyond death. The thoughts that surround a powerful being at the time of physical death lie with the being, beyond death."

Taking a moment to think about what Beladon has communicated, I try to make sense of this cryptic message. "If the power and the thoughts at the time of death remain with Elias's essence, then those thoughts could be magnified, uh, increased, by the power beyond the resting place of the essence, is that what you are telling me?"

"Yes."

I expand on the hypothesis that I'm compiling, "If the thoughts are negative, evil, like the thoughts of the people that executed him, then energy from those thoughts could reach beyond the ground he is buried and influence humans that were near to the essence?"

"Yes."

"The Danforths, people living near the essence, could have been changed by the evil thoughts that lie with Elias Doever's essence, enough to make them kill?"

Beladon then ends my inquiry and boldly makes a new statement. "Dorian Leeves, there is another task you must complete. When the three bloods are united, there must be a sacrifice of a beast that gives birth to a live beast."

"What! I don't understand?"

"To summon your power, the life of a beast that gives birth to a live beast must be sacrificed. You must prepare this sacrifice when you have the essence of Elias Doever."

Contemplating this statement, I arrive at a horrible conclusion. "I have to kill a beast that gives birth to a live beast? You don't mean a human! I can't do that!"

Beladon does not answer.

Quickly, I think of an alternative idea. "Could it be another mammal…like a lamb, or a goat, those have been the animals that have been sacrificed throughout the ages?"

"Yes, they are beasts that give birth to live beasts."

I breathe a sigh of relief at his response. However, I'm left with the uncomfortable feeling that I'll have to kill a defenseless animal to secure this power I've been promised. Suddenly, I remembered that sacrifices in the Bible and Pagan worship typically involve the spilling of blood, so I approach Beladon with an alternative.

"Can the blood be used if the beast is not killed?"

"A life is sacrificed to summon the power of the three united bloods."

"I can't bring the blood of an animal? The animal has to be killed at the time of the summoning of the power?"

There's no answer. I feel the serene energy dissipating, but I continue to wait a few minutes for a response. Beladon's presence has left. The last response is the one I'm left with: I will have to sacrifice an animal, a mammal, to receive my birthright. I've only killed animals in a laboratory in the name of science, like rats or frogs. But I still feel remorse. I've never killed an animal for sport or fortunately, for food. The better question is more perplexing and disturbing. Why am I thinking that I will do this? Why do I feel compelled to do this when I know it is wrong?

The uneasiness of this revelation keeps me from sleeping for several hours, even though I'm exhausted. Eventually, my exhaustion conquers me, and I drift off to sleep.

Chapter 22

112 Old Salem Highway
4th week of October 1992

Driving on Old Salem Highway, about a half mile before the 112 address, I slow down and turn the headlights off. Turning slowly into the entrance immediately after the driveway, the sedan barely fits into the space between the entrance from the road and the metal slat gate. I'm slightly concerned that another car could hit the back of it on the dark road. As I get out of the car, I close the door quickly and quietly to reduce the exposure of the car's interior light, leaving the car running as I approach the gate. Holding the padlock attached to the chain wrapped around the gate, I concentrate on turning the gears inside the lock. With ease, the lock springs open. Pulling the lock off, I gently lower the free end of the chain so it drapes along the metal fence. Pushing it open, I secure the gate with the chain onto another post erected next to the fence, then proceed to the car and slowly drive until I clear the gateway.

Moving very slowly up the driveway with the headlights off, I limit the sounds that could alert the neighbors of my illegal presence. I pass the dilapidated barn on the right. It's a dark-looking structure that could've been here for decades or centuries as the architecture of barns in this area has not changed significantly for hundreds of years. The car approaches the Cape Cod-style house. There's little moonlight tonight, so it's difficult to make out anything other than the general silhouette of the building. I drive around the northern corner of the house onto unpaved ground and park behind the back of the house so that no one can see the car from the road.

Walking toward the shed with a flashlight in hand, I feel the presence of extraordinary waves of energy radiating from the shed like I did when I approached it yesterday. However, unlike that experience, I don't feel the disorientation or disequilibrium I felt on the beach. I surmise that I won't be having any overwhelming, debilitating visions tonight, at least, not for now. Peeking in through the window next to the door, the interior of the shed is pitch black. Checking to see if there's any animal activity inside the shed, I shine the flashlight through the glass panes of the window in a circular motion, exposing the interior structure and contents of the workshop. The structure appears to be uninhabited as I don't see the reflections of any eyes staring back at me. Shining the flashlight on the chain and padlock on the door, I concentrate on moving the gears in the padlock as before. With a minimal amount of effort, the lock springs open. Immediately, an absurd thought pops into my head: if I fail at becoming an academic, I can always become a cat burglar.

Removing the padlock from the chain, I open the door. The intense energy waves flowing from the shed are vibrating against my feet as I walk across the wooden planks of the floor, each board creaking loudly with every step. Moving the flashlight in front of me, I explore the one-room structure. It's exactly as I'd seen in my vision, only everything is blanketed in cobwebs and dust. The iron stove is present but there are piles of wood stacked upon it and part of the smokestack is broken and hanging from the ceiling, creating a drafty hole. The long workshop table is present with tools and other instruments I don't recognize, covered in mounds of dust and debris. There's a simple wooden straight-back chair next to the table. Picking it up, I bounce the legs on the ground to see if they're still sturdy. Passing this test, I sit on the chair. Shining the flashlight onto the floorboards, I try to identify the initial location of the pulsating light I saw in my vision, but I cannot discern one area of the wooden floor from another. Closing my eyes, clearing my mind, and using my psychic ability, I envision the location of the source of the energy waves presently bouncing into my body. Abruptly, I open my eyes and direct the beam of the flashlight toward the floor again. A current of swirling translucent energy, distorting the view of the floorboards beneath is now visible. Swirling above the floor, the energy waves are emanating from a source in the middle of the invisible whirlpool. Shining my flashlight into this swirling fountain of invisible energy, I detect a faint light pulsating beneath it. A weak humming sound that was not audible a few seconds ago is also emanating from the upwelling of energy. Although these stimuli are weaker than in my visions, this is the pulsating light and humming sound that I experienced yesterday. Elias Doever is buried below this well of energy.

Standing up, I wade slowly into the swirling current of energy so that I'm looking down at the source. Imagining that I can loosen the wooden planks of the floor where the energy pours from, I concentrate on the nails securing the planks. Slowly, the heads of four nails, one at each of the four corners of one board rise from the wooden surface, making a creaking sound as if they were being pulled by a hammer. Nails popping into the air, the plank propels above the swirl of energy and crashes to the floor. I peer into the space created by the missing floorboard—the pulsating light is now brighter. The humming sound is also louder.

Redirecting my eyes to concentrate on another adjacent board, the nails in the plank repeat the same action, and the plank rockets into the air as before. Repeating this process several times, widening the space of light and sound, I can now see the earth that lies beneath the whirlpool of energy and pulsating light. The soil is bubbling, pulsating, trapping something that wants to escape to the surface. Concentrating on this particular ground, I imagine a digging action, separating the soil into piles to create a chasm. As if an invisible shovel were tilling the earth, the ground's surface fractures. A jagged opening appears and widens slowly as if a force were pushing from beneath. The light rays pulsating through the crack in the surface illuminate the soil with an intense yellowish glow. The humming increases in volume. The radiating beams of light are bouncing off the ceiling and walls, making it difficult to look directly into the abyss I'm creating.

As I continue to imagine the soil moving to the sides to create a deeper hole, the light rays become filtered, as if something were blocking their trajectory out of the hole. An object is rising from the earth through the beams of light. As it levitates higher above the pit, the shape is now identifiable—a human skull. The surfaces of the cranium and the facial bones are gleaming, the yellow light reflecting off the clean bone, absent of any dirt or organic residue. The bony architecture of the skull is perfectly preserved, unmarred by 300 years of being hermetically sealed beneath the surface. I reach for the skull with my hand and grasp it from its levitation. Holding the skull of Elias Doever, cradling the braincase in the palm of my hand, I admire its perfection while the pulsating waves of energy that resonate from it dissipate into my hand.

A series of images flash in my mind's eye…

****

A handsome man with long blond hair and blue eyes is lying naked on a primitive-looking mattress of a crude wooden bed. In the dim candlelight of the room, he's staring at me, smiling, laughing, and then he says, "I do love thee, Elias Doever, with all my heart."

A wooden cart filled with a harvest of different types of root vegetables is being pulled by a black horse, traveling along a dirt path in front of a Puritan-era house that I recognize as the house on Doever Farm.

Suspended above a round structure holding water, a well, I'm surrounded and illuminated by people holding torches, screaming, "Die! Evil one, die!" The sensation of being lowered into the water, steam rising to the surface of the water simultaneously burns and soaks my body—the excruciating pain relieved only as my body is lifted out of the well.

Submerged in a watery environment, as I look toward the water's surface, an intense pressure mounts in my chest, pushing against the rib cage, increasing in force as if something is trying to escape. The agony of the force destroying the bones and flesh as the force leaves my body. I'm gasping for air but only sucking in water pouring into my mouth and down my throat.

****

The shocking sensation from this last image causes me to involuntarily drop the skull. However, as though an invisible hand was present, the skull doesn't hit the floor but levitates just above the surface of the planks. Another object rises out of the abyss of light and sound. A long, large cylindrical object emerges from the pit and floats above the surface. It is a femur, the longest, strongest bone in the human body. I grasp it from its levitation among the light rays.

More images flash in front of me…

****

An older man lying in a large four-poster bed, his skin grayish in tone as though ill. With great difficulty, he whispers, "Elias, beware of William Putnam. He means to do you harm."

A creature resembling Beladon is floating above the water, riding the spray, and speaks, "You are the chosen one, Elias Doever. It is a prophecy that is your name: you wield great power." A commotion in the water, a swirling rising vortex rises next to Beladon, a larger darker being whose features are indistinct. The unrecognizable being incites fear in me as soon as I see it perched above the waterspout.

I drop the femur involuntarily, again from the shock of the contents of a vision, but this time the femur does not levitate above the wooden floor. It lands with a thud onto the wooden planks. Staggering back to the chair, I sit. Suddenly, the light rays begin to dim, retreating into the pit; the humming sound decreasing in intensity with the light's disappearance. The piles of earth move independently of my thoughts to cover the underlying light, sound, and remains of Elias Doever. The opening in the pit is sealed. The whirlpool's current of energy gradually slows and then dissipates, the distortion of the floor beneath has vanished. The planks jump from their resting places into the original configuration of the floor. The nails find their respective entries into the wooden floorboards, and then as if an invisible hammer was at work, the nails are driven into the floorboards, tightly securing the planks into place. Within a matter of seconds, my work to expose the bones of Elias Doever has been reversed, and the burial place of Elias Doever is concealed again.

Amazed at what I just witnessed, I quickly gather the skull and the femur. The skeletal remains are still emitting the strange powerful waves of energy, but there are no images attached to the bones lying against the naked skin of my hands. Placing the bones into my knapsack, I exit the shed, loop the chain around the door handle to the door frame, and secure the door with the padlock. I move rapidly to the car, fire up the engine, and back the sedan carefully around the corner of the house, keeping the headlights off. Within ten feet in front of the gate, I hastily but quietly exit the running car and remove the chain and the open padlock to open the gate. I drive to the other side of the gate, and with lightning speed, swing the gate back and padlock the chain to the gate. In the dark, I scan the highway for other headlights. With none present, I slowly pull out of the driveway onto the highway. The headlights flash on when 112 Old Salem Highway is out of sight in the rearview mirror.

Returning home slightly after 1:00 a.m., I quietly enter the house and go directly to my bedroom. Placing the knapsack on the floor next to the bookcase, I sit on the bed. Faint vibrations of energy are emanating from the knapsack. I wonder if this will affect my ability to relax and sleep.

Lying in my bed, I contemplate all that has happened tonight and all the things that could have gone wrong. A major flaw of mine, I do this after every "adventure," whether that be a long road trip or a new experience with some possibility of injury. This practice can, in some cases, contribute to the logic of not partaking in future risky quests. But this time it's different, and not for the obvious reasons of breaking and entering. Nor was it the witnessing of the extraordinary power that Elias Doever's remains contain, an incredible demonstration of the power that Beladon spoke of. And it wasn't because I essentially became a grave robber tonight, something that I won't be adding to my resume any time soon.

Something or someone stopped this discovery and exploration when the visions became too disturbing to me. Could it have been Elias Doever's spirit? Beladon? This force determined that I had seen and experienced enough. If it was Beladon, perhaps it was preventing me from being overwhelmed by all that I had undergone in one evening. Which was a lot, I won't argue with that. Still, I feel there's another facet to this that hasn't been revealed to me…yet. This is what I fear will keep me awake tonight.

There's something else keeping me awake: Where is Beladon? I'm sure *he* knows that I have the bones because it senses when I have questions. And I have a lot of questions swirling in my brain. I expected to be contacted by now after such a discovery. The three bloods can now be united. But Beladon has gone "radio silent." There have been no answers, cryptic or otherwise. Where is Beladon?

Chapter 23

Provincetown, Massachusetts
Bell, Book and Candle Bed and Breakfast
4th week of October 1992

It took us more than four hours to get to the end of the Cape to arrive in Provincetown at noon, hitting most of the weekend traffic crossing the Sagamore Bridge into Cape Cod. As we departed this morning, I thought about the car ferry that leaves from Boston, but I was shelling out a steep amount for one night at a bed and breakfast the weekend before Halloween in P-town, also known as *the weekend*, where every gay man that ever wanted to dress in drag has the license to do so without any judgement. Hell, there are plenty of straight men that like to do that in P-town as well!

I was able to get a single Saturday night reservation at my favorite bed and breakfast: The Bell, Book and Candle, a kitschy B/B named after the famous movie that starred Kim Novak as a witch belonging to a modern-day coven in Greenwich Village during the swinging 1960s. I met the hosts/owners in Boston during a particularly wild weekend when I turned twenty years old. They're a cute British couple who immigrated to the Cape after they fell in love with P-town on holiday. Our meeting prompted an invitation for a weekend at their B/B and we've kept in touch ever since. Miraculously, they had a cancellation immediately after I called to inquire about a room. I had nothing to do with the circumstances behind the cancellation. At least, I don't think so.

As we drove down Commercial Street in the Mercedes, it turned more than a couple of heads. It isn't your typical car that ventures down the rough pavement of this repurposed Portuguese fishing village. As we coast toward our destination, I can't help but look over to observe Toby's face as he gets his first impression of the denizens of P-town. His electric smile and accompanying laughter, reinforced by the squeezes of his hand lying on mine, relay the wonderment and joy he's experiencing. The drag queens were out in full force advertising their shows for the Saturday before Halloween, one of the biggest nights in P-town. Not known for shying away from anything political, there were plenty of Hillary Clintonesque and Barbara Bush look-a-likes (the election was only two weeks away) amongst the usual bevy of Chers, Judys, Lizas and Barbras pedaling their acts. Focusing on two men our age holding hands out in public as they walk along the street, Toby leans over and kisses me quickly on the lips.

We park in the lot designated for our accommodations, the envy of many who are desperately trying to find parking in a town not known for its vast parking spaces (most of the fishing villages in New England originally relied on the ports rather than the land for transportation). Checking in, I introduce Toby to our hosts, expats Nigel and Russell, who have been together for over twenty years, a rare sight in the gay male community. As rare as unicorns. Although they have an "open" relationship, which seems to be the key to success for long-term gay male relationships, AIDS has made this a more dangerous lifestyle choice.

I can tell that Nigel and Russell are taken with Toby. Why wouldn't they be? He's the perfect example of the All-American boy that so many gay men lust over, including me of course. I'm not a unique gay man; I'm not a unicorn.

As we make our way to our room, paraphernalia from the film that the B/B is named is strewn throughout the converted sea captain's house: movie stills of Kim Novak, Jimmy Stewart, Jack Lemmon, Elsa Lanchester, and Hermione Gingold in various scenes of mod club life in Greenwich Village along with props from the movie that Nigel and Russell acquired from auctions at Sotheby's in New York. Their prized possession is a signed movie still of Gillian Holroyd (Novak) posing with Pyewacket, the Siamese cat that's her familiar in the movie. The movie is a favorite with gay men as the parallels aren't hard to discern: an artistic, creative subculture with a belief system that's not accepted by society. But instead of being discriminated against because of whom they love, they're discriminated against because of the false perception that they gain their powers from being in league with the devil and their highly misunderstood relationship with the supernatural realm. The world of magic in the film has no connotations to worshipping Satan. Their naturally acquired powers, inherited through familial lines, require no obedience to any deity, rather, an appreciation and the ability to manipulate the natural world.

Our accommodation is a tastefully decorated room

and private bath with a decidedly nautical décor. I notice that we've been supplied with masks for the festivities tonight. I appreciate this gesture from our hosts as the costume requirement of the weekend had completely slipped my mind. I'm also surprised to be supplied with this essential item as it's expected that every queen in P-town plans for their Halloween costume months in advance. Then I notice a note next to the masks addressed to me:

"Dorian love, we know you will enjoy these. We remember that weekend in Boston and how much you like to…play. Enjoy! Love, N and R."

I'm smiling and tittering as I read their note. Toby inquires as to what I'm giggling about. I hand him the note to read. After reading it, he looks at me and then asks, "Play?"

"Long story. I'll tell you sometime when I'm good and drunk, which probably means this weekend!" I respond coyly.

Toby smiles and bobs his head. "Cool."

It's an unusually warm day for the end of October, so I suggest we go to one of the beautiful beaches of Provincetown. If not to go swimming, we can sunbathe. I avoid mentioning the gay nude beach because this is not the locale I want to see Toby naked for the first time, nor do I want anyone else ogling him. I'm not that secure in our relationship…yet.

Eating at restaurants is infamously pricey here. To coin a local phrase, "It is wicked expensive!" So, I suggest that we shop at one of the local markets to get food for a picnic and then ride out to Race Point Beach on the mountain bikes that Bell, Book and Candle provide for their guests. Toby agrees to my plan, and we ride out on one of the many bike trails that honeycomb the state-protected seashore. The hilly topography creates challenges when climbing the upgrades, but the ride is a good workout and makes the reward of relaxing on the beach that much more enticing.

Race Point is gorgeous today. The late afternoon sun reflecting off the water and the brown coarse sand is picture perfect. The dunes creating interesting shadows in the mid-day sun would be the only source of natural shade on an intensely hot day. However, due to the autumnal breeze and the reduced strength of the sun at this time of the year, becoming overheated is not an issue, and we lie in the sun's rays without any protection (besides our sunblock). I glance at Toby while he lies there motionless on a towel under the warming rays of the sun. He looks sexy in his tan cargo shorts. His naturally brownish, year-round tan produces only a faint tan line at his waist. He lies with his arms folded behind the nape of his neck, displaying his massive upper arms, and highlighting the perfection of his muscular physique. I look at him and wonder what it is that he sees in me. I know that I'm attractive in that pale, dark-haired English schoolboy sort of way, but what's this blond sun-god doing with me?

As if he can read my mind, knowing that I'm thinking about our relationship, Toby moves his left hand toward me so that it lightly bumps my right hand. I take it graciously and enclose my fingers around his hand. It's hard for either of us to believe that we can hold hands together on a public beach without any threat of being harassed or abused for being a same-sex couple expressing their affection. This openness is what makes P-town such a unique place in the world for gay people, like the beach communities of Rehoboth Beach in Delaware or Key West in Florida.

We bought a freshly made seafood salad of shrimp, lobster and whitefish and sourdough bread from the market to make sandwiches, and with homemade coleslaw on the side, we had a picnic. It was a perfectly delicious late lunch to complement our perfect day at the beach. As the sun moves further toward the western sky, and the air starts to become chillier, we decide that it's time to ride back before it gets too late so that we can take a "disco nap" before we go to dinner and out to the bars. Pedaling back to town is infinitely easier as most of the hills are on a downgrade, allowing us to coast more on the way back to town than we did on the way to the shore.

After we check the bikes back in, we head up to the room. Peeling our semi-sweat-soaked shirts off, both of us collapse on the full-sized bed after our five-mile workout. It's not long before both of us pass out, on our backs, into an effortless slumber. Later in our napping, sensing that there's another being in the bed, I roll onto my side and wrap my arm around Toby's muscular waist, squeezing to gain a tighter grip. He acquiesces, rolling onto his side and leaning his back into me so there is no daylight between us. We slept for over an hour. Our first disco nap together.

After we shower (individually) we dress for the evening: black shirts, a button-down long sleeve for me and a polo-style short sleeve for Toby, designer blue jeans, black belts and casual shoes, brown Docksiders for Toby, and black Chelsea boots for me. Donning our masks, simple but elegant satin black guises that tie with black ribbon, we're ready to face all that P-town can offer on the Saturday before Halloween. Tea Dance is first.

Tea Dance is the quintessential event that most gay men in P-town start with for any evening. The most popular Tea Dance venue has a good-sized pool and a large deck for mingling while drinking expensive cocktails. At any given time of the year, every type of gay man can be found here including porn stars, drag queens, regular queens, businessmen, young men looking for Daddies, Bears, Cubs and Otters (big, small, and tall/skinny hirsute men), leather/BDSM aficionados, Abercrombie and Fitch/surfer boys and academics. Typically, Tea Dance begins in the early evening and lasts until early dinner time. Then you have the choice of going to dinner, and most likely make it an early evening, or you go home for a disco nap or sex, especially if you meet "Mr. Right Now," shower, change, have a late dinner, and then visit the clubs. I purchase two famously pricey Rum Punches for Toby and me, without either of us being carded, which is a relief in Toby's case but annoys me that they assume I'm twenty-one years or older. Handing the drink to Toby, I explain to him the "Devil's Tongue:"

"The straw is filled with a shot of dark rum, so that first sip is extra special and potent. I affectionately refer to it as the Devil's Tongue, because after a few of these, you are ready to tongue anyone! Cheers!"

I watch Toby's face as he takes that first sip through the straw. "Whoaaa! That is strong!" he belts out in his usual dude-like voice. With a decidedly adorable grimace across his face, he continues, "I don't know if I'll be able to finish one of these!"

"Like I said, the first sip is the most powerful, the rest is just spiked Kool-Aid. You'll be surprised how easily they go down."

I was right. We each have three in two hours, a bar bill that is nearly half of one night's stay at our B/B. But we're having a great time, making small talk with the populace. The people-watching is especially amazing, as some of the clientele have already donned their costumes for the night, or at least the first costume for the night. Most of them had participated in the make-shift Halloween parade that had happened while we were napping, so who knows what they'll look like by the wee hours of the morning.

As per usual, drinking in mass quantity leads to urinating in mass quantity. The bathrooms at any of the bars in P-town are large enough to accommodate the needs on a regular night, but on special weekends they are obsolete, and you can find yourself waiting in line for twenty minutes to piss in a sink if need be. Luckily, Provincetown is surrounded by water, so if you aren't too drunk, you can slip out near the "dick dock," P-town's infamous cruising zone under a pool terrace and wade out into the surf and do your business. Of course, one must watch out for the police who are patrolling for men cruising the beach, but at night, it's much more difficult to see beneath the terrace.

Slightly tipsy, I inform Toby of my intentions. "Hey, the line at the bathroom is ungodly, I'm going to slip out to the beach and relieve myself in the ocean. Do you need to go?"

"Nah, I'm okay. Drinking alcohol doesn't have that effect on me for some reason. The guys on the team think I have a bladder as big as a rugby ball," Toby nonchalantly informs me.

"Good to know," I say, slightly slurring my response.

I proceed to walk around the pool and out the side entrance. Walking down Commercial Street in the darker areas of the street, searching for a pathway to the water, I find a narrow space between buildings, partially obscured by a large bush. I stealthily maneuver my way to the water, kick my boots off quickly, and wade into the water up to my ankles. I unzip my fly and relieve myself into the waters of the Atlantic or Mass Bay, as it could be either.

Suddenly, the water about ten feet further into the surf from me begins to churn and bubble as if something is rising to the surface. I pull up my underwear and zip my fly. As the bubbling becomes denser, increasing in surface area, the water surrounding the bursting air bubbles begins to swirl. The swirling action is now a fully formed whirlpool; I know what to expect. Through the bubbling medium in the center of the whirlpool, I see the shiny exposed head of Beladon breaking the surface of the water, followed by the naked, gleaming scale-covered human-like body, upright on a column of water rising through the swirling water. The glowing aqua lights that beam from the irises of the entity find me in the darkness, directing my attention toward it.

Defying gravity, as this entity stands upon this waterspout, Beladon addresses me, "Dorian Leeves, the time of ascension is near. You have the three bloods. You will summon your powers when the moon is its most powerful."

Slightly incoherent, but understanding the gist of

what Beladon has told me, I clarify the statement, "Do you mean the full moon? The next full moon?"

"Yes, when the moon wields its greatest power on the earth."

"So, let me get this straight. I'm to sacrifice a mammal of some sort using the bone of Elias Doever, doused in my blood, which contains your 'essence' on the next full moon. Any particular time?"

"No, Dorian Leeves must bring the three bloods, a beast, and a mortal witness," Beladon informs me.

"A mortal witness? Why?" I drunkenly inquire as the rum is beginning to catch up with me.

"The mortal realm. The immortal realm. The sacrifice. Ascension," Beladon instructs me.

"Well, who is this mortal witness?" I simply ask.

At this time, the waterspout begins to descend into the surf, carrying Beladon down into the depths. Soon, all that I can see is the glowing aqua lights of the eyes and then complete darkness as the last bubbles disappear. The water, losing its circular vortex, returns to a wave-like pattern breaking on the shoreline. Beladon did not answer my question, again, and it didn't give me any time to ask the many questions that I've had since the night I found Elias Doevers's remains. This encounter adds more to the count of unanswered questions. Then there's the new task: Who will be my mortal witness? Immediately, Toby comes to mind. But this means that I'll have to tell him everything. And soon, as the next full moon just happens to be in three more nights, on Halloween. I know this because part of our research with the snails involves the tidal current, which is influenced by the lunar cycle. I'm now sobering up because of this revelation.

I find my way back to Toby, armed with a new task. But we're in P-town, and we're here to have a good time. He greets me with a big kiss on my lips; open mouth and plenty of tongue. Finally coming up for air, I joke, "Someone is feeling their oats tonight!"

"What?"

"It means you are feeling uninhibited, free, carefree…good."

He responds, slurring his words, "What's not to feel good about? This is a perfect place, a perfect night, perfect drinks, and a perfect man!" The rum punch is catching up to Toby as well.

With that last statement, Toby wraps his bulbous arms around my neck, pressing most of his weight against me as well. Toby has a good forty pounds on me, and because I'm also feeling the power of the rum punch, it is all I can do to keep the both of us from crashing to the deck. But I manage, hoisting him up until I can get him back into a standing position. I also recognize what this posture and this loss of balance means: Toby has precious time before he's going to be incapacitated, sick, passed out or all of the above. I decide that we need to get back to the room for a breather, another disco nap maybe, before the rest of the night, if that's possible.

Supporting him with my shoulder most of the way to the B/B, we make it to the room where Toby passes out on the bed, as if on cue. Normally, if I had a gorgeous man in this condition, I would be in full seduction mode: removing clothes, foreplay, and then the main event, hopefully, if he was willing and able, with a shower before (the Virgo thing I mentioned before) if the dude wanted to and was capable. But this is my boyfriend and we have resisted sex because we want it to be special, and his being drunk and incapacitated are not the conditions for consensual sex, special or not. I decide to take off his docksiders and jeans so that he can sleep more peacefully. Taking my boots and jeans off, I slide next to him on the bed. Preventing him from aspirating on his vomit if he gets sick, I prop him up on his left side. It's also a good position for spooning. Wrapping my right arm gently around his waist, applying no pressure to a distended belly, I fall asleep quickly.

I awake to the sensation of lips pressing against mine. Opening my eyes, I see my golden boy peering at me with a Cheshire-like grin on his face. The lights are still on in the room as we passed out together. He moves his mouth back onto mine, and I close my eyes to enjoy the tactile pleasure. His lips and tongue exploring my mouth, I'm becoming aroused. I can feel Toby's hardness through his boxer briefs on my hip. He stops kissing me. I immediately open my eyes and stare into his. Toby then moves his head to the right side of my face and whispers, purring into my ear, "I'm ready…I'm ready to do… whatever you want to do."

I initiate a long, passionate kiss. Toby breaks away from me to pull his polo shirt over his head and then resumes to kiss me full on the lips. Placing my hands on his chest, massaging the mounds of muscle, I lightly brush my fingers over his already taut nipples, eliciting a deep-throated moan of pleasure from Toby. This cues me to concentrate on the gum drop-sized masses of sensitive flesh with my thumbs. Circling the tips of his nipples with the tips of my thumbs, a more vocally responsive whine escapes from the back of his throat. Grasping them with the tips of my index fingers and thumbs, I roll the sensitive nubs of flesh in between my fingers. Toby is whining and moaning at the same time. My hands then move down to his flat stomach. Using my fingertips to explore the crevices in between the cubes of abdominal muscle, outlining them with my fingertips, my fingers move lower until I feel the crevice of his naval and the wisps of long curly hair that descend toward his pelvis. I slide my fingers inside the waist of his boxer briefs, pulling the elastic band back, and entangle my fingers in the thick patch of blond, coarse, and curly hair. Toby's breathing is accelerating, guttural sounds escaping from the back of his throat as I pet the mound of tight curly hair. Expectedly, a roundish mass of spongy flesh pushes against the side of my hand. As I unfurl my fingers to grasp it, I stop.

"Wait, Toby, before we go any further...I have to tell you something," I say as I remove my hand from the elastic of his briefs. Moving my body away from Toby, I sit up and lean against the headboard. With a perplexed expression on his face, Toby also sits up, cross-legged on the bed.

"Dorian, what is it? What's the matter?"

"Before we have sex...become intimate, I have to tell you something about me," I state nervously, barely able to speak, my mouth completely dry from the anxiety I'm feeling. Toby continues to look at me with those confused, big puppy dog eyes of his. Finally, I just blurt it out, "I'm a warlock!"

"What?" Toby says incredulously and quietly, still harboring that same confused look.

"I'm a male witch, a warlock, I have supernatural

abilities. I can move things with my mind... I, I have visions...I know when things are going to happen before they do...I can read minds...I can manipulate water..."

Toby's expression changes from confusion to surprise, some might even say fright. The face of someone afraid of the crazy person next to them who told them essentially that they were delusional.

"Here, I can prove it!" I exclaim, quelling his doubt. With that statement, I look around the room. Seeing a candlestick holder with a snifter attached to the bedside table, I point to it. I concentrate on moving the snifter. The snifter moves slightly, unhooking itself from the base of the candlestick holder, levitating until it reaches the top of the taper and then lowers itself onto the candle. Turning to look at Toby to see his reaction to the feat of levitation I performed, his eyes are wide open.

"That was amazing. How did you do that? I can't see any wires. It must be a projector or something. You didn't tell me you were a magician!" Toby exclaims.

"What? No, it's not a magic trick, I really moved that snifter onto the candle!" I bellow.

By the look on his face, I can tell that Toby is not buying it, still confused as to why I did a magic trick when we were about to consummate our relationship. I resolve that I'll have to show him something else. Water. I get up from the bed and walk into the bathroom. I can feel Toby's eyes trained on me as I disappear behind the door. Lifting one of the glasses provided for guests, I fill it with water from the faucet, return to the bedroom, and place the full glass of water on the bedside table.

"Here, drink from this glass," I say as I hand it to Toby. He picks up the glass, brings it to his mouth, hesitates for a moment, then places the rim of the glass against his lips and drinks. "Now put the glass down," I instruct. Toby puts the glass down. Concentrating on the water, I imagine it moving in a circular motion. Slowly, a swirling current evolves inside the glass, gaining momentum until a mini whirlpool is present. Turning my head to observe Toby's reaction, he has the same look of astonishment on his face as the candle trick.

"Dorian, you're really good. I didn't even see you put the tablet into the water."

"What the hell are you talking about? I didn't put anything in the water!"

"Whoa, dude, calm down! I just gave you a compliment on your skills. I saw this same trick at a magic show at my old school last year, and that dude was up on a stage. I'm right here, and I didn't see anything!"

Exasperated, I blurt out, "It's not a fucking magic trick! I'm doing this with my mind! I am a warlock, for Christ's sake!"

Toby backs away from me on the bed slightly. Looking at his expression, it is obvious my outburst has made Toby visibly afraid of me, of what I might say or do next. "Dorian, do you hear what you're asking me to believe? If this is the way you are when you drink, because if this is something that I'm to accept; my dad is an alcoholic, and I can't—"

"I'm not drunk!" I exclaim loudly. Realizing that I'm scaring him more, making the situation worse, I calm myself down, "Okay, okay. I'm going to calm down now. I'm not angry at you, Toby, I'm frustrated. I'm trying to share something with you that is very difficult for you to believe, I understand that…"

Then it hits me. I need to show him something more personal, rather than manipulating water or a candle holder. Staring into Toby's eyes, I concentrate on his thoughts. He continues to look at me as I stare at him, but I can tell he's feeling uncomfortable with my intense glare.

"Dorian, dude, you're freaking me out right now!"

"Your mother's name was Pamela. She was a petite woman with strawberry blond hair and blue eyes and liked to wear pink, especially pink sundresses made of cotton."

Toby's mouth is agape after my statement, but then he closes it. "I don't remember telling you anything about my mom. How do you…"

I'm suddenly possessed by one of Toby's most important memories of his mother, reliving it. "Toby, honey…don't listen to what your father says…you are handsome, strong and good, like the prince in this story, my little prince, my Prince Toby, my lovely Prince Toby…and one day, like in a fairy tale, you will find your Rapunzel, or Cinderella or…maybe another prince, Prince Charming, and that would be fine too…I will always love you, my Prince Toby."

I break from my trance-like state and look at Toby. He's staring at me with watery eyes, tears spilling from the corners of his eyes and streaming down his cheeks. He wears a pained expression on his face.

Gasping for air in between sobs, to produce any sound from his throat, he quietly and gently asks, "How? How did you know that? I have never told anyone about that."

"I read your mind. I had to prove to you that I was telling the truth...I had to find the most special memory to you...the most special memory you have for your mother," I compassionately explain, placing my hand lightly on his arm. Squeezing it gently. "And what a lovely memory that was. Your mother loved you and accepted you for who you are. You can't ask anything more from a mother."

Hearing this statement, Toby completely breaks down. Falling into me, I take him into my arms, supporting him as he cries into my shoulder. Shouldering his weight, I lightly smooth the hair on his head with my fingertips, gently stroking the blond locks from the top of his head to the base of his skull, repeating the gesture, soothing him. Wrapping his arms softly around me, he embraces me tightly as he continues to cry aloud. Slightly rocking him back and forth, I comfort him for what seems several minutes. Rising from my shoulder, Toby looks at me, only breaking his trance to wipe the tears from his eyes and face.

Gaining his composure, Toby utters a single sentence to me, "I believe you."

With that pronouncement, I lean into him, wipe the tear from his left cheek with my hand, and then place a soft kiss on his mouth. Resting my hands on both of his shoulders, I gently guide him to lie down on the bed, as I fall toward the bed as well. We're on our sides, looking at each other. I hug him, wrapping my left thigh around his right muscular thigh, as I continue to stroke his head. I whisper into his ear, "I'm sorry I had to...make you relive that memory. But I didn't know how else to prove to you what I am."

Silence. Stroking the curls on the side of his head, I'm feeling drowsy. Toby isn't moving except for the consistent movement of his massive chest against mine as he breathes. "Toby," I whisper. Silence. He's asleep in my embrace. Holding him closer, burying my head in his shoulder and chest, I close my eyes, inhaling his scent. I'm asleep in seconds.

****

I awake to feel pressure on my chest and abdomen. The sensation of bare skin against my chest, abdomen, pelvis. Muscular arms lie on either side of my chest, cupping my sides, hands buried beneath my shoulder blades. I open my eyes to see Toby's handsome face hovering above me, his eyes trained on mine. He gives me a long passionate kiss, exploring the inside of my mouth with his tongue, my tongue meeting his as we massage them together inside our mouths. My hands are now creeping over his naked broad back, circling over the well-defined muscles of his shoulder blades. Moving my hands along the contour of his back toward his waist, I am pleasantly surprised that there is no band of clothing strapped to his waist—it is completely bare. I move my hands to smooth and cup his muscular glutes, squeezing them. The round globes of musculature are taut and silky to the touch. He is completely naked, resting on top of me. Realizing that I can feel his naked skin against mine, I conclude that Toby has not only stripped himself but has also stripped me of the clothes I was wearing when we passed out together. I'm now aware of a familiar hardness pushing, slightly gyrating against my pelvis, touching, caressing the tender flesh of my inner thigh. Staring at me with those gorgeous baby blues, Toby whispers, "I'm ready. I want to do whatever we want to do."

Chapter 24

Provincetown, Massachusetts
Bell, Book and Candle Bed and Breakfast
Three days before Halloween, 1992

The following morning, basking in the afterglow or
whatever you want to call it that comes from having sex
for the first time with someone special, while we ate
our breakfast of home-made blueberry muffins,
scrambled eggs, chicken sausage, coffee, and blood
orange juice in the common dining area, we
contemplate the previous evening. But first, we talk
about typical topics like the outlook of the weather for
the day (it's going to be another atypical beautiful day
in late fall for our ride back home), the tastiness of the
meal (Nigel makes the sausage by hand and freshly
squeezes the blood oranges he has specially delivered
from Boston via the ferry), the chicory-flavored house
blend coffee that's reminiscent of the Café du Monde
(New Orleans is another favorite American destination
of our hosts), and the latest headlines from the
newspapers Sunday Edition (Clinton is gaining in the
polls). After we ran out of the typical topics and eat
most of our breakfast, our light banter became more
difficult, as we had more pressing topics we needed to
discuss. After a period of uncomfortable silence in
which neither of us knew how to ask questions of the

other about the events that unfolded the night before, that were not proper "pillow talk," I finally broke the solitude. "So, what made you want to have…sex after what I told you about me?"

I observe a sense of relief coming over Toby after the ice is finally broken. "Well…when we were making out before you told me about yourself, we could have continued and that would have led to…but you took the risk of telling me about…what you are, knowing that I could've been so freaked out about it. By the way, I still am…sorry, and ended it between us…but you were willing to take the chance of losing me, to be honest…I knew that you really cared about me…sounds cliché, but that's what I felt."

Slightly surprised by his confession, his use of the word "honest" catches me off guard. I instinctively grab his hand, holding it in this safe public space as I respond, "I saw you there, lying on the bed, looking so beautiful and ready to…and I knew that I couldn't keep something that important from you before we…became intimate." Toby squeezes my hand. "God, there really are no appropriate expressions for having sex besides 'having sex' are there? Anyway, you know what I mean. There would've been no going back."

Toby kisses me sweetly on the lips. Kissing openly in a public space, in a room with other guests, the lack of awareness of typical social norms and the safety that comes from a special place like Provincetown has sunk in for the both of us. Feeling this sense of safety, I decide to broach another difficult subject.

"Toby, I need to ask a favor, but I don't know how to ask it. So, I'm just going to say it. I need you to be a witness. Very soon, I'm going to have the opportunity to increase…my powers, dramatically. An ascension, if you will. A birthright, that was predetermined before I was born, because of my lineage, to acquire powerful abilities…abilities that I want to use to benefit mankind…I don't know, I haven't thought that much about it but like maybe, the cure to cancer, if I can…but there's a process, a ritual, before I can gain these powers…and I need another human being to be present. I want you to be that person. I want to share this with you."

"What?"

"All right, I know that didn't come out well, my tendency to ramble when I'm nervous didn't help." I try a different tack. "Basically, it's like puberty, instead of the body going through tremendous physical changes according to a genetic plan, I'm going to go through a change that will enhance my supernatural abilities according to a genetic plan. The abilities that I showed you last night. But it requires a process, a ritual, involving the power of the full moon to alter my body and I need another person there for it to happen."

Toby stares at me for a few seconds, which feels longer. I can see that he's thinking of a response. Suddenly, he gets up and walks away. He's going into the bathroom connected to the breakfast area. I sigh as I start to think of what I'm going to say next.

I check my watch; five minutes have passed since he disappeared into the bathroom. A sense of unease washes over me as I contemplate the possibility that our relationship may have been irreversibly harmed. He finally emerges from the bathroom, his hands absently rubbing together as he takes a seat at our table. His gaze is fixed on me, mirroring the serious expression he wore when he confided in me about being kicked out of his dad's house.

"I trust you, Dorian. I trust you with my life, which you have saved twice. But does this 'ritual' have anything to do with worshipping Satan? Wearing a black robe, or some other kind of weird shit? I am a Christian, I don't go to church very much, but I'm still a Christian!"

"What! Who the hell said anything about Satan?" I tersely respond to his inquiry.

"Well, you tell me you are a witch, sorry, a warlock. What else am I supposed to think when you say that you are coming into your power, and you need another 'human being' to be there? Do you hear how fucking nuts that sounds?"

I take a moment. Processing what Toby just said, trying to keep myself from blowing up, I consider his point of view and answer calmly, "I hear you. It sounds crazy, believe me, if I wasn't experiencing this, I would have a hard time believing it. But everything that I've been told about this ascension has been true so far, and I don't need to share the details yet, but trust me when I say that none of this has anything to do with the Devil or worshipping the Devil. My powers, my supernatural powers are a result of inheriting DNA, just like any other trait, but there are certain 'conditions' involving the 'natural world' that have to be met before they are fully realized. I will admit, if I'm being completely honest, I don't completely understand it myself. But I can assure you, there has been no mention of Satan, the Devil, demons, or any shit like that. I wouldn't be involved in this if there were, and I certainly wouldn't involve anyone I loved either!"

I managed to keep my anger under control until that final statement. As I reflect on the situation, a realization dawns upon me—I had just used the "L" word for the first time. Toby realizes it too. Staring with a bewildered expression, I can see the machinations of Toby's thought process through his facial expressions as he tries to sort out what I just told him.

Finally, he speaks, "You love me?"

"Oh my God! Yes, I love you! Is that all you got from that!" I shout.

Quickly realizing where we are, acceptance, or not, it isn't "kosher" to yell in a public dining room. Drama. Of the gay variety.

Toby then takes a deep breath, exhales, relaxes his broad shoulders straining against his polo shirt, grabs my hands in his, and speaks, "I love you, too."

Feeling more relaxed, because Toby seems to be more relaxed, I continue, "I'm not sure what will happen in three days. Did I mention that this will all happen on the night of the next full moon? Which just happens to be Halloween. I know. But there will be no coven of witches, not that I'm aware of anyway, and there will be no raising of the dead or…well, you get the point."

In an attempt to avoid overwhelming Toby with all the particulars of the ritual, I neglect to reveal that there will be a small animal sacrifice using the bone of a 300-year-old warlock doused in my blood on the night of my ascension. I've decided the sacrifice will be a common lab rat, a beast that gives birth to a live beast. My reasoning? Hundreds of thousands of rats have been sacrificed in the name of science, so what's the difference?

"Halloween, Tuesday night. What time? Please don't say midnight!" Toby pleads.

"No, I was told that it will happen when the full moon exerts most of its power on the earth. Presumably, when it is dark, but not necessarily midnight?" I say sympathetically after hearing what my full moon comment sounds like.

"Okay, I don't have any exams this week. I didn't really have any plans for Halloween outside of this weekend. I can come over after practice."

"I'll pick you up around six, six-thirty p.m. and we can get some dinner before we go back to Doever Farm. That's where this will all take place."

Toby looks at me with the same serious expression and asks without any emotion, "Doesn't this sound strange to you?"

"Yes, but I was also skeptical of the abilities that I was told that I had inherited, which have become stronger every day, the powers that I showed you last night," I answer factually. "Everything that I was told would happen, has happened."

"Dorian, I trust you but…"

"But what?"

Toby looks at me in silence for a few seconds, frozen, as if he's in a daze. "Okay, I'll do whatever you need me to do."

"Good. We should get going. We have a long trip back and everyone will be bugging out soon, and if you thought the traffic was bad yesterday!"

We pack quickly. After thanking Nigel and Russell for the accommodations, squeezing us in on such short notice, we hit the road. The drive off the Cape is long and arduous, but it's a beautiful day, which makes driving easier and less stressful. With the windows down, the breezy salt air refreshes while the mid-morning sun warms us. Waiting in the traffic that courses through each small town, the time provides us with the opportunity to have many long and meaningful conversations. Getting to know each other better. It's wonderful, but something keeps nagging at me when I look into Toby's soulful eyes during our discussions: Why did he agree so quickly to being there for my ascension after he clearly opposed it? Did I influence him with my psychic ability somehow, a new power I never knew I had?

Or was there another force that changed his mind? Love?

Either way, it left me with an uneasiness that put me on notice.

****

Crossing into the Bedfordshire corporate limits, not far from the turn-off for the road to Doever Farm, Toby points out the open passenger window toward the side of the road and exclaims, "Hey, look. Don't those two deer look like the ones we saw at your house?"

Turning my head quickly to look where he's pointing, I see an eight-point buck and a six-point buck standing majestically in the wooded area about ten feet from the edge of the road. Their heads are turned in our direction, eyes trained on the Mercedes as we approach them. Tracking us as we pass them, I've a perfect view of the eight-point buck as it glares at me, motionless, except for the subtle movement of its powerful neck musculature. Quickly, a strange feeling comes over me, not like the debilitating symptoms I experience before a vision, but an intuition, a foreboding. As if this magnificent creature knows something and is trying to communicate it to me. Looking in the rearview mirror, I can faintly see the head of the eight-point buck, turned in our direction, still tracking us. As it is becoming harder to distinguish the body parts of the bucks, mere brown-colored shapes impossible to identify from this distance, I notice the silhouettes moving and disappearing into the wooded area. A sense of relief comes over me as I realize that they didn't try to cross the coastal highway.

"Hey, Earth to Dorian," Toby asks as he snaps his fingers near my face. I turn to look at him, still slightly dazed.

Toby repeats his earlier inquiry, "You didn't answer my question: Do you think those are the same bucks that we saw on your place?"

"Oh, maybe. I'm certain there are other eight-point and six-point bucks in the Bedfordshire town limits, but we just passed the turn-off to the road to Doever Farm, so we are close enough that it could be that pair. That would explain why I haven't seen them in a while on the farm," I answer logically.

"That makes sense," Toby confirms.

As we approach the gates of the college, I turn left into the parking lot of the Presbyterian Church. It is Sunday, but later in the afternoon, so all the church-related activities are over for the day and the parking lot is empty. I park so that I can give a proper farewell to Toby. "So, if I don't see you tomorrow, I will see you in lab Tuesday and then I'll pick you up for dinner after practice. Meet me at the gates, like before, for my…ascension, that seems to be the best way to describe it."

"Yeah, I should be done with practice around six o'clock. Are you going to be in your lab before you pick me up?" Toby queries. I nod my head, affirming his query.

"Okay, I'll call you at the lab office from the locker room before I hit the showers to give you a fifteen to twenty-minute warning." Continuing to look at me, he pauses and then speaks in a quieter, more thoughtful tone, "I had a great time this weekend. Thank you for everything. It was…really special to me." He pauses again, but I notice his eyes tear up before he bows his head.

Feeling the need to break the silence and spare Toby, I say, "I know that we have a long way to go, and considering our 'unique' circumstances, to say the least…I think we're off to a great start." Toby lifts his head and smiles.

Trying to lighten the mood, I continue, "We cleared a big hurdle Saturday night: we're great in bed!" Toby laughs as he wipes a few tears from the corners of his eyes.

"You laugh, but I have seen more than a few possible relationships 'crash and burn' because of incompatibility in the 'boudoir.' Lack of flexibility, versatility whatever you want to call it…it is the 1990's. If we have learned anything from the AIDS crisis, it is that life is short, and we can't mess around because of what we think is expected of us…"

Toby smiles. "I agree, dude, do whatever feels good." Giggling, he continues, "Man, that sounds like something I would say stoned."

Undoing my seatbelt, and leaning over the seat toward Toby, I place my hands gently on either side of his jawline, cupping his face in my palms. I softly overlap his lips with mine, feeling the contours of the lower and upper lips as I press my mouth harder against his. I resist releasing my tongue, thinking this isn't the time or place for a kiss that could lead to illegal activity in a church parking lot. Toby resists as well. It remains an old-fashioned, early Hollywood type of kiss, one that would have made the audience watching a movie from this era slightly hot under the collar. The type considered mild for our generation but typical of soap operas that flood the weekly afternoon television schedule.

Breaking away from each other, still tasting his saliva on my lips, I fire up the sedan and drive across the street to let Toby out a hundred yards from the gates, an arbitrary distance we have agreed is far enough from the prying eyes of students/faculty on the campus grounds.

Entering the driveway to Doever Farm, part of me was hoping to see the two bucks we had seen along the highway to make sure they were safe and had not tried to attempt to cross the busy coastal road when we were out of sight. Alas, there was no sighting of the bucks as I parked in the circular driveway. Gathering my knapsack and walking into the house, I'm confronted with a delicious smell coming from the kitchen. It's unmistakable—the smell of bread baking and clam chowder.

"Oh my God, that chowda smells wicked good! I'm starving," I bellow in my best rural Massachusetts accent.

"Hello, honey. How was the Cape?" Mother shouts from somewhere upstairs.

"Great, as per usual. Halloween in P-town was full of…surprises. Nigel and Russell send their love." I lay my knapsack on the kitchen table.

"That's sweet. I'm baking sourdough rounds for bread bowls for the chowder. Should be ready in ten minutes or so. Can you set the table?" she instructs.

Starving, I stir the creamy white soup loaded with clam pieces and potatoes with the ladle; the smell wafting from the cauldron is overwhelming. I scoop a ladle full and lift it to my mouth. Carefully sipping the steaming hot soup, the buttery, creamy seafood flavors overrun the taste buds of my tongue. My belly bellows from the coming attractions. I notice a Halloween-looking card attached to the refrigerator by a magnet advertising the local supermarket. The front of the card is a cartoon rendering of the proverbial haunted house with several stock creatures smiling and appearing in windows and doorways: various ghosts, the Werewolf, Dracula and Frankenstein, and the Bride of Frankenstein. Pulling the card away from the magnet for closer inspection, I open it and realize that it's an invitation to a Halloween party from my mother's closest friend, Belinda, who throws a masquerade ball every year on Halloween, regardless of the day of the week. It's one of the biggest events in the quaint suburb of Mendham, about 20 minutes from downtown Boston; the town where my mother grew up and where my aunt still lives.

I shout to Mother while standing in front of the refrigerator, "Hey, are you going to Belinda's party this year?"

"I wasn't planning on it."

Startled by her sudden appearance, I jump back.

"Shit, you scared me! I didn't hear you come down! Don't sneak up on me like that. You could give me a heart attack!"

She responds drolly, "Slightly dramatic, Dorian. But you were in P-town all weekend; maybe you haven't gotten it completely out of your system yet."

"Why not?" I ask about her earlier answer.

Continuing the sarcastic tone in her delivery, she answers, "Really? Okay, let me list them: it's on a Tuesday, and I have classes on Wednesday. I'm single, unless you want to go with me. And I don't have a costume, and you know how much Belinda likes her masquerades. Shall I go on?"

Realizing that this party was the answer to getting Mother out of the house on the night of my ascension, I need to push her further. "I know, but you always have a good time. And you haven't had too many of those since you and Dad split up."

She doesn't respond. Concentrating on convincing her to accept the invitation, I physically turn to Mother, looking directly into her eyes. "Mother, Belinda is one of your dearest friends, and you are only an hour away, and she did think to invite you. Think of how disappointed she'll be if you don't come."

She pauses, blinking several times before saying, "All right, I think I will go. My classes aren't until the afternoon, and I don't have office hours that morning."

Walking out of the kitchen, just as the buzzer on the stove goes off, she states, "I have that Betsy Ross outfit I wore to the Independence Day pageant. Let me go and see if it needs pressing." She continues to walk away.

"Mother, don't you hear the buzzer, your bread is

done," I shout to her, removing the bread pan from the oven with an oven mitt, laying the hot pan on the counter to cool.

She returns to the kitchen, shaking her head as she enters, as if she were struck in the head, and turns the buzzer off on the oven. Observing the cooling bread on the counter, she speaks slowly, "You're right, I don't know what I was thinking. Why don't you unpack and wash up for dinner? The bread will have cooled by then, and I can scoop out the centers to make the bowls."

"Sounds like a plan." Feeling concern for her state of mind, I ask, "Are you okay?"

"Yes, don't be silly. Now go do what I said," she sternly barks.

After placing my knapsack down on the floor in my room, I sit on the bed. Contemplating what I have done, feeling an uneasiness at how powerful I have become when I do the "mind trick," I take a moment to reflect. After seeing her trance-like state after I wished her to change her mind about the party, thoughts of brain damage begin to seep into my mind. I quietly verbalize my inner thoughts. "I have to be more careful."

Chapter 25

Bedfordshire College
Halloween, October 1992

I've decided to use a rat as the sacrifice (God, I hate that word!) for my ascension. Because "the beast that gives birth to a live beast" must be killed with the sharpened end of the femur bone levitated out of the grave with the skull, I knew that the animal had to be a certain size. Big white rats, the kind that labs use for experimentation, would be a perfect specimen. Experiments using rats are so ubiquitous in the research community that a lab in our research facility at Bedfordshire specializing in determining the environmental factors for spinal cord birth defects to develop was using rats to conduct their research. This lab subject presents me with the perfect opportunity to obtain/steal a lab-quality rat.

I began to stake out this lab to learn their methods of operation a week ago: the hours of operation, the security equipment/protocol, the lab personnel, hours they worked, and the barriers to access the animal facility. It wasn't difficult to obtain the information because the security in the animal facility is minimal. The room that holds the rats is divided into two areas: individually labeled glass containers with wire mesh roofs for the rats that were involved in actual experimentation and a larger glass and metal container for rats for future experimentation.

During lunchtime, I infiltrate the facility and steal one of the rats from the large container. First, through my telekinetic powers, I disabled the video security feed in the hallway and the animal room out of the sightlines of the cameras, which I learned were hardly monitored during lunchtime. I open the locked door (no alarm) to the animal facility using my telekinesis as well. I sneak into the animal room with a container I obtained earlier.

Not being a fan of handling rats (picking them up by their long, scaly tail), I wonder if I can levitate one of them out of the larger holding container into mine. Observing an isolated specimen, I concentrate on the image of lifting it from the floor of the container. Focusing on the rat, imagining that my hand is cupping the underbelly and lifting its body, the rat starts to squeal as its feet slowly leave the floor, squirming and convulsing violently as it levitates out of its enclosure.

Without warning, I start to feel the intense sensation of pulsations racing through my body! The rate of the pulsations is increasing rapidly as I direct the rat toward the smaller container. I deduce that the pulsations are somehow coming from the rat's heart, pumping wildly, blood coursing through its body as it senses it is being placed in danger. The pulsations racing through my head are becoming disorienting, making it difficult for me to concentrate on the levitation. Once the rat is floating a safe distance above the floor of the smaller container, I visualize its release. The rat drops to the floor and the pulsations cease. Quickly, I close the larger container and leave the facility. Locking the door with the mind trick, I use it again to engage the security cameras once I'm out of range of the animal room.

In my lab office, I prepare the empty container: filling and attaching the water holder, spreading wood litter on the container's base, and placing plenty of food pellets. I then hide the rat and the container in the storage closet of our lab behind several large boxes of paper.

Sitting at my desk, collecting myself after the deed is done, I realize that I was experiencing the rat's sympathetic reaction, its "fight or flight" response while levitating it. I had never experienced anything like this before, but this was the first time I used my telekinesis on a living creature and not an inanimate object. Wondering why it happened, I chalk it up to another question that I would ask Beladon.

****

It's now 5:55 p.m. Expecting a call any minute from Toby, I'm working after hours on the lab computer, crunching statistical data. Dr Hayden is packing up his briefcase and knapsack, preparing to leave for the evening.

Dr. Hayden stops next to me on his way out the door. "Dorian, burning the midnight oil?"

"Huh? Oh, yeah, I had some data I wanted to finish computing."

"It's Halloween. Don't you have a party or trick-or-treaters to get home to?"

"No, I don't have anything planned."

"Well, your dedication is noted, but try and have some fun tonight. You are only young once. Believe me, I'm reminded of this every day. Good night,

Dorian." Dr. Hayden leaves just as the phone rings.

"Dorian?"

"Yeah, it's me."

"We just finished, so give me about twenty minutes to shower and walk to the gate."

"Okay, make sure you clean all your nether regions."

"What? What are my nether regions?"

"Nothing, not important; just trying to be funny, lighten things up, and obviously failing. I'll see you soon."

"Okay, I love you."

Taken back, this is the first time he or I have used this word in this context. I'm speechless.

"Hello?"

I finally answer him after several seconds of silence, "I love you, too."

Gathering the container from the supply closet, I turn off the computer, place the container/rat in my empty knapsack, turn off the lights, and lock the door to the lab behind me. Stealthily, I walk to the parking lot. Meeting Toby at our usual location, a hundred yards north of the gates to Bedfordshire College, I'm anxious about what's going to happen tonight. Once Toby is in the car, I lean over and give him a quick kiss on the mouth in the dark; the headlights are still off, and we're far from a streetlight. Turning to him in the passenger seat, I demonstrate my usual behavior when I'm nervous: I ramble.

"Hey, so what's everyone doing tonight? Are there any parties? Are the frats doing anything special? Is anyone going to Salem? I mean it is Halloween, if you're going to party, why not do it in the spooky capital of Massachusetts?"

"Hey, slow down, take a breath," Toby says as he firmly lays his hand on my shoulder.

Somewhat breathlessly, I respond, "Okay, you're right, I'm just a little nervous."

"Understandable," he says in a comforting tone.

"Get a hold of yourself, Leeves," I say to myself as I try to calm down. "So, where do we want to go eat? Besides candy, do you have any favorite foods you like to eat on Halloween?"

"I like pumpkin pie this time of year, if that's what you're asking."

"Great! Let's go find a place that has pumpkin pie!" I exclaim for no reason.

Abruptly, Toby plants a closed-mouth kiss to quiet me. Holding his mouth on mine for what seems like minutes, he caresses my face with his big but gentle hands, stroking it lightly. My breathing rate starts to decrease. Calming me when I can't do it myself. Realizing what he's doing, I gently pull myself away to look into his eyes. "Thank you. I think the diner has pumpkin pie. Sound good?"

"Let's do it," Toby replies, smiling with that crackerjack smile.

Chapter 26

Doever Farm
Halloween, October 1992

Pulling into the driveway of Doever Farm, the only thing I'm looking for is the presence of Mother's car. She said she was going to Boston, or rather Mendham, for Belinda's party after my psychic intervention, but I didn't know if my "spell" would last. Spell. I guess that's what it would be called if a warlock uses his mind to persuade. It sounds very old and Shakespearean, à la *Macbeth*, or kitschy, like *Bewitched*. Mother isn't here; one of the reasons for my anxiety is now relieved.

After parking the sedan, I retrieve my knapsack from the back seat, and we walk into the house. I head straight to my bedroom door. "I gotta go to the bathroom," I yell, to keep Toby from following me. I watch him secretly as he walks toward the kitchen. Placing the knapsack on the bed, I quickly pull the container with the rat out of the knapsack. Laying it on the bed, I check the condition of the rat. It's racing back and forth inside the container. It's obviously disturbed, but still alive. Closing the bedroom door, I run into the bathroom, flush the toilet, and head straight to the kitchen. Making a beeline for the cabinet, I remove two rocks glasses and walk to the liquor cabinet.

"I need a drink, a stiff one. Want one?" I ask while pulling a decorative bottle of Wild Turkey Bourbon Whiskey from the cabinet.

"Sure, what are we drinking?" Toby inquires as he looks at the blue ceramic bottle with a painting of a turkey in flight, a rare sight immortalized in robust color.

"Wild Turkey Whiskey—it was a gift. As you can see it's almost full as we don't typically drink hard liquor. But I think this night warrants a departure from the norm, don't you?"

Filling each glass about a quarter full of whiskey, I hand one to Toby and then lift the other in the air to toast. "Bottom's Up!" We both drink the shot quickly and react violently.

"Oh shit! That's strong!" I bellow.

"Woah, it's still burning my throat!" Toby exclaims in between explosive coughing fits. "Why the hell does anybody drink this shit!"

"To get messed up quickly. I know guys who sip it slowly on the rocks. I don't care for the taste, not even when sipping it slowly. But it does take the edge off quickly."

After our recovery, which takes a few minutes, Toby asks, "So, what do we do next?"

"We wait for further instructions."

"From whom?"

"Beladon."

"Excuse me?"

"Be...la...don," I repeat with difficulty, stressing each syllable as my mouth is completely dry from the nervousness I'm experiencing.

"Who is Be-la-don?"

Swallowing hard, trying to produce saliva in my mouth, my "fight or flight" response is at full capacity. I'm not able to speak at all. Pouring another shot into the rocks glass, I quickly suck it down, hoping to stimulate my salivary glands. Feeling that I have some lubrication in my mouth again, I nervously explain, "Beladon. I have learned about my powers from Beladon…Beladon has been guiding me through this process…telling me about who I am and what I am to become."

"Does this Beladon dude live near here?" Toby innocently inquires.

I pour another shot and down it quickly, summoning the courage to answer the question, "I'm not sure if he is a…dude. I don't know what he is."

Toby is staring at me, his eyes wide open, mouth agape. I take a deep breath. "All right, Toby, I'm just going to tell you, because I'm freaking out so badly right now, I don't know how else to do it. He's an…immortal, an entity that lives…in the bay, water in general. He represents himself as a…merman-looking creature. He has translucent skin covered with scales, aqua-colored eyes that glow underwater, and a tail that looks like a dolphin or a shark, I'm not sure."

Toby's eyes and mouth are still wide open. "Dorian, what the fuck? You expect me to believe this is a good thing? That you are going to receive some kind of power from a…a sea creature? …And, and if this is true, which I have a really, really bad feeling that it is, I'm just supposed to go along with it? Why didn't you tell me this before?"

"Because I knew that you would have this kind of reaction…and I needed you to be here…"

Toby stares at me, his puppy dog eyes are wet with tears, but his facial expression still reads anger and confusion. Shaking his head, he's trying to make sense of nonsense.

After several long seconds of silence, he says, "Dorian, I love you…but I don't have a good feeling about this. I'm outta here. Come with me," he pleads.

"I can't…I don't know why…but I just can't."

Toby picks up his jacket and walks toward the door. Following him, I race to place my body against the door to prevent him from opening it and leaving. I lean on the door. "Wait, you're right. I should have told you…I'm sorry."

Noticing my car keys on the end table next to the door, I pick them up and hand them to Toby. "Take my car. It's a long way back to the college, and it's Halloween. You never can tell what can happen on a night like tonight, right?" Realizing the irony of what I just said, I chuckle slightly, and continue, "I'll get it back tomorrow, hopefully."

Toby then moves toward me and kisses me lightly on the mouth, grasping the back of my head in his hands. After several seconds, he stops kissing me. Pressing his forehead against mine, he holds it there while massaging the back of my head. He's crying. Retrieving the keys from my hand, he backs away from me. Tears are streaming down his face. I slowly move away from the door. Toby pulls the door open and walks through it. I close the door, leaning my back against it, feeling like I'm going to collapse.

Suddenly, I see a bright aqua-colored light stream through every window in the house. Pulsating, as if spreading, one wave after the other, bouncing rhythmically against the walls, the furniture…me. I hear the Mercedes engine revving up in the driveway, and then, unexpectedly, a booming voice echoes in my head, canceling out all other sounds.

"Dorian Leeves, it is time to summon your power. Come to the water with the essence of Elias Doever, the beast that gives birth to live beasts and a blade and the witness. Come as you came into this world."

With this command resonating in my head, I retrieve the skull and the femur that I had hidden in my wardrobe beneath a pile of sweaters and place them on the wire mesh roof of the glass container. Picking up the container with the skull and femur bone lying on top, I walk into the kitchen and retrieve a knife from the wooden block that holds our sharpest knives. I place it on top of the mesh lid next to the skull and use both hands to lift and carry the container with the precious items on top of it. Concentrating on moving the door handle with my thoughts, the ancient knob turns with ease. Kicking the door open, realizing that I could probably have moved the door as well using the mind trick, I clear the doorway.

As apprehensive as I am about tonight, I'm feeling the power, like a warlock in my own movie. Like Nicky Holroyd in *Bell, Book and Candle*. For whatever reason, most likely because anxiety is playing with my sanity, the spell used in that movie to remove a witch/excommunicate a sinner, comes to mind as I'm walking to the shoreline of the bay: "Ring the Bell, Close the Book (Bible) and Snuff out the Candle." As I get closer to the berm, the aqua lights pulsating, radiating from Beladon's presence, the scene becomes more vivid. Reaching the crest of the berm, I partially shield my eyes with my hand to reduce the intensity of the display, to fully realize the scope of the impossible, magnificent image before me.

Beladon, in the usual guise of a beautifully sculpted merman, is surrounded by the aqua light pulsating across the beach and the property. The intense, fluorescent aqua-colored light, not only beaming out of the extraordinary irises, emanates in waves from its entire body as if this creature were decaying radioactive, glowing bioluminescence. Beladon balancing upon a column of water, the human-like appendages and the scale-covered tail flipping back and forth within the fountain of water, atop the watery pillar that rises from the depths of an eye of a great whirlpool circulating below. The entire scene, the halo of aqua-colored rays emitting from this creature's entire being, is reminiscent of the golden, holy light that emanates and surrounds Christ, Mary, and the Saints in Renaissance paintings. The tableau before me is a living, breathing work of art. My mesmerizing, trance-like state is interrupted by the voice that beckoned me in the house.

"Dorian Leeves, you do not come as born into this world."

Overcome by all the stimuli, I barely find the words to verbally respond, "I don't know what you mean?"

Beladon offers another cryptic message. "That which binds."

"Binds?" Abruptly, the image of a naked man appears in my mind. "I need to be naked, is that what you want?' I ask tepidly.

Beladon does not answer; I read this as an

263

affirmation. Placing the container with the precious elements on the firm sand, I unbutton my shirt, remove it from my torso and toss it carelessly onto the dune. Kicking off my boots, I quickly unfasten my khakis, pull the zipper down, and slip my pants off one leg at a time while balancing on the firm shoreline. Standing on the beach in my boxers, feeling self-conscious about stripping and being exposed on the land, as opposed to being covered in the water when swimming nude, I finally grasp the elastic band of my shorts and pull them down quickly, kicking them to the side. Standing completely naked on the shore, vulnerable to the world, images of nude men on the banks of bodies of water come to mind.

Beladon's telepathic instructions interrupt my thoughts of modesty and embarrassment. "Dorian Leeves, to summon the power, it is the time of the sacrifice of the beast that gives birth to a live beast with the three bloods."

Taking my cue, I remove the skull, femur, and knife from atop the container and place them on the sand. Picking up the femur, I grasp it so that one hand is holding it on either end of the bone. Resting the middle of the long bone against the kneecap of my bent right knee, I pull the femur toward me, hoping to snap the ancient bone in half. The resistance of the tissue is impressive as I exert my will on the bone, but it finally cracks and then breaks in two, revealing the jagged edges and the round cavity filled with dust. Not hearing any further psychic instructions from Beladon, I surmise that I'm doing what's necessary. Placing the piece of the bone with the femoral head on the container, I pick up the knife. Standing above the container, I make a shallow cut along the side of my right forearm, allowing the blood to slowly drip onto the jagged end of the bone. The ruby red liquid sliding into the crevices of the jagged bone, I squeeze the skin and muscle around the self-imposed wound to drench the lacerated surface of the bone. The white, gleaming surface is thoroughly stained with my blood, the blood containing my DNA and Beladon's "essence."

Removing the wire mesh roof from the container, I grasp the large white rat by the tail with my left hand. Lifting the squealing rodent out of the glass container, I dangle it in the sea air as it violently squirms in vain, attempting to loosen my grip. I pick up the femur with my right hand. Not hearing any more direction from Beladon, I close my eyes momentarily. Opening them, looking at the rat, I repeat the hunter's code: "I honor your life and the sacrifice that you make for me." Plunging the blood-drenched jagged end of the bone into the side of the rat with my right hand, piercing the soft flesh, blood spurts from the wound onto my right forearm; the initial high-pitched squealing from the rat is silenced as I direct the sharpened bone further into the viscera of the chest cavity, macerating the heart.

Beladon's voice echoes in my head, "The sacrifice is done; the Master approaches."

Confused by what Beldaon has said, I say aloud, "The Master?"

Unexpectedly, there is a disturbance in the fountain of water next to Beladon. Within the aqua-colored aura of the water display, another being rises from the whirlpool, darker than the serene blue water, rising into the column of water, a mass of dark matter approaches. Emerging from the fount, the dark, shadowy cloud levitates above the column of water. The sight of this sinister, formless being immediately elicits uncontrollable fear in me. This is the presence that I saw next to Beladon in my vision at the burial site! The evil presence that I feel now! Shaking, I lose all unnecessary motor control and drop the blood-drenched femur and the carcass of the rat onto the beach.

Beladon makes a pronouncement, "The Master...the light-bearer...Lucifer."

I want to ask Beladon what this terrifying revelation means, but I can't speak. I'm in shock. Beladon answers the question in my head.

"Beladon serves the Master...the sinful men that die at sea...they serve the Master...for eternity."

Still unable to speak, Beladon continues to read my mind, answering the questions that I'm thinking.

"The prophecy...to serve the Master...the Devil Noer Sea."

Gradually, my motor functions return, and I gain the ability to speak, "I...I d-don't understand, B-Belad...don w-what is the...Devil Noer Sea?"

"Devil Noer Sea, the servant through the waters."

"Beladon serves the Master...Elias Doever, Devil Oer Sea, serves the Master...Dorian Leeves, Devil Noer Sea, serves the Master."

Unable to understand what Beladon keeps repeating to me, my confusion contributes to my overwhelming fear, petrified by what is to happen next. I stare at the black presence floating above the fount of water, it still has not assumed any shape; an evil void of darkness, swallowing the aqua-blue light that envelopes the watery tableau.

"The summoning of the power of the Devil Noer

Sea is at hand, come forth witness," Beladon proclaims.

Remembering that Toby departed earlier, a sudden relief comes over me that perhaps not having a mortal witness as Beladon had instructed me to bring will stop this ritual. I also think that I'll have to pay the price for disobeying Beladon. Most likely…with my life.

Suddenly, the aqua light behind Beladon condenses into a denser concentration, forming a ray of light, a beacon that blasts from the dais of water onto the shore to illuminate a patch of beach and a dune. Then my heart sinks as the head of a figure appears above the crest of the dune. A figure with fair hair that reflects the aqua light. The face and the bare shoulders are now visible in the beacon's glare. It's Toby. As he ascends the dune it is now apparent that he's naked, his magnificent physique bathed in the aqua light, he is a Greek hero personified. Standing at the crest of the dune, the aqua-colored radiance highlighting every contour of every muscle, Toby is motionless, a blank expression on his face. His gaze does not stray from the source of the beacon of light, as if it had drawn him out, leaving the place where he was hidden during the summoning of the dark spirit. He's in a trance, obeying whatever Beladon commands.

The beacon of light then becomes more diffuse, spreading out and illuminating more of the shoreline, moving toward my position on the beach. Toby walks toward me, following the direction of the light. As he comes closer, I feel both comforted and terrified. This stunningly beautiful nude man is coming toward me. This would have been, in any other circumstances, the prelude to a physical encounter, a meshing of our naked torsos as we embrace, skin on skin, as we stood on the firm sand beneath us. A statue of two classical heroes enfolding each other as if it were their last night before some battle. But this was not to be. Toby stops a few feet from me and stands waiting for his next command. I feel an instinct, an urgency to protect Toby, to shield him from what is to happen next.

Mustering the courage, I speak aloud, "Beladon, what is the purpose of bringing Toby here, naked?"

Beladon ceases to communicate telepathically, its voice now echoing through my ears and not my mind as before. "To summon the power of the Devil Noer Sea, there must be a sacrifice…the witness."

Horrified by what Beladon is proposing, I nervously interject, "But, but you told me that the sacrifice of the b-beast would summon the power, you said nothing of the witness…"

"Sacrifice of the beast summons the Master. Sacrifice of the witness summons the power."

"You lied to me! You said nothing of human sacrifice!"

"Toby Blessing the sacrifice…Toby Blessing the sacrifice…of the blood of William Putnam…the sacrifice for the death of Elias Doever…the Devil Oer Sea."

Petrified by this revelation, I'm speechless. I don't know how to respond to what has been said, overcome by what Beladon has revealed. I sense the tears spilling into the corners of my eyes. Finding the bravery to address this pronouncement, I try to clarify what has been told to me.

"You are telling me…that Toby is the descendant of William Putnam, the man responsible for Elias Doever's execution? That he was destined to be…the sacrifice for me to summon my power?"

"Toby Blessing would have died in the sea...Beladon saved the sacrifice."

"You saved Toby from drowning that day so that he would be here for me to kill him!" I shout to Beladon, tears streaming down my cheek in anger.

"The sacrifice must be killed with the three bloods to summon the power."

I'm silent. Pondering another terrifying disclosure, the horrifying options I'm left with. I make my decision.

"I will not do this. I will not kill the man I love for any reason. I will accept the consequences of my decision," I scream into the night.

Beladon's facial expression changes from indifference to anger. Suddenly, narrow beams of light project from his irises into mine. As my eyes are exposed to the searing radiance, I'm unable to move my hand to shield my eyes from the damaging light. Baring the exposure to the intense light sensation, I accept my fate. I prepare for my death. But the light is not burning, not destroying my eyes. I'm not dying. The light is spreading from my eye sockets, enveloping my body. As the aqua-colored beams continue to enter through my eyes, my body is absorbing the wavelengths of light. Realizing I'm not dying, I try to move something in my body that does not require as much energy as raising my hand. I try to close my eyes, but I'm unable to move my eyelids.

Abruptly, my body moves, but I am not in control. My view is shifting, changing from the focus on the watery platform; I now recognize that the light beams have stopped beaming in my direction. My view has shifted to the sandy beach, tracking the narrow strip of land, searching for something. My body is moving along the beach. With this involuntary movement, it finally dawns on me that my body is being possessed by Beladon, and that the light rays that infiltrated my body have now allowed Beladon to control my actions. The broken femur bone drenched in my blood is now in focus. My body moves to pick up the bone. Horrified by this action, I come to the sobering realization of what is happening: Beladon is possessing my body so that I will stab and kill Toby with the broken femur containing the three bloods. My cognitive dissonance at this prospect places me in a panic I have never experienced: I'm going to kill another human being, someone I love, and I can't stop it!

Approaching Toby with the bone in my hand, he is still motionless, unable to react to the danger he's in. I see my right hand holding the bone so that the jagged edge is facing outward. I helplessly watch my arm rise above my shoulder, unable to stop what I'm about to do!

As I near Toby, suddenly, in the distance, two figures appear in the background, running with great speed toward me. The figures are not running on two limbs, but four. The silhouettes of the beings are approaching me, stampeding toward me over the dune, getting closer to me as I come within feet of thrusting the bone into Toby's chest. In the aqua light, I instantly recognize the shapes. Two bucks are charging at me, their heads bowed, antlers facing me.

As the sharp end of the bone connects with the flesh of Toby's pectoral muscle, the power of the thrust into his chest is stopped by the plunging of the antlers into my chest and abdomen. I'm being gored by the points of the antlers, and the momentum of the bucks slamming into my torso pushes me away from my target. I fall to the ground. The bucks back away from me, removing their antlers from my chest and abdomen. I can see that I'm bleeding profusely, but there is no pain. My heart races and my chest heaves. The bucks stand over me, their kind, innocent eyes now look angry, observing me for any more movement. My body is in shock, frozen in place. They have incapacitated my mortal body from carrying out Beladon's wishes. The eight-point buck lowers its head toward my face and licks my cheek. Unexpectedly, I feel a tremendous force leaving my body, aqua light diffusing out of my organs, muscles, skin; Beladon's presence is leaving my body.

Instantly, the exquisite pain of the multiple lacerations across my chest and abdomen causes me to writhe and convulse on the beach. Curling into the fetal position, lying on my right side, the watery dais supporting the immortals is in my sight. Through the excruciating pain, I continue to keep my eyes open, watching the display, unable to anticipate what is to happen next.

Abruptly, the dark mass next to Beladon expands as if it were going to swallow Beladon. A low-pitched angry roar emanates from the void as it pulsates. Beladon's blue aura begins to fade. Its evil glowing blue irises trained on my eyes as his blue halo disappears. The bucks lay down in front of me, blocking Beladon's evil stare. I hear another unworldly, blood-curdling scream, but I can't see which entity is making the sound. I extend my neck so I can see around the buck's body. Beladon is contorting as if in pain.

Suddenly, I'm receiving a series of images and messages telepathically. Faces of various men flash in front of my eyes. I recognize one of them as the man from visions that I saw deformed in pain in the well: Elias Doever. I see the men, part of a vast crowd of people, and an enormous dark void moving toward a great mass of dark clouds opening. A blinding light pierces the scene, obliterating everything in the image.

I'm looking at the beach again. In the flash of an eye, the black mass disappears, descending into the depths of the bay through the water column. It collapses violently into the surf, waves crashing on the shore. Beladon's form is now writhing, changing as the fountain he floats upon subsides. The body of the beautiful merman-like creature is covered with eruptions, round nodules of grayish-green tissue spreading across the delicate scale-covered skin of the tail and human-like torso. The fine, delicate bone structure of the handsome, youthful face is slowly and methodically replaced with blunt, grotesque features: exaggerated projections of bone over the eyes reduce the size of the eye sockets into thin cylinders encompassing small black eyes with the tell-tale aqua-blue irises; large masses of sharp bone penetrating the cheeks produce blunt monstrous tissues that collapse the face into an ugly grimace; the nose disappearing altogether, leaving room for the expanding mouth, shaped by hideous bulbous lips; and the neck now displaying profound jagged slits between the ugly masses of erupted flesh, the gill slits it uses to breathe underwater. Beladon's true form, the monster that I saw in my vision, is before me. As the column of water lowers and becomes level with the dissipating whirlpool, the hideous creature turns its head in my direction. As I suffer on the beach, I watch it descend into the depths, a great waterspout rising into the air to herald its departure. The final sign of the end of Beladon's presence.

As I lay on the sand in excruciating pain, observing that my breathing rate has decreased while my heart rate has increased dramatically, I feel the sensations of several streams of liquid dripping across my chest onto the sand. I lie still, gradually falling asleep, accepting, and expecting my death.

Without warning, something touches my left shoulder. Reflexively, I convulse away from the unexpected sensation. Then it becomes apparent it is a human hand. Slowly rolling over in the direction of the tactile sensation, opening my eyes, trying to focus them on the moonlight of the darkness, I see it is Toby who is gently rubbing my shoulder. Elated he is still alive, a weak smile forms across my mouth. He is kneeling next to me. Tears stain his handsome face. Remembering that I stabbed him, I quickly look at his chest and see the wound; there is no blood oozing from the laceration on the left side of the chest. The blood has dried to form a preliminary scab. Apparently, I merely gave him a flesh wound.

Sobbing, Toby manages to speak to me in a quiet, comforting voice in between sobs, "Dorian, Oh my God, you're alive."

"Toby," I whisper, using as little air as possible, "I am so sorry. I love you."

His handsome face leans toward mine. My eyes remain open as he gently places his lips on mine. In the near distance, there are two figures peering over his shoulder as I kiss him; the bucks are staring at us. Their kind, concerned eyes have returned. The images of the deer and Toby's face begin to fade. I'm losing consciousness. I'm dying. Toby's weeping dies away as my eyes close.

Chapter 27

Puritan-Bedfordshire Memorial Hospital
November 2, 1992

A splinter of white light penetrates my closed eyes. Is this the white light that I have heard of when you die? The white light that firm believers, those that have technically died and then brought back to life, have sworn is the light that leads to Heaven and God? I command my eyes to open wider to take in this glorious light. As my eyes adjust to the luminescence, the light is not glorious, nor is it "heavenly," by any stretch of the imagination. The light is fluorescent, as in long, industrial-sized, commercial fluorescent bulbs hiding beneath plexiglass. Moving my eyes from the harsh glare, I scan the rest of the environment. It's a plain white room, with painted cinderblock walls, two large windows covered by two rows of Venetian blinds, a countertop with several cabinets above, a large stand-alone closet, a door to a bathroom (as I can see the toilet) and a doorway, in which the door is partially ajar. There's also a large bed with rails next to me, similar to the one I'm lying on. As I move my head slightly to the side, I now notice a long plastic tube attached to my left forearm. It's obvious I'm in a hospital room, and something is pumping intravenously into my arm.

Sounds of the hospital suddenly become louder, redirecting my eyes and my semi-conscious state of mind to focus on the door. A group of people are processing through the doorway. The first person I do not recognize, but the uniform identifies the individual as a nurse or some other hospital personnel. But the next two people filing through the doorway with big smiles on their faces are people I know and love: Mother and Toby. She rushes to the side of my bed and immediately places her small delicate hands gently around my face and kisses me softly on the lips. Tears trickle down the sides of her nose. "Dorian, sweetie, you gave us such a scare. You have been unconscious for two days. The doctor was going to give us the prognosis today if you didn't…but you are awake now! Everything is going to be fine."

By this time, I can see that Toby has situated himself next to the bed. He's also smiling and tearful, although more subtle about displaying his emotions. Wiping away his thin tears quickly with the back of his hand, his mega-watt smile lights up the room more effectively than the cheap fluorescent bulbs. He covertly places his hand on my knee covered by a sheet and coverlet and softly squeezes it. He removes his hand quickly.

At this time, Mother turns to her right and acknowledges Toby. "Dorian, this is Toby Blessing, the young man who found you when you were being attacked by the deer. He's the one who saved you and who was wounded when he fought the deer off you. You were very lucky that he was running near the house when he saw those bucks trying to kill you."

Comprehending the events that Toby has invented

to explain my injuries, I play along, "Yes, I know Toby, Mother, he is a student in my lab section."

Lifting my arm slowly, as any muscular movement connected to the flesh and sinew wounded in my chest and abdomen is exquisitely painful. Even subtle movements of my chest and belly during normal breathing are painful. I extend my hand toward Toby to shake his hand. Speaking to him in the cheesiest, most cliché manner, reminiscent of the old movies where heroines in peril were saved by dashing heroes, "Thank you, Mr. Blessing. I don't know how I will ever repay you for your bravery and kindness."

Toby silently mouths, "We'll think of something."

Not missing a beat, Toby verbally responds in his best Dudley Doo Right vernacular, "I'm just glad that I was there to help you…the right place at the right time. I would hate to think what could have happened to you if I hadn't been there." This is all becoming too comical.

Then another voice, a voice in a lower register interrupts the conversation. "Mr. Leeves, begging your pardon, I'm Officer Nolan. I was the officer on duty when Mr. Blessing called your attack in. I just have a few questions, if you feel up to it?" Officer Nolan, standing in the corner of the room, advances toward my bed. He's an attractive, middle-aged man of average stature wearing a gray and black policeman's uniform complete with a gray wide-brimmed felt hat. I can clearly see his silver badge on his chest, conjuring up thoughts of a role play I did with an old boyfriend to spice up our sex life. I blame the inappropriate thoughts on the pain medication pumping into my arm.

"Sure, if I can remember anything," I say, continuing

the charade.

"Now, Mr. Blessing says that he saw the two bucks stampede toward you before they gored you in the chest. Did you provoke them in any way?"

"No. I was coming home from working late at the lab. I'm a graduate assistant at Bedfordshire College in Dr. Hayden's lab, when these two enormous deer came charging at me through the yard, and then bowing their heads, so that their antlers were prone to stab me, they attacked me!"

"That is the darndest thing! I've served on the Bedfordshire Police Force for over twenty years, and I've never once heard of an incident where a deer attacked a person. They are so timid they rarely attack anything, only when their young are threatened, and only if they're threatened by much less dangerous animals. I've had plenty of incidents where deer hit people and cars when they were running from something, usually a predator like a coyote or a wolf, but I've never seen one attack a human being, much less two. But your wounds are consistent with those caused by the sharp point of an antler, and the pattern suggests that it was a large number of antlers responsible for the multiple lacerations in your chest and abdomen."

I offer a plausible but false explanation. "Maybe they ate something that made them psychotic, like psychedelic mushrooms with Psilocybin."

"Maybe," Officer Nolan states with reservation in his voice.

Mother interjects, doing her best protective lioness routine. "Is that the only question you wanted to ask my son? Because if you don't have any further questions, I think we all need to leave so that he can get his rest."

"Oh, yes, no, that was the only question. Mr. Blessing filled me on everything else in his report. Okay, well, I'm glad to see that you are better, Mr. Leeves. If you remember anything else later…anything that could help us to prevent this from happening again in the future, we would appreciate it. Good night, Mrs. Leeves, Mr. Blessing," Officer Nolan states as he bows his head to us and leaves.

"Well, I think we should all take our cue from Officer Nolan and leave so that Dorian can get all the rest he needs to heal. Is there anything I can bring you when I come back later, sweetie?"

"Yeah, even though I haven't tried the food here yet, I'm sure it's going to be…well, hospital food. Could you get me some—"

"Twizzlers? Cherry flavored? Dark sea salt chocolate?" Mother interrupts.

"You read my mind, Mother; you always could," I say, smiling, with some irony in my voice.

"I'll get it before visiting hours are over tonight," she says as she leans down and kisses my right cheek. "I love you."

"I love you too," I answer. "Oh, and, Toby, could you stay behind for a minute," I ask. Mother looks at me in confusion at my request.

"I want to ask him something, in private, Mother. You know, guy things."

"Oh, okay, but don't be long." Mother saunters out of the hospital room.

"Guy things? Are we going to talk about jock itch?" Toby muses.

"I know, but it worked. Okay, you need to fill me

in on the story you told the police so that I can corroborate it, if necessary."

"The true story or the fake one?"

"The true one for now, the fake one later."

"First, after you passed out, I checked to see if you still had a pulse and were breathing. Your pulse was weak, so I knew I had to get help soon. So, I picked you up off the beach and carried you back to the house, naked, and so was I. I didn't want to waste any time getting help. When I got you back to the house, I put a blanket over you to keep you from going into shock. I called 911 and reported that you were gored by two bucks, and you were bleeding profusely from your chest and stomach.

"While I waited for the ambulance, I went into your room, pulled a pair of mesh shorts out of your dresser, and put them on you. I didn't want to bother your wounds, so I didn't put a shirt on you. I told them that I ripped the bloody shirt off you and used it to apply pressure to the cuts bleeding the most and then threw it away because it was soaked. Which was true, but I used one of your bath towels instead of a shirt. After I dressed you, I went in search of my clothes. I went to the car, that was the last place I remember being before I 'woke up.' I don't know how else to describe it, on the beach naked, and there were my clothes lying next to the driver's side of the car. I guess I stripped there before I walked to the beach."

"So, you carried me back to the house? You have forty pounds on me but I'm six inches taller than you. How did you do that?"

"I dunno, adrenaline? I just knew that I had to get you to the emergency room, whatever it took." Toby raises his hand to caress my cheek. Getting lost in his big blue eyes, our moment is interrupted by an announcement over the P.A. The mood is broken, and Toby moves his hand away.

Still staring into his eyes, a question pops into my head. "So, what do you remember before you were drawn to the beach?"

"After I started the car, I remember I was about to put it in drive, when this crazy aqua blue light came through the windshield, blinding me, and then the next thing I remember is seeing that crazy scene in the water…what was that?" Toby exclaims quietly.

"Long story…another time."

"All right, but I have a lot of questions."

Toby continues talking, changing his tone, "Before I forget, here is the fake story. To explain my wound and cover the story about my trying to stop the deer from goring you, I ripped a hole in my shirt approximately where the cut was on my chest, picked my scab to get some blood, and then smeared it across the ripped area. Of course, this was after I had figured out the most logical story to explain what happened to us. I was told that when you are going to lie about something, you should try to stick to what really happened as much as possible.

"To explain why I was near your house that late at night, I said I was going for a run, that your house is only three miles from campus. I ran to your house one time to see if you were home, so I knew that the running story would make sense. It was kind of late in the night for a run, but I couldn't think of anything else that wouldn't incriminate me…or you. Besides, I knew the police wouldn't doubt that you were struck by deer antlers when they investigated your wounds, rather than suspecting me stabbing you multiple times…like a serial killer."

I'm astounded at Toby's story-telling abilities. "Wow! That story was brilliant thinking on your part. I didn't know you could be that devious; that could come in handy in the future," I say, smirking.

Toby smiles back, raising his right eyebrow, owning his deviousness. "I need to go so you can get your rest and your mother doesn't kill me. I still have a lot of questions, but they can wait until we have more time…when you're better."

Toby then looks over his shoulder toward the door, scanning the scene through the doorway; I presume he's looking to see if the coast is clear. Satisfied, he quickly bends down and kisses me. His lips feel so good, I don't want it to stop. But as soon as he touches his lips to mine, they are gone.

"I love you, Dorian Leeves, no matter what you are," he whispers.

"I love you too, Toby Blessing."

Toby then stands up and walks out of the doorway purposefully, looking back and forth in the hallway to confirm no one was lurking or eavesdropping on our conversations. Turning to look at me, he flashes that million-dollar smile and then disappears. Feeling exhausted, I rest my head on the multiple pillows beneath my neck. I'm asleep in seconds.

Chapter 28

Doever Farm
November 12, 1992

I've been home at Doever Farm for five days now.
I'm on powerful antibiotics taken three times a day to
control the infections that caused the fever that knocked
me out for two days after I was almost fatally wounded.
My graduate assistantship duties will resume next
Monday.

Toby is visiting me today. He comes over
whenever he's not practicing or studying. Sometimes,
he comes here to study. Mother now knows we're
involved romantically. I spun a tale that after he saved
my life, and we learned that we were both gay, I fell in
love with him. She told me that it was called
"Nightingale Syndrome," wherein patients fall in love
with their caregivers. Even though Toby is not my
caregiver, Mother uses this psychological condition as
the rationale for accepting our relationship, even though
I'm a graduate student, and he's an undergraduate. I
learned it is also called "Damsel in Distress Syndrome,"
whereas Toby would be Prince Charming, and I
the…damsel. Enough said. Even though Mother does
not approve of faculty/student relationships, she has
made an exception in our case because of the
circumstances. Of course, she doesn't know the truth

and we have sworn to never tell her no matter what happens in our relationship in the future. Mother insists that we keep it a secret as the college would most likely not be as accepting, and Toby's scholarship and possibly my Graduate Assistantship could be in jeopardy. She has become quite fond of Toby and includes him in most of our family events, even requiring him to do chores on the farm when she sees fit.

Toby and I have had many discussions about what happened that night. I explained everything I knew about Beladon, the quest for the bones of Elias Doever and the night of my ascension. How I acquired Beladon's DNA through the "Happy Showers," the encounters with Elias Doever's spirit at Witch Well Park, and the shed at the James Corey farm, ending with that fateful night when Beladon demanded I kill Toby to ensure the inheritance of my ultimate power from Lucifer.

I told him about the "Devil Noer Sea" and that I still don't know why Beladon kept referring to me using that moniker. After researching the word "noer," we learned that the word is an old English word that means "swim or travel through water." The verb makes sense when next to the noun "sea," but why Beladon kept referring to me as "the devil swims through the sea" when he's the actual demon or demi-god or whatever that lives in the sea is still a mystery. We also discovered that "Devil Oer Sea," the term that Beladon used to describe Elias Doever translates as the "devil above the sea." These translations would define Elias as the "devil above the water" and I would be the "devil in the water." I have tried to hypothesize what these terms mean besides the literal translation.

When Elias Doever died in the well, was that Beladon's DNA in the guise of Elias Doever's corrupted soul that rocketed out of the well and into the bay, the "devil above the water" returning to the sea to be reunited with Beladon? How did Elias Doever come to possess this "essence," DNA, soul…or whatever you want to call it, from Beladon? Were there others before Elias with the same birthright from the same bloodline? Is that the legacy that I've inherited in my DNA, only transformed, or reincarnated as the "devil in the water?" Is that it? Am I the reincarnation of Elias Doever? Is that the reason why I ignored all of my instincts that there was something wrong, very wrong about all of this? Why I acted the way I did without any regard for anyone else but myself?

Beladon's evil DNA transformed me into his servant. Evil, yes, that is the word. Any creature that associates with Lucifer is evil. A servant that would carry out Beladon's evil deeds. I suspect that the evil "essence" had the same effect on Elias Doever's demeanor when he acquired it. An evil presence imprisoned in his body only to explode from it when soaked in holy water. In retrospect, that should have been a detail to have examined closer.

We have researched Toby's surname "Blessing" as well because Beladon kept referring to Toby as "the witness Blessing…sacrifice." In addition to learning that Toby's lineage to William Putnam is on his mother's side, there is significance to the origin of the last name Blessing: "blessing" refers to "being consecrated with blood" and its origins come from non-Christian, Pagan practices. Consecration with blood means to draw blood from an animal/organism, and typically that would translate as sacrifice as the animal gives its life to the cause as it loses its blood. So, in a sense, because Toby was a descendant of William Putnam, the accuser and executioner of Elias Doever, and his last name literally meant to be sanctified with blood, it was pre-destined that Toby Blessing was to be the sacrifice to not only raise Lucifer for my ascension but to avenge Elias Doever's murder. Interestingly, when we were researching the surname Blessing, we also discovered the meaning of my last name Leeves. The origin of the term "leeves" is Anglo-Saxon. An Olde English word derived from the term for "dear or beloved one." The irony that the man whose last name meant "beloved one" and the man whose last name meant "being consecrated with blood" was a loving, romantic couple was not lost on us.

Through our discussions, we figured out most of what happened the night of my failed ascension. Besides the "Devil Noer Sea" mystery, there is one very important component of this story that we can't answer: the involvement of the bucks, and how their appearance was crucial to how we survived the night. After many conversations, we hypothesized that the powerful animals were preordained to prevent the ascension from happening. From the initial sighting of the stag, which coincided with Toby's first visit to Doever Farm, to subsequent sightings on and around the farm, the timeline of us being together as a couple on Doever Farm concurs with the stag's presence. As if the bucks' steadfast devotion to each other to survive in the world was foreshadowing the same kind of dedication that would be needed for what we were to encounter in the days ahead. As to why they were so powerful in our fight against Beladon and Lucifer, I uncovered some very interesting research.

The stag is a symbol of Christ and/or Christianity in early European Christendom. The powerful pointed antlers growing, falling off, and growing again is a symbol of regeneration, like the regeneration of the soul that Christians believe happens from acceptance of Christ as your lord and savior and the ultimate reward of life after death with Christ in Heaven. The traits by which deer live their lives have also been associated with the values Christ taught in the Bible: honor, love, kindness, mercy, grace, and piety. The stag, the masculine, virile, courageous creature is a symbol of Christ himself, who battles and destroys the Devil daily. In the constant fight of good versus evil, the stag represents the being that is equipped with the virtues to ward off the temptations of Satan and its followers.

After I shared those passages with Toby, we were convinced that we were the beneficiaries of the stag's ability to combat and win against evil. That it was a pair of bucks, one protecting each of us, that made this possibility even more relevant to us. They were watching after us from the beginning as they knew we would be encountering evil forces. Our deer brethren would protect us and do battle when the time came. When I was possessed by Beladon, it was the symbol of the regeneration of Christ that stopped me from killing Toby, and from sacrificing him in the Biblical sense. As unbelievable as all this sounds, an animal regarded as the symbol of all things good in the world was there to fight for us through an authentic good-versus-evil scenario where my soul could have been lost to Satan. I shudder to think of the evil deeds I would have had to carry out in the Devil's name in return.

As a result, Toby and I have a new outlook toward our deer brethren. Not only do we revere the stag as creatures of virtue but have actively become stewards of these animals, whether that means being part of the movement to protect their habitat or being involved in campaigns against their destruction. The hunting and killing of bucks are of particular importance to us, as their antlers are regarded as the ultimate prize for deer hunters. When we see the stag, we are humbled by their presence. Just short of worshipping them, we know that they were placed on this Earth for the ultimate benefit of man, and his constant battle with temptation and evil.

****

One night, several days after being home from the hospital, I'm awakened in the middle of the night by a bright light in my room. I quickly jump out of my bed and look out the windows. There's a flashing light coming from the beach, an aqua-blue light. I hesitate, not sure of what I should do. There's nowhere to hide. Instead, I rush to put on my shorts and dash out of the backdoor in the kitchen. I run to the berm, my heart beating a mile a minute, not knowing what I will do if I find Beladon waiting for me. As I make it to the top of the berm, there is no light beaming from the calm bay waters. I walk closer to the shoreline to see if I can see the sparkly head of a youth or the grotesque countenance peering above the tide. The moonlight is weak this night, but I can still discern the reflection of the quarter moon on the glassy water. There's nothing immortal there. I continue to search the bay. After several minutes of surveying the shore and water, I'm convinced nothing is here. I go back in the house and climb back into bed. I don't get any sleep that night.

Epilogue

It has been several months since the night of my failed ascension. Toby's no longer my student. He earned a B in my lab section (I don't play favorites, even if you are sleeping with the teacher). We're still not out publicly as a couple, but we're not as cautious in our public interactions as we were when there was the reality of favoritism during the fall semester. We both have become active in an LGBT (lesbian, gay, bisexual and transgender) group which includes allies (i.e. heterosexual students; I hate the term "straight") on campus known as the Bedfordshire College Rainbow Coalition, the BCRC. Toby's involvement in the BCRC made headlines as he was the first male athlete in Bedfordshire College history to come out of the closet while he was a student. Of course, this broke a lot of hearts in the female population, but some of these women became our best allies. Unfortunately, he faced a lot of pushback from the male athletes: not including him in non-official school events like road trips and fraternity functions. However, he found solace in the Coalition, and of course, me. I can say that we, individually and as a couple, are weathering the challenges of being out in a mainstream world that is just starting to acclimate to a rising subculture that has been present for a long time.

As for my abilities, they have returned to pre-

Beladon levels. I would be lying if I said that I didn't miss my powers. Oh, I can still move a small object a short distance by thinking about it for a long time, but I no longer have the ability to do more impressive feats like open doors or move quadrats via telekinesis. The psychic abilities for flashbacks, predicting future events, and reading minds are mostly gone. Occasionally, a vision will pop into my head, or I'll have an intense dream about something that eventually comes true. If I can read anyone's thoughts, it's usually restricted to Toby. I miss this ability the most, especially when I want to know what Toby's really thinking about what I'm wearing when I decide to go out on a limb and try a new fashion trend or style. The one power I do not miss is the power to influence people with my thoughts. I still worry about Mother and the possible brain damage I could have caused. She seems to be fine, but when I detect any sign, no matter how insignificant it may seem, associated with traumatic brain injury, like forgetfulness, this always puts me on guard.

I'm not sure why I lost my powers. After approaching the problem using the scientific method, I have come up with two hypotheses: both of which are impossible to prove as the powers in question cannot be experimented upon. First, the powers Beladon bestowed on me are only active when Beladon is present. Like an energy source, Beladon's DNA, which has become part of me physiologically, and the encoded abilities are only active when the original source of DNA is present. When Beladon disappeared that night, so did my powers. The second hypothesis is that when Beladon possessed me and then extracted itself from me when the bucks intervened, Beladon extracted all its DNA. The abilities I now possess are those that generate from the DNA I've inherited, without the amplification of Beladon's powerful DNA.

Having Beladon's DNA assimilated into my physiology and then violently extracted has also raised another concern for me. Will the presence of Beladon's immortal supernatural DNA have a deleterious effect on my mortal body? Will I develop some type of weird cancer or debilitating condition later in my mortal life? It's a real possibility. Mutations that result from the presence of Beladon's DNA would be no different from when someone inherits a debilitating or fatal genetic disease or condition, like Huntington's Disease, for example.

I can worry about developing telltale symptoms every day, or I can live every day as if it were my last. As a wise man once quoted:

"We all have to play with the cards we are dealt."

Amen.

February 21, 2020

Lackawaxen, Pa.

A word about the author…

Patrick Field has a Ph.D. in Anatomical Sciences and Neuroscience and this knowledge informs his writing, a unique blend of scientific knowledge with supernatural storytelling.

You can find more information about the author and his books at:

www.patrickfieldauthor.com/

Thank you for purchasing
this publication of The Wild Rose Press, Inc.

For questions or more information
contact us at
info@thewildrosepress.com.

The Wild Rose Press, Inc.
www.thewildrosepress.com